ST. ORPHEUS BREVIARY I.

MARGINALIA
ON
CASANOVA

MIKLÓS SZENTKUTHY

ST. ORPHEUS BREVIARY I.

MARGINALIA
ON
CASANOVA

MIKLÓS SZENTKUTHY

TRANSLATED BY

TIM WILKINSON

Contra Mundum Press   New York

Szent Orpheus breviáriuma, Budapest © 1973 by Mariella Legnani and Mária Tompa ⚜ Translation of *St. Orpheus Breviary, Vol. 1: Marginalia on Casanova* © 2012 Tim Wilkinson

Translation of Zéno Bianu's "Boudoir and Theology" © 2012 Rainer J. Hanshe
Republished with permission of the author

First Contra Mundum Press edition 2012.
This edition of *Szent Orpheus breviáriuma: Széljegyzetek Casanovához* is published by arrangement with Mariella Legnani & Mária Tompa

Originally published in Hungary in 1939 by Kecskeméti Hírlapkiadó

Library of Congress Cataloging-in-Publication Data
Szentkuthy, Miklós, 1908 – 1988
[Szent Orpheus breviáriuma: Széljegyzetek Casanovához. English.]
St. Orpheus Breviary, Vol. I: Marginalia on Casanova / Miklós Szentkuthy;
translated from the original Hungarian by Tim Wilkinson.

—1ˢᵗ Contra Mundum Press ed.

360 pp., 5 x 8 in.

ISBN 9780983697244

I. Szentkuthy, Miklós. II. Title.
III. Bianu, Zéno. IV. Introduction.
V. Tompa, Mária. VI. Afterword.
2012946494

Contra Mundum Press would like to extend its gratitude to the Hungarian Books & Translations Office at the Petőfi Literary Museum for rewarding us with a subvention to aid the production of this publication.

HUNGARIAN BOOKS
AND TRANSLATIONS OFFICE

INDICATIVE
TABLE OF CONTENTS

INTRODUCTION

BOUDOIR & THEOLOGY

V AST LYRICAL SELF-PORTRAIT, colossal historical scrapbook, odyssey of travesties, inventory
of human feelings, polyglot entropy... hyperbolic
phrases naturally surge to mind as soon as one risks a
definition of the utterly unclassifiable work of Miklós
Szentkuthy (1908 – 1988). Struck by a perplexing fasci-
nation, critics seem incapable of going beyond the level
of enchanted stupor — and evoke pell-mell, by way of
prudent delineation, the names of Rabelais, Proust, Joyce,
Borges, or even those of Gadda or Lezama Lima. Szentkuthy, moreover, contributed greatly to impose this image
of a demiurge, who intended in the serenest of manners
to "melt all in a single universal time." Solitary, splendidly
isolated, long confined to silence, he continued building
after the eruption of his first novel, *Prae*, an emblema-
tic constellation without parallel in European literature.

Prae, or general pre-figuration, or else alchemical
precipitation. Published in 1934, this inaugural book
contained the foundational elements of what we must
call an *illuminated rhetoric*: a romanesque structure pro-
moted to the level of character, a burlesque marriage of all

antinomies, an exhilarating science of pastiche, dizzying culture deployed as rustling, haughty, and playful, "a classicism of dissemination" — in short, a completely fragmented narrative no less comparable to the dynamiting advocated some years previous by Joyce (whose work, incidentally, Szentkuthy introduced in Hungary). Despite the lucid support of some inspired criticism (László Németh, Antal Szerb, and Gábor Halasz), the "thing" — a monster block of six hundred dense pages, naturally published by the author — was declared by the good spirits of time as "unreadable," and its major fault "non-Magyar," that is: "cosmopolitan."

But it was in 1939 that an even more unexpected fireball landed on Hungarian literary ground: *Marginalia on Casanova*, nothing less than the first book of the *St. Orpheus Breviary*, to which nine other volumes would be added: *Black Renaissance* (1939), *Escorial* (1940), *Europa Minor* (1941), *Cynthia* (1941), *Confession and Puppets* (1942), *The Second Life of Sylvester II* (1972), *Despair Canonized* (1974), *The Bloody Ass* (1982) and *On the Trail of Eurydice* (unfinished).

The careful reader will observe a break of thirty years in the accomplishment of this ambitious project. During these long years of suspension, mainly from 1947 to 1957, Szentkuthy adopts the mask of the "internal refugee." Between the translation of a communist Greenland hack and the compulsory study of the *Grammar* of Stalin during joyful seminars destined to deaden thought, he wrote, according to the Hungarian expression, "for the drawer." He published nevertheless some "invented biographies" — and as many veiled self-portraits — devoted to Mozart, Haydn, Dürer, Handel, and Goethe. The latter, brilliantly entitled *Face and Mask*, was well worth the wrath of his publisher, who criticized him — oh sweet retrospectives of history! — for not conforming to the image that the German Democratic Republic had of Goethe! For good measure, this professor of English, elected by his peers, peremptorily refused an important position at the university and chose — the thing is rare enough to be reported — not to write a single line honoring the regime up close or from a distance. So much for a minimal biography of this singular temperament: purity and stubbornness ... [1]

But let us return to the great work: *St. Orpheus Breviary.* Basically, this opus can be read as a long mythos of the *marginal.* From his room-library with some twenty-five thousand volumes, Szentkuthy annotates and revisits history. Mixing with ease and joy hagiography, literary study, fiction, narrative, the lyric poem and the aphorism, this *roman-cathedrale*, whose denomination "breviary" must not mislead, with the humor of his antiphrasis, offers an unprecedented recrossing as unheard-of as much as it is ironical of all literary and artistic forms cultivated by the West, from early times

[1]. For further consideration, the reader can refer to the magazine *Caravan* № 2 (1990), which published the first five chapters of the *Frivolous Confessions* — an extensive protean autobiography now being translated by Éditions Phébus.

to the twentieth century, with major milestones: Rome, Byzantium, Venice, the Italian Renaissance & the Spanish Baroque. As archivist buffoon, Szentkuthy feeds the extravagant theater with his rigorous bulimia of a thousand networks of burgeoning stories, palimpsests in abysses and apocryphal pitfalls. Appropriating countless masks, pacing the epochs, this emotional athlete has no other aim than to break time until it stills the whirlwind of history into one continuous present.

Lord of illusions or exhibitor of shadows, there is something of the devourer in this man, who cannot bear to live cramped in one body, one life, one language. He prefers to cultivate double replicas of being, invest all fates — saints, libertines, popes, musicians, emperors, writers, eunuchs, painters or biblical girls. "I always wanted to see everything," he confessed, "read everything, think everything, dream everything, swallow everything."

From whence the art and manner of travelling across languages and playing the Argonauts of Planetary Writing (is it a coincidence that Szentkuthy was the translator of both *Ulysses* and *Gulliver?*). In truth, this stubborn survivor of the Enlightenment seems motivated entirely by a furious encyclopedic desire. A simple glance at the table of contents of the *Breviary* suffices to show the profligacy of this inner odyssey, where a few characters who were never in search of an author marched pell-mell: Casanova, Mozart, Adonis, Toscanini, Turner, Rubens, Brunelleschi, Keats, Herodotus, El Greco, Pythagoras, Voltaire, Puccini, Ariosto, Tintoretto, Shelley, Abelard,

Monteverdi, Tacitus, Messalina, Theodora, Akbar, Lao Tzu, Palladio, Mary Tudor, Donatello, Philip II, Buddha, etc.

As many roles as Szentkuthy assumes in the manner of a comedian or an absolute dreamer, writing thus a sumptuous *catalogus amoris*. Here truly resides the infinite song of an Orpheus with Apollonian harmonies, god of metamorphosis, "being whose role it is to celebrate," in the words of Rilke.

In an age where anyone — even under the sign of the worst conformism — prides oneself on marginality, Szentkuthy appears, all in all, as the writer of the absolute margin. Throughout his life, he continued to write in the margins of his books, covering and recovering — maniacally, scrupulously — volumes, newspapers, journals, and other documents. An infinite mosaic of notes, footnotes, keywords and various doodles, continuous shuffling between reading and writing — one without the other is here inconceivable — interminable bubbling of the library-universe in the heart of the Opus Magnum. Borges reminds us: "Another superstition of those ages has come to us: that of the Man of the Book. On some shelf of some hexagon, we reasoned, there must exist a book which is the key and summary of *all the others*; there is a librarian who has read this book and who is like a god."[2] If there is a writer who is a Man of the Book, according to the wish of the Argentinean master, it is

2. "The Library of Babel," *Fictions*.

VI

Szentkuthy, in relentless pursuit of a *magnum opus* that would contain and even restore all creation.

Such was his passion, and his method as well. A process inaugurated in the first book of the *Breviary*, precisely titled *Marginalia on Casanova*. Strangely — but can we talk of strangeness when discussing a man who claimed to "work in co-production with chance"? — the structure of this founding volume owes much to theology. In 1938, Szentkuthy read the *Römerbrief* of the famous Protestant exegete Karl Barth, a commentary that is based on an analysis, phrase by phrase, even word by word, of the Epistle to the Romans. Literally enchanted by the effectiveness of this method — "where, in his words, every epithet puts imagination in motion" — he decided to apply it on the spot to Casanova, whose memoirs (a German edition in six large volumes) he had just annotated with gusto.

Simultaneity of all epochs, anachronistic audacity, chaos erected into a system ("the order of the random," as defined by the same author) — was what this flamboyant opus quietly gave to read. The reception? Actually, there was none, since as soon as it was published — and even though Szentkuthy dutifully went to the church to "give thanks to all competent authorities of Catholic Heaven" to have authorized this iconoclast publication — the Royal Hungarian Court condemned *Marginalia on Casanova* for blasphemous profanity and assault on decency. Enjoying the protection of a prosecutor of the crown, the accused barely escaped trial — but all copies of the work were immediately confiscated. Thus was inaugurated the series of "Orpheuses"... [3]

Let's measure once more the eternal stupidity of the censor. What are we really being told about in *Casanova*? Of literature, of metaphysics, and of sensuality ("the thought is as sensuous as the smell of a rose," T.S. Eliot already noted about the Baroque poets) — certainly all things scandalous, but that would not likely undermine the social order of the country, which stood so strong in the bounded zeal of the régime of the censors. [4] Our "blasphemer," known for his obsessive taste for transvestism, borrows in the space of a book the panoply of the Venetian, and makes a breathtaking inventory of forms dear to the eighteenth century. Through one hundred and twenty-three notes radiating around these cyclical themes (the mask, the ball, the bath, impossible youth, Venice, the boats, the night, autumn, lethal romanticism, intoxication, the asceticism proper to dandyism, gardens, opera, etc.), Szentkuthy reinvests, with his unique, playful, and tragic tone, the *Memoirs* of the perfect lover. Anxious to break down barriers between genres (here the scholastic treatise and the fashion magazine),

3. It was not until 1973, thirty-four years later, that the book finally saw the light of day, on the occasion of the reissue of the first six *Books of Orpheus*. An opportunity that Szentkuthy would take to re-compose and unify once more the *Breviary* by opening each volume with the "life of a saint."

4. At the time when the book appeared, Hungary was subject to the dictatorship of Admiral Horthy, a great admirer of fascism.

associating baroque crests flowing together like endless rows of pearls, multiplying the set pieces (we recommend the *l'"inédit"* of Abelard, namely the portrait of Heloise reconstituted in macaronic Latin, also a bewildering description of Tintoretto's *Susanna*), he locates the metaphysical ideal in Casanova, able to reconcile elegance and bestiality — or, if one prefers, boudoir and theology. In short, beautiful as the encounter of Leibniz and Gloria Swanson on the stage of the Fenice!

Zéno Bianu

Tr. by Rainer J. Hanshe

ST. ORPHEUS BREVIARY
I.

MARGINALIA
ON
CASANOVA

I.

Vita (Life of a Saint)

Alfonso Maria di Liguori (1696 – 1787)

Saint Alfonso died at the age of ninety-one, but at the age of eighty-three, after writing uncounted books and letters, he was prohibited from writing for health reasons, because, although he was able to formulate with the greateſt ease, he never amended, or even tried to correct himself; thoughts and sentiment juſt poured out of him like incessant rain, now simply, now in a baroque fashion, but behind his matchless ſtyliſtic flair raged huge passions, both sorrows and joys, regarding the fate of God, the soul and unfathomable body of men, the purpose or unacceptable purposelessness of hiſtory. Scholaſticism, Freudian discoveries, Marxiſt observations, exiſtentialiſt deſperations likewise tore his body and soul to shreds, like the winged beaſt of deſtiny Prometheus' liver, he was chock full of foot-tapping impatience and brain-dizzying fear that he was late with his autobiography, his portrait of God, his scrutiny of hiſtory, the writing of the *Summa Summarum* of his research into nature & the soul. And juſt when these favored topics had achieved a final maturity inside him in the unſtable proportion of queſtions or answers, he was barred from writing.

This well-meant hygienic prohibition arrived from several quarters: on one occasion he had been feeding doves on the window-sill of his cell from a tin, but a dove did not wish to eat and alighted on his shoulder, and Alfonso, with sinful lack of modesty, was under the belief that the Holy Ghost-Muse had come in person to give him inspiration — not that there would have been a problem as regards the Holy Ghost, only it had not come to give him inspiration, but to snatch Alfonso's quill with its bill and carry it off for fun, perhaps like some kind of silver arrow of Venus to the dancing girls of the Catholic Parnassus among the boughs of the monastery garden. On another occasion, half the College of Cardinals, all *cardinale* in purple, turned up at his ice-cold studio (already wilted but still treasured tulips and bouquets huddled the same way in the ice box of the kitchen corridor) so as to prohibit him from writing, but those were more in the way of scarlet Tartuffes: they were not interested in Alfonso's health but in some of Alfonso's politically risky theses (of course, they also brought along doctors in fancy dress to expound their accumulated tommyrot of lengthy eras). And in any event they advised that Alfonso be excommunicated (therapeutic foresight lacking, alas, any effect either) as he occupied himself with the most fantastic facts of the whole body and the deepest soul, whereas (according to them) body and soul lie at an inexpressibly far remove from the philosophically circumscribed province of medicine.

Alfonso also noticed that the extraordinary intellectual tension evoked late temptations from his organism: the penitences of old penitents flourishing like the *Arabian Nights* in his imagination; adolescent memories were as if they had been the healthy spots of sick puberty in his soul, so that he (as the rascally lexicographers used to express it), "the greatest confessor of all confessors": he himself went off to confess, but no one dared to undertake that holy operation until in the end — why had it not occurred to him before! — he trudged off, neck pulled into his chest, to one of his greatest foes, who then heard the catalogue of the senile Alfonso's sins with Luciferian or barracks of Hades lust, took indescribable delight in proscribing writing, and, not feeling bound by any confidence of the confessional in "this special and typical case," the company in the glass palaces of the Neapolitan king cranked out stale jokes about the doddering exhibitionist satyr which required no wit at all.

When he had still been at liberty to write, his head had ached so badly, he felt dizzy and fevered (damn & blast these not so rare conjunctions of radiant *raison* and all kinds of abominable morbidity), he would clutch an ice-cool marble tablet to his left temple with the aid of a contraption that was the brainchild of a nun's head. He had acquired the marble tablet out of the lavish classical collection of Pope Benedict XIV from an ancient villa, and it depicted the scene when Orpheus has to leave his wife in the underworld — every thinker's thought is his wife, and he always has to leave her behind in the

underworld —, and it stands to reason that Alfonso
did not rest his head on the embossed side. In any case,
he had several of these temple-cooling marble tablets,
& when (having been forbidden to write) he piled these
up in a corner and contemplated them in turn, in a fine
symbolic act, in the manner of a philosopher and poet,
in much the same way as one can suppose with the tilers
of stoves, varying what can be varied: when he had done
that, not giving a hoot for the thieving pigeon, the traveling political circus of cardinals and cynical slanderers,
he declared in the Roman manner: "One doesn't have
to live, one has to write." He summoned a very old,
very intellectual 'nun' (a fairly alarming character
sketch thus far) from whom heavenly & earthly beauty, 'sacro-sexy' features radiated along virtually angelic
set-squares, and — sss! sss! ssss! — in a chapel in
the woods, dictated to her in great secrecy — no question
of any true or trashy storytelling Boccaccio novella, nor
could or can it have been. And yet, something... but *not*
in the aforementioned sense. That 'something' is (our
story does not run to punch lines, so we can divulge the
ends of several novels in advance): the nun was none
other than the duchess whom Alfonso's father had selected for his son "a century ago," but, as we shall see, nothing came of the marriage, the duchess became an
enemy of Alfonso's forever (with jealousy being perhaps the least cause), and now here she was anew, a
sham nun in sham costume, though lost time, *'temps
perdu,'* was her best disguise. It was to her that Alfonso

dictated the memoirs from which this present outline was prepared.

Alfonso and Casanova, unless my old head is calculating as badly as it normally does, co-existed for sixty-two years. When Casanova was born, Alfonso was already twenty-nine — while Casanova lived another eleven years after Alfonso died. They met in Italy under the most diverse imaginable circumstances, with each other's memoirs often being turned over in each other's heads, and if not always in the way that this *Breviary* demands, one can always shove the years forwards or back a bit in the interests of a symbolic moral. Which has nothing to do with either historical error, or the paltriest commercial anachronism, let alone with lying — just as the prodigal, pervading scent of elder in May or jasmine, drifting far and wide, is neither a lie nor a close-lipped kaleidoscope of perfumes, for after all the elder bushes stay in place, a solid positive (to someone who is a connoisseur), and even in those most far-lying areas the straying scent of elder is still that of — elder.

Casanova lived in the Bohemian castle of Count Waldstein, in Dux, between 1785 and 1798 as 'court' librarian; those were the last thirteen years of his life, from the age of sixty till his death. A librarian with every good reason, because, as you will be able to see in the following saintly reading, Casanova was (admittedly with slight St. Orpheus exaggeration) an intellectual of the 18th century: far more interesting than he was a sexually and otherwise oriented chameleon daredevil.

One would probably not be far off the mark in presuming that the count was not solely interested in the historiographer, philosopher, and mathematician in Casanova. He was solitary unto himself, working on his memoirs, though he never did get round to writing the remaining parts, and of what there was some fifty percent was lost — academic historicism loves to employ such episodes as the pedestals for broad-brimmed hypotheses, in diametrical opposition, of course, to our own methods. Now he is getting on for seventy. The library is partly composed of the interiors of huge, baroque churches, theatre auditoriums, and ballroom associations, with snaking balconies, sky-high windows overlooking the grounds, crushingly heavy velvet curtains cascading from a cornucopia, ceiling frescoes teeming with a potpourri of theology and mythology, the books themselves near-invisible — seeming like tiny organ pipes and panpipes behind soap-bubble glass doors. On the other hand: the library is also composed of the most intimate little boudoirs, the lascivious trysting rooms of the mind, with a tightly packed splendor of books instead of walls. The latter reminded Casanova of love, the former of the throne rooms of the Vatican and empresses. Now he is working in a large room, very hot, his upper body naked, though with the order of the Knights of the Golden Spurs hanging round his neck amidst the runnels of perspiration. (Was that where it was originally worn? Of what matter could that be to him in his old age, in this Versailles-like hall of mirrors!) The order of the Golden Spurs had

been bestowed on him by the pope, and this is important
to us from the point of view of the *Breviary* because on
the order, apart from the Maltese Cross and the spurs
symbolizing sadism, is: an image of St. Silvester I — a
life of whom can be read at the start of the seventh chapter of our prayer book. Pope St. Silvester I interested
Casanova from a Voltairean angle because this pope (in
the fourth century AD) almost had a stroke and became
transfixed by the bronze gate of St. Peter's Church in
Rome (it was painted bright green) when he saw that
St. Helena, during her lengthy pilgrimage to Palestine
to recover the True Cross, had nearly became an avowed
Jew, so that Europe had been within an ace of convert-
ing to the Jewish faith, and St. Peter's Church of becoming a synagogue. Casanova has no great desire to reflect
too much right now, in the heat, on the alternatives of
Providence and Nonsense and would far rather gaze on
the attractive marble relief inserted into the wall that he
had been given by Cardinal Aquariva, combined with a
splendid post, though he had been kicked out of the latter the next day on account of the routine amusements
that he had committed during the unveiling of that very
antique relief.

The title given to the relief in Count Waldstein's
catalogue (Casanova reworked & explained away with
the greatest solicitude) is *"Musikalische Unterhaltung,"* or
musical diversion, though, for all its Hellenistic-rococo
charm, in it were lurking the most ancient myths of
death & orgy, about which Alfonso wrote in the depth-

psychological book *Theologia Moralis*,[1] intended for those who take confessions, and which continues to live on — even today, as may be discerned with the greatest ease — in people, in children, in puzzling animals and puzzling flowers, in primitive peoples indeed in our Catholic ceremonies and the most formal court ceremonial — to say nothing of so-called neuroticism —, being covered by no more than a gossamer-thin shroud or by mendacious iron masks.

On the relief is an intimate bacchanalia — with beds, semi-wedding night consummation, mandolin-strumming hetæra, a homosexual lute-god in unmistakable 'boy for sale' pose, a Neapolitan lemon-cynic, the chest approaching the loveliness of a bodice. While writing the explanatory catalogue, Casanova often broke into gusts of laughter at the various descriptions of the world of Antiquity, its stillborn afterlives in various periods of Europe, in the circus Renaissance, neurotic romanticism, puritanical moralizing, and Biedermeier-bourgeois psychoanalysis. He found the most acceptable imitations in certain gargoyles of Gothic cathedrals and the art of his own Mannerist-rococo century, though the eternal clumsy, wholesale contrasting of art, comparative religion, myth, and rationalism bored him *"en gros"* (and whom do they not? when not? where not?).

In his whole life Casanova only ever met one person who professed a similar notion, with similar undying irony and humor, not just about progressively tenacious and dormant Greek mythology, but also about Europe stolen on the back of a cattle, and that one person was Pope Benedict XIV. If you by any chance glanced at the Table of Contents for this chapter before looking at this "Life of a Saint," then you may have seen the heading 'Benedict XIV: symbolic sculpture of the 18th century.'

The process before he was elected dragged out over six months (What a legal brainwave it would be were it to carry on until doomsday: could it be that even the Protestant issue might thereby possibly achieve some form of temporary resolution? — Casanova asked Benedict XIV, Falstaffian both on the outside and in). Precisely the opposite came to this soon-to-be pope's mind. When the electoral college of cardinals attended what happened to be a most joyous garden party in Tivoli (they were joyous because these were the ones who had no chance at all), the soon-to-be and still chuckling pope raised his glass to say: "Why the ridiculously long deliberations over the naming? If you are looking for a saint, there's Alfonso di Liguori — and he pointed towards the depths of the gardens, with respectful pantomime gestures to imitate eating roots, falling into a trance, rapture when praying, and chasing a squirrel under his arm. — If you are looking for an open-minded diplomat (though sometimes the narrow-minded type would be a better bet in this zodiac), then you have Aldobrandini, who by no chance at all contrived the world's sneakiest-snakiest labyrinth on the grounds of his residence. If you want a wise old head, a laughing Christian Democritus, then there's always me. Choose me." They elected him.

The Pontiff was very fond of the classics (Alfonso di Liguori, a researcher into souls and hormones in his confessional, never forgot the quote that the pope had cited from *Oedipus* at the Tivoli banquet: "I am who I am. Why should I fear to trace my birth? Nothing can make me other than I am."). In the evenings, liberated from the daily run of religion and politics, he arranged great debates (using his own canon-law slippers to send fanatics to where such toads and howling monkeys belonged), and on one such he held a long discourse based on his experiences in Istanbul. Casanova spoke against Turkish fatalism (even though he was much attracted to it), whereas Alfonso presented a dramatic account about the death of a similarly fatalistic, theologically disposed Jansenist nun.

Our *Breviary* would fall into a sin of omission if we failed to remark that Benedict XIV wrote lives of saints — with Casanova delivering the political dirt in towering stacks of files and Alfonso his flowering bunches of legends. Both had free access to the pope at any time. The Vatican's entire army and its Amazon horde of nuns did not dare go within ten rooms of Benedict's studio (Hush! hush! the Holy Father is working!), meanwhile the pope could barely wait for someone, anyone, to enter and tell him a good joke with the relish of *genuinely spiritual* people.

Benedict's teeth were set on edge, to use the vernacular, by the wrangling, like the braying of flea-bitten asses, that went on over the conversion of the Chinese

— maybe because he was far from convinced that this could be accomplished in practice, maybe because he did not consider it to be one of God's heavenly intentions: thinking of the main protagonist of the gospels, "Go into the world, and preach this unto peoples of all nations," he was not thinking of global population statistics or world geography, but with simple sketchiness meant only to spread the news, "insofar as it is possible, to the widest possible audience." There was also a particular reason for the irritation, in that here in Europe, with its frequent humbug, missionaries were attacked for making the *maximum* possible concessions to Chinese converts to retain much, a very great deal, of the ancient customs of Brahma, folklore, and Buddha. Yes, retain! That was applauded by enlightened Casanova — Alfonso: profoundly silent, because this did not particularly appeal to him, and (in this exceptional case, this is *not* an authenticated fact) the pope put his bishop's miter on an inkpot and crossed his legs in a Buddha-like pose.

Skipping the Buddha-like pose, Alfonso might have acted exactly the same when the pope allowed the Spanish king to confer bishops with their sees and other benefices (albeit in exchange for the king paying a huge church levy on the basis of a cross-eyed 'that makes us quits' law). Benedict explained as follows to the grimly black and blue Alfonso: "I would be crazy to reopen that sterile and bloody Investiture Dispute! An emperor bestows the tiara on the pope, the pope crowns the emperor, kiss of peace, murderous war to boot, emperor chops tiara to bits, pope crushes crown, antipopes spring up like mushrooms. Ugh! There's been enough of that!" Whereupon Alfonso again turned hermit, Casanova clapped again (that's laid-back liberalism for you!), but five minutes later, out of defiance himself turned hermit because the pope delivered such a sound cuff to Venice, the state so loved by Casanova, that the whole Byzantine junk-dealer-antiquarium all but slid under water, along with St. Mark's, the ghetto, its Moorish palaces, its senators perching with faces like funeral weepers on their sacks of money.

Alfonso, like many of our saints, did not set off as a saint but a lawyer (Casanova's start was no different). In this brief *vita*, we can only touch on the mental nourishment: Casanova survived the French revolution by nine years, living in the baroque hermitic surrounds of Dux, whereas Alfonso died one year before the revolution. What manner of thoughts could have been going through the heads of these two lawyers, one cum-saint, one cum-adventurer, in the company of wigs crawling with lice and bishops' miters that resembled a leather-bound wine list? It is no surprise that a series of attempts were made to expel Alfonso from law school in his very first year, because he puzzled over the *foundations of law*, its final causes, which attracted general hostility from all university chairs and courts. What is the contribution of Christianity and the gospels to European law? What is the Roman heritage? What did the Goths and other Germans contribute to the mixture? How about those who paved the way for the French Revolution? What about his father's grandee family? The money-grubbing, rapacious, sophistic shysters. Here *all* possible ethics had to be examined in space and time, and only *after* that could one slap an only half-legible skew-whiff stamp of a *nullus nullificatus* on an enacting clause (full of subclauses). When the father learnt about his son's investigations, viler than even the curse of leprosy, into 'final causes,' it was all he could do not to run him through in the university's assembly hall (a fine gentry comedy): whereafter Alfonso followed his intellectual dabbling in secret, in the same way as fellows pursued their sexual lives, and already as a law student he was an unbeatable legal adviser to a range of products across the social scale, from the Vatican to Don Quixote feudal puppets.

A big trial brought a decisive change in his life. In much the same way as physicians call spectacular operations carried out before a big public 'music-hall surgery,' this was a music-hall hearing, if only because millions hung on which way it went, with Alfonso's father himself being involved as well as, to add further romantic spice, the fabulously beautiful woman (picked by family) to whom Alfonso was affianced. In the trial Alfonso spoke on behalf of his father and his fiancée. He always spoke without notes, with a sea of documents, an ocean of tiny bills strewn before him on his table, but all he would do is occasionally point to one or another — knowing the whole thing off pat. In one of the 'boxes' was his father, now swollen up from barrel-size into an even bulkier barrel in the knowledge of a certain win, while on another balcony was the fiancée, quite deliberately attired in such a stunning costume that, in its blossoming-bejeweled whiteness, it was hard to tell apart from a wedding dress, with its liturgical piquancy flickering from the Madonna of the myrtles to the maenads.

Alfonso cited from memory a last will and testament of around six hundred pages, as was his wont, but he stopped short at one particular article, thought about it, then unexpectedly tossed in four different directions the four paperweights which served to prevent the file from curling, and exclaimed — "back to the beginning!" — with almost a fishwife's lack of grace, the thing being? the thing being what? The thing being that at that moment — he came to realize that he was representing a flawed and false case that, in all good reason and conscience, he held to be incompatible, and he stormed out of the courtroom, decorated as it was in the style of a Handelian opera.

Gigantic theatrical upheaval, and after the chorus and counterblast of bawling lawyers had calmed down slightly, a mercenary commander's wolf howl — "After him!" — unleashed an even greater infernal chaos, and people did in fact rush out after him, like policemen on the tail of a regular gang of regicides, with the subtle difference that one of the groups (as it happened, the one in which the barrel-father was riding, and the fiancée, half-naked in rent garments of 'seminude snaky curves,' as twittering sculptors who are imagined to be ultramodern are in the habit of labeling their half-baked jokes), well anyway: one of the groups did indeed come upon the decamping advocate in the Church of the Holy Cross of Jerusalem prostrated on the altar steps in front of the Most Majestic Holy Sacrament locked in the tabernacle. The halfway-trial-losing-halfway-winning horde stopped short, not daring to go as far as the altar, and the father rushed over to the priests flowing out from the sacristy, his sword clattering as it got caught up with the collection box, to demand that they drive his 'sacrilegious' (but then on what grounds?) son away from the altar.

The very next moment, however, the risk of 'sacrilege' drew perilously near: Alfonso ripped off the door to the tabernacle as if it were a badly glued gold-paper poster, then grasped the Sacrament with the strength of his sword-wielding ancestors and raised it on high above the paralyzed herd of legal eagles. "No question about it, here one must kneel," muttered a dwarfish lawyer with a head like a dried fig, and in a trice all that could be seen were bowed heads, in the manner of a Goya painting, and all that could be heard was the asthmatic, muffled holy-mother-of-God stirring that is part of the technique of kneeling. (Casanova as a lay child parishioner once preached in a church in Venice, as you will soon be able to read.)

If a very large portion of Christian medieval painting, or medieval biblical myths about the Jews, often the finest part, happened to treat topics which are *not* in the gospels or the canonical Old Testament, then this

Breviary too: for the sake of their novelistic or instructively symbolic delight, may also record similar *un*official data, in this case relating to precisely the trial in question.

Since by the time he was born Alfonso was already twenty-nine years old — the infant Casanova can play no particular part in the foregoing comedy. However, there is one apocryphal tale which maintains that while the discussion was in full swing Alfonso's duchess-fiancée (to take her mind off the excitement) played ball in the grounds with her woman friends — the nun-Astartes of Botticelli's *Primavera* —, and Casanova jumped over the fence, giving rise to the normal screams, the normal joy at having such a gallant playmate drop in out of the blue, and the normal amorous conclusion amidst the impenetrable scenery of the darkest bushes, the whitest statues, and the greenest fishpond mirror. When Alfonso unexpectedly flung a falsified law book at another wall — like Moses the tablets of the ten commandments —, and repudiated his role of 'defense' counsel in the suit, being pursued by his father & his fiancée, then — according to this unofficial version —, Alfonso did not race to any church, but his father grabbed him by the scruff of the neck (in all likelihood, just symbolically), took him home to his palace, and there, before the eyes of a huge throng, had it established by doctors of theology and medicine that his son had suddenly — been possessed by the devil.

When the exorcists who were on duty at the palace tried out various artifices on Alfonso in vain, in the most

unfrequented chamber, a jovial little, wise cardinal-Socrates whispered in the furious father's ear that these artifices were anyway poppycock with Alfonso, everybody
knew that: a much smarter thing would be to lock up
Alfonso with his glorious intended, this lady (learning
greatly from the utility of Salome's dance) would persuade him to continue representing his father's and her
own interests in the trials.

Still glinting on the duchess, in an almost literal
sense, were what from all quarters are recognized to be
the dewdrops of love — so it was with natural merriment and like a juggler directing balls that she listened
to the advice offered by the little cardinal-Socrates and,
locking up (having herself locked up with) Alfonso, in-
stantly set about a replay of the stage work that had been
learnt from Casanova. But as, thank goodness, that was
all in vain the duchess returned to Casanova in the park
grounds, Alfonso showed up as a priest at the monastery and university, while his father was able to trifle
for a time with lame apoplexy.

In the next episode factual truths and (one suppos-
es) imagination commingled in the healthiest way; moreover they connect with the epic grace of an apoplectic
fit. When Alfonso preached the sermon as an ordained
priest, in a most tattered soutane, under the prayer-lined
palmette vault of the Gothic vaulting of a church at daybreak on Ash Wednesday, immediately after carnival:
the father saw his son again for the first time as a beggar
dragged out of a rubbish bin — whereas father and his

family, clad partly in Spanish royal costumes, partly still
in the harlequin fancy dress of Shrove Tuesday, reeled
half-drunk or else formed a guard of honor at the foot of
the pulpit (a broad Italian stage made to run about on).

Grandees detest that dissolute breed of clowns &
virtuous proletarians (in his son's eyes he was now one
of the latter and nothing more), so the father swooned
away in aristocratic dismay, which was tantamount to
an earthquake there, among the reed-thin columns with
their vine-leaf capitals. After the homily: taking confessions (whether a person was of the street or quality or
a drunken jester, just one church rule applied, and that
was: join the queue), supposedly (out of diabolical vengefulness and a perverse delight) the duchess also confessed
unimaginable imagined sins to her ex-betrothed — with
Casanova, in the disguise of a Capuchin friar, standing
behind to prompt her. Apocryphally, that is where the
idea of the *Theologia Moralis* occurred to Alfonso (this
is the long-forgotten term by which 'Freudianism' was
known in 18th-century rococo jargon). When, on one
of his thousand missionary trips to a nunnery, Alfonso
was received with evidently hostile feelings because
a rumor had spread through half of Italy (true, by the
way!) that on the occasion of that memorable confessional Alfonso had treated the jesters with much more
forgiving tolerance than he did the so-called decent or
honest folk.

The mother superior was the most vulgar combination of the customary princess plus sadism plus small-

mindedness plus sexual repression and set about Alfonso, the meekest of souls, like a bullying female figurehead, squawking out to him some tale of a French Cistercian convent (Port-Royal as it is referred to in guidebooks) where the nuns were so strict to their rule — fatalistic, deterministic, fanatics of eternal guilty conscience — that even the saintliest among them kicked the Holy Sacrament out of the window at the time she was being given extreme unction because she sensed that she was not in possession of salvation and divine grace — and she was still laboring in the original guilty conscience of original sin. "The lady was very much mistaken, indeed committing sacrilege — commented Alfonso with a drawing-room gesture of dismissal —, it's good luck Jesus couldn't care less about caviling bitches of her sort."

One can just imagine the frame of mind in which, after the mother superior's dogmatic yapping, both bestially self-lacerating and therefore lacerating to others, he received the poor, meek, modest, and innocent little scullery-maid of a nun who (sincerely and by way of solace) recounted to Liguori by the washtub a vision she had had that he would be: a great saint, the founder of a great clerical order, a plumber of souls for the Church to outdo all the old theological doctors. To start with Alfonso flew into a hysterical rage but then gave the girl absolution at the end of the confession with a kiss of peace — she skipped out of the kitchen, a song on her lips: "In spite of everything, I know what I know!"— something of that sort was blazing in her stubborn, ironic eyes.

Alfonso did indeed become a founder of the order, but from beginning to end he just acquired enemies — evil men, imbeciles, dullards and interested parties (drovers and slaves of the Bloody Ass of fate) left him in the lurch, accused him, ridiculed him, denounced him, misunderstood him (it may perhaps raise a smile to learn that in the end even the old Casanova felt himself to be a martyr, some kind of awkwardly modern negative saint, especially after hearing Mozart's *Magic Flute*, in the cushioned womb of his curtained Viennese landau following an 'escape' from Dux).

Heretics reveling in the blind rigor of blind fate crowed against his infinite understanding — philosophers distorting an almost nihilistic anarchy out of the French enlightenment, lords with millions of acres to their name who saw worse in the saint of the poor than they presumed in Robespierre — the bigoted (which is to say cowardly-aggressive) adversaries of psychoanalysis, strict legal machine and geometry minds, presidents of Supreme Courts of the Judicature — the Vatican (Clement XIII and XIV) initially idolized him, but subsequently, the King of Naples, as a matter of policy, didn't give a damn for Liguori's tiara or beggar's clothes, & "in the Church's interest" unleashed what was almost a crusade on Liguori's Jesus and his congregation — a bunch of adventurers sided with Liguori, thinking that they would be able to procure rich pickings from his order — envious people who brewed a witches' cauldron of hatred almost just for the heck of brewing it, *l'art pour l'art*, closet homosexuals who deemed to have hit upon a safe place, neurotic visionaries, tunnel dwellers, the superstitious.

When he nevertheless managed to cobble together his order, Clement XIII compelled him to accept a bishopric — and Alfonso embarked on his high pastoral activities (having demanded that much from the pope), having sold off all the treasures in the bishop's palace at a memorably Eyetalian-style auction (a play! novel! this *Breviary* has a job denying itself of this plum!) — he had the gates barred with huge locks and he put it under military guard while he moved into a more modest villa (though it was not so modest in its dimensions). It was not so much the high-key work of missions, more the gilded vilifications of diplomacy which made him ill, his distress over the shady sides of the human soul, the impending atheistic revolution ('deism' he regarded as an atrociously badly-cut mask of unbelief) and for now disenchantingly inept clashes of the extremes of pathologically rabid reaction, and his wish, his longing, to be back in what he imagined to be the beautiful, reformed congregation — those are what made him ill. He asked the pope to be allowed to return home, if necessary on a stretcher, by litter (the sweet coffin of a walker in woods?) — but taken back to his congregation to look at the heavens and write his memoirs.

Closing scene in the wood. Stout-hearted monks carried him slowly, carefully in the ceremonial litter of the resigned bishop ("if those crazy papists like drapes, fasts, and mannerist opera scenery then, damn it all, let them feast their eyes on it; by now I will gladly be a flashily beribboned May Day nag for them"), when all of a sudden, amid the dark bushes, at the head of a small army, Queen Maria Carolina of Naples, Marie Theresa's daughter, jumped out and began bawling & cursing and laughing hysterically like a hyena — all of this directed at Alfonso just when he was sleeping peacefully on his fevered bed-sheets. The queen & her spouse (Ferdinand IV, long a nervous wreck through orgying) lived more in fear and trembling of the French Revolution than possibly anyone else in the whole of Europe — with Ferdinand being the royal house's domestic jester and alcoholic, now wasted into a harem-voyeuristic eunuch, his consort (who brought in women of any kind by the wagonload!) reigned in his stead and she fancied she could discern a French revolutionary spy network in, of all things, Liguori's Congregation of the Most Holy Redeemer.

On a playground suited to Jesus and children (a grassy clearing among the bushes), the queen barked that Alfonso had written his *Theologia Moralis* for the benefit of revolutionaries, and every piece of information that it contained regarding perversions (unfounded slanders, of course) had been drawn from the life of Ferdinand IV in order that Paris might snigger, gloat, and take up arms against Naples. Alfonso sat up in his bed, wove the ribbons of his miter into droll bows, and although his chin had long sunk to his chest, he was still able to nod — for it seemed as if he was still nodding affirmatively after each and every shrieked charge. It was at this point that the Angelus bell rang out from a nearby village. With the assistance of two friars, Alfonso climbed from bed and kneeled in the grass (begging pardon of the blades of grass) and prayed, with the soldiers also kneeling because they saw a celestial light above Alfonso's head — whereas the queen in her fury flung one of her bloodied pencil-heeled shoes at Alfonso and raced off into a thicket. All along their way, Alfonso toyed with the shoe with childish and urbane expertise — before giving it to a peasant girl when they were at the monastery — "Royal sale! Look after it; it will be useful for the dowry. The reverend fathers will explain all. What are you loitering about for, *fratres et patres*? We'll be late for supper. Presto, presto."

2.

Lectio (Saintly Reading)

1. He is a descendant of actors. That is decisive and important before all else. When I was still such a child that I sought to pursue philosophy and physiology in German, the sort of book that I constantly had in my mind's eye had the title: *Innerste Theatralik aller Wesenheiten.*[2] The most primal principle of life is theatrical: the jellyfish in the fairylike-fatal underworld of the sea, the coconut periwigs in the Gothic fan-towers of palms, the fetid head of an embryo at the end of the umbilical cord, jasmine, horseradish, sicknesses: these are all theatrical, colorful, simulating and subterfuges. Not lies, just masks, mimics. That is what history is too; that is the darkest instinct of life. That and art. The darkest and also the loneliest. If I were not myself descended from an actor ancestor, I would not believe in my existence. Reality and theatre: unambiguous. Which is why it is so much an absolute law-book and Domesday Book that Casanova's memoirs open with that alpha and omega without which there is nothing: actor, actor, actor.

2. But the other 'ontological prelude' is also perfect — the fact that two things light our way: the name of Locke and *Hexerei*.[3] If you wish to live, then you can only be an actor, a comedian, like the gods and the cosmos; once you have started to live, then you must forthwith bear a duality of life, of humanity, that can never be elucidated: the clarity of meaning and the eternal hocus-pocus of meaninglessness, Locke and the witches, wise women, exorcists and evil spirits of the Venetian suburbs of Murano and Burano. That is the 18th century *par excellence*, but the whole of human life is eternal. This duality underlines Casanova's entire eroticism: the sobriety and commonsense grayness of the atheism of "*Experimentalphysik*," the spirit of the demons, Roman "*Irrlichter*,"[4] and ineradicable wizardry. But could man be intelligent any other way? Life can exist somehow without witches, but not 'human understanding.'

3. After that two-step humanist prelude, the *codex amoris* can begin. The first, the pre-love, pre-narcissism, pre-lust, pre-mind, pre-moral, pre-everything 'papillonage':[5] young Bettina washes his legs, and she does so with such scrupulous thoroughness that little Casanova's semen is loosed for the very first time into the world. If we wished, we might choose this *pre*-love as an eternal fate. This clearness, cheerfulness, ignorance, creepiness without horror, delight without nervous pathos, this asexual, anonymous, pre-narcissistic narcissism. Light colors — everything is creamy white.

It is *morning*. This is so important in the whole of Casanova's youth — the all-obliterating victory of morning, dew's primacy over the night. Love is a morning activity, adventure, beatitude — a gift of the fading Moon and silver mists on the park. A white washbasin, then skinny white child's legs, white pillows, white towels, white children's stockings, white milk, white milk jug, white apron, white soap bubbles, white flowers in the garden, white moon, white pollen.

What is soap, what is body, what is flower? What is dream, what is morning butter? What is sin, what a tickling sensation? What is washing and what nuptials? What is a twinge of conscience and what is joy? What is innocence and what perversion? What is tiredness and what strength? What is virginity and what eternal breeding? All this, and more, is as yet unequivocal, all this anything at all — this bud, this one and only happiness, the threshold of thresholds, Casanova's youth codex is a book of nostalgia: by the time we first understand it, we are definitely no longer eight years old, and therefore we are excluded forever from the one and only paradise.

We are not youngsters anymore: this first melancholy underlining in itself already lends otherworldly magic colors to Casanova's first volume. 'Perdu,' but so definitely and absolutely *perdu* that youth, that definiteness of non-existence, is already god. It is also symbolic that love, or præ-præ-præ-love: begins with a bath. The bathing is the secretive, spleen-sugared 'center' between love's form of anarchy & love's form of civilization.

This secretive 'center' is the essence of the whole Casanovan experience — for a moment an era, or perhaps even just one person, and he *perhaps* only in his book: managed to reconcile the animal and ceremonial sides of love. Love was never so depraved, so golden-aged, so libertine, as here — never so elegant, so neatly turned and masked, as here.

Nowadays one can sense only one thing: such animal protoromanticisms and protochaoses as feelings of love can only die, be lost in caricature agony within civilization. Though one may also suspect that it was perhaps just this very civilization that made it so chaotic and romantic — might love without civilization be a — platitude? It is true that there is no problem of that kind in Casanova — here people can 'bathe' blithely, naked that is to say, but they are playful, they can blithely mix up the Eve era with the era of Molière's doctors. The bath is an eternal European compromise-grimace: at times with nymphal charm, at times in desperation, but we can never renounce it as a compromise form of love. It is a hedging of bets, not a solution, even in Casanova's time; but as a hedging of bets it succeeded better with him than anyone else.

What a marvelous 'bath' scale it is — from the washbasin of boyhood, through the peasant girl's tub to the pool of the harem in Constantinople, where Turkish odalisques splashed in the nocturnal moonlight. The bath is cleanliness: at once baptism and hygiene. The bath is vanity: women use a lake's stilled surface as a mirror.

The bath disrobes and thus is an erotic game. Nymph myth and civilized hygiene frolic. How right medieval nuns were, to be sure, to consider cleanliness and love as being one and the same.

4. Casanova writes a note to his love. Will it truly always be so? Without letters, without the compulsion to write, would there be no love? Is the spirit always cowardly? Or will the body's archetypal erotic cowardice always pass itself off as mind, and this mind again as literature? Mind out of cowardice, literature out of mind: is that inevitable circulation not touching?

What preludes: unselfconscious body-zither-playing and love letter — some bodily ignorance, nervous error, and some '*littérature*' about the moonshine mind, dreams, myths. All literature 'as such' is charmingly here, but eternally and lethally compromised.

5. But this moment when the taste of the breakfast milk and diabolical sin still mingle in a single sweet uneasiness does not last long; even in the moment that is youth it is but a moment. The elements separate out; adolescents, whether girls or boys, make a start on the 'mind's' great paradox harvest. Very much in the grand style, very crudely. Raw nervous disorders, raw mythologies, raw lies make their appearance — and moral insanity makes an appearance in all its consistent vividness.

Bettina is possessed by the devil. Now is that Catholicism or Freudianism, one may ask? Or is it just sober and calculating hypocrisy: who can decide, and anyway who would care? This is love's indigestibility to itself, man's natural impossibility for man. Over time, an adult gets used to the fact that he is, in point of fact, a self-contradiction and loitering absurdity, but not, as yet, a child — a child is still logical —, and for precisely that reason becomes neurasthenic or possessed by the devil or a liar: these little prepubescent liturgies are the *sole* adequate expressions for life's inner self-contradictions. If Casanova and his young girlfriend for a moment were *'Narcisse blanche,'* they subsequently also had to accept this Satanism.

6. And while saints and charlatans tussle with the devil in Bettina's body, what sort of thought is hovering in the air? That of the *ball* to come. A ball is the same eternal hedging of bets as the bath, from its Hellenic sources to the *plagues* of Deauville. Naïve superstition though it may be, I insist that dance, the ball, was only truly dance, or ball, in the 18th century. This is the most central center in the entire Casanova myth: a ball is a good deal less than Dionysian, but much, much more than a social refinement or game. Evening dress is: half a ritual garment, a priestessly pose, half a hetæra advertisement.

The dance: half nuptials, half an artless Vestal tourney. If anyone wishes to know and feel the impossibility and nonetheless-affectation of European love, just take a look at a dancing couple: the subtext of tragicomedy is written in garish letters. For us, but not our Casanova. This is his element — he knows that this is the maximum in the sex history of Europe, so he plunges in and, with a laugh on his lips, salvages what can be saved. There is no 'Christian morality' or 'pagan freedom' here — instead it is some mysterious, iridescent third party: the dance. There is no brutal vegetation and refined society — here is a blissful third party: the ball, the carnival.

If there is no love without 'littérature'-cowardice and conjuring up of the devil, all the less can it exist without the ball. What is so splendid about Casanova is that these "Urphenomena" are nowhere else than with him to be found interwoven in the epic with such nonchalance and yet ontological weight (rococo and ontology? yes, and how!... Mozart).

7. Adolescents, hence their milieu too, may sometimes be seized by pedantry: since Bettina was possessed by a devil, she switched to the other logical stance — became mad. A kind of intermittent madness. This game between child madness and ballroom mood is pleasant: now doctor, now hairdresser; now a straightjacket, now a periwig; now Beelzebub, now Pulcinello.

There is and will be nothing other than these two, says the most reliable gospel: madness and ball, agony and dance. Here it is not a matter of some kind of game of romantic opposition, but of two things in themselves, *Dingen an sich*. Apropos of Casanova one feels most of all that any commentary is, in the end, risible windiness — this is simply the point at which an entrance is made by fundamental facts without which there can be no love within civilization, and one has done one's job by pointing a finger at these fundamental facts. A fact illuminates solitarily, like a lonely but eternal lamp in the depths of a blind lagoon. If it were possible to comment sensibly it would no longer be a fact but a thought or, God forbid, some other such litter.

8. The nicest thing in Casanova is the absolute certainty with which he puts his finger on the essential features of love (not the ideal love, maybe, but the possible, 'relatively still the best' love). He started before all else with acting as primary matter, following that with the kinship of 'Locke' and '*Hexerei,*' then he flashed a light on the butterfly charm of dawn-time chance pollution (something so fine as to be almost, but not quite, impossible), then after that on the grand and irrefutable logical monumentality of adolescents when they pump themselves full of the devil and hysteria, and their every desire is that the 'ball' should go on 'forever': now, after all that, he gives "the dogmatism of the ages of life" with just as much declared accuracy. In Venice he connected with a seventy-year-old nobleman, white Senator Malipiero. 'Connected': we can already remark here that this 'connecting' is no lazy epic

platitude but just as much dogma as everything else in this book.

The *sine qua non* for love is wandering, continual 'connecting,' from palazzo to palazzo, from bordello to bordello, from seminary to prison, from ship's cabin to harem, from park to maid's room, from pontiff into the Venetian night — irresponsible throwing into a milieu is the essence of love. Malipiero is seventy, Casanova fifteen. Both are in love with a young girl living in the house opposite. This is the dogma: love is a thing of the senile and children — an adult man's love is *nulla*. The essence of love is: the boundlessness of sensuality and the boundlessness of dream-dreaming; only here does it exist absolutely: in the pre-spring snowdrop & the last post-autumnal yellow leaf. In immaturity and in "ripeness is all." [6]

Just as in art the finest works are those of extreme youth and extreme old age, March and November; summer be hanged. No one suggested this as categorically as Casanova did in the next scene. In one of the palace's boudoir dining rooms, elderly Malipiero & child Casanova are taking supper under a candle which burns with a sputtering reminiscent of a large tidal swell in a lagoon — and they are talking about the actors' offspring who lived across the way. They have a perfect understanding of one another: they are on a shared level of impossible sensuality and impossible dream. Love as *sweet* impossibility, not apocalyptic nonsense: that is something only the two of them understand. The melancholies of renunciation, self-denial, disappointment, doubt, paradox, infidelity and forgetting: to bestow charm, a flower, a scent, a smile, melody — those are things only Casanova understood. That in essence crude adventurer. Was it perhaps writing, after all, which made him tender?

But there is something here even more important, of prime importance, which swallows up even Casanova, love and everything in its colorful darkness: the appearance of *Venice*. Casanova's first volume is a big self-hypothesizing of youth and Venice: youth as a Mozartian phantom of transitoriness and Venice as reality itself; a *primum mobile*, a mainspring, which renders gods and loves superfluous. Europe is a poor word and superfluous reality — there is just one word and one reality: Venice. Venice is no 'beauty spot,' it is not a paradoxical opal of history and aquatic vegetation; Venice is reality.

Casanova does not speak about Venice — for everything is Venice. In the end that has to be expressed dogmatically: Venice is an article of faith and unappealable reality, the one thing, after all has broken down, for which it is worth living, but then forever. If a mother loses her only son, all I can do is say with Casanova: Venice. If all gods are dead for anyone, I have just one response: 'Venice.' Because if love is in part what, and only what, it is to *aged* Malipiero and the *child* Casanova: a sweetly blazing unreality — then love is something else besides — a *place*; it is always identical with some scenery, town, house or shore.

In love the word milieu is useless; Venice is not some backdrop to love. Venice is itself love. How exclusively decisive it is in Malipiero's love that the streets of Venice are narrow, the windows are vast, and consequently it is possible to spy in quite mystic comfort (comfort is always mystical, perhaps the one thing that is!) on a woman: into her home, her boudoir, her soup and her wash basin. 'Narrow street' — life hinges on things like that, always on such bare, nothing-more facts on which no commentary is possible: which is why art & philosophy are superfluous.

Naturally, Venice's aspects are inexhaustible; on the day we die we shall be just as falsetto-toned amateurs in other-worldly polyphony as we were to begin with — but here, out of this infinitude, for example, Casanova shows one thing: the identity of the civilized city, aristocratic caste-pigeonholes, and the jungle in the era of primordial ferns.

Everybody is infinitely close to each other, it is not possible to get closer, yet the contour map of social chasms is still huge. That too is 'central': between town and forest — only there can love be optimal. The house walls are terracotta colored: not vermilion nor brown — that too is *already* the *height* of love. The windows are longish, slim, almost curved in their Gothic lankiness: that is the reality (not just some version among a million others) and thus, of course, immediately love itself. The windows are in stone frames, the houses are decaying but they are from the Renaissance: for me they are not 'travel reminiscences' but the only thing in which I have faith. Casanova in the end solved everything with this Venetian beauty-ghastliness: no more was there a need for myth, no need for thought, no need for love, no need for art. After that Casanova really can become easy, can be a dancer here, where we have long been dead, because at the bottom of everything seethes and whispers in midnight lilac the discovered metaphysics: Venice. That is also the only aspect of tragedy in it, the all-excluding swampy eternality of Venice.

9. From then onwards, of course, everything is different; floating behind everything in the colors of ice-spring the city's death-gentian. The dogmatizing tone remains — with next being: a loose, finely decayed Catholic milieu. Casanova himself is a young abate — who in that era was free to wear ecclesiastical garb as he wished, no one was checking. There is no question that his entire erotic career was not based on Geneva but Rome.

Only in Roman Catholicism would the eerie proximity of St. Ignatius Loyola and Don Juan be possible. In any case it would be interesting (if it were possible to believe in anything other than reality, for example in so-called thoughts) to juxtapose three figures: Don Juan, Casanova, and Cagliostro. It would be just as exciting to compare the Casanova of *Venice* and the Casanova of *Rome*. *Venice* is always the Atlantic tragedy of the whole of existence, of reality — *Rome* is no more than the joviality of the gods, the ephemeral splendor of Elysium.

Protestantism recognizes neither the penitential frenzy of lonely eremitism nor the swaggering purple of Roman simony — therefore it does not recognize Casanova. Just as within a short space of time in the course of his travels Casanova sets eyes on the Arabian aridity and ascetic poverty of Calabria, then the easy-going harems of Constantinople: so the background to the whole mental possibility is this Catholic duality — a Baroque ermine and Toledan (Grecoesque) self-torture.

That is the psychology which operates in him: it derives from the psychology of confession, and it returns to that notwithstanding any cynicism. The hypothesis is thus: a Protestant cannot be in love. Of course, nor can a true Catholic either — only this maneuvering Counter-Reformation-era, peripheral Catholic, shuttling between hypocrisy and superstition.

As an abate he had access to young girls: he is familiar with the pleasure of uncertainty — part friend, part-lover, part priest; all and none of these. Civilization wanted *that*: obscure, glossed-over roles. Casanova was well aware that by then civilization was just as eternal an entity as any 'virgin nature' and so could be counted on. He was aware that an out-&-out priest, an out-&-out adventurer, or an out-&-out lover is just: comic — so he will be an absolute cocktail.

The marvelous thing is: precisely that this is a complete, unstinting acceptance, a brave and winning affirmation of the self-contradictions of civilization. Making a supreme pleasure out of all that on which others go romantically to rack and ruin. Another adolescent in the same situation contracts nothing less than a *comme il faut* neurasthenia and becomes a writer: Casanova makes civilization's lie healthy, a sport. There are already many who made art out of lies; Casanova knows how to produce *joie de vivre* as well.

10 "Ging ich in *Maske* aus" [7] — that is the logical culmination of civilization as an affirmation of self-contradictions. That culture: a *mask* culture, the reality of the 18th century, the reality of the mask. 'Psychology' here is a mistake arising from the mask, games of *quid pro quo*; sensuality only becomes truly great through the secret of the mask. Behind the mask lurks nihilism — a mask is almost as much a possibility of tragedy as Venice is simply by virtue of being Venice.

Neither Sophocles nor Shakespeare wrote a sentence as tragic as Casanova's: "*Ich ging in Maske aus.*" A colored mask? A black one? With a long, corkscrew freak's nose or just a simple covering for the forehead? Life is only tolerable in a mask — in this daring gesture civilization makes use of all game of games, a paradox from which it follows, but at the same time its nostalgia for non-civilization is quite tremendous.

A masked head is a death mask. In this disguise are preluded the two or three adventurous Venetian midnights which play a part in Casanova: when he has his revenge on an adversary; when a senator faints in a gondola; when marble tables are thrown together on resounding stone and he drunkenly tolls the bells with his musician companions.

11. As a small baby abate Casanova delivers a sermon in church. What is important above all else is that there is a world in which such a thing is possible, historically speaking. A world in which no one gives a damn about whether a person wearing a priest's garb is a priest; a world in which a young boy can make a debut like a little ballerina. If that is the milieu then a thousand other things are self-evident. Yet Casanova's entire intellectual mission (because he has none other in life) hangs on this: that a milieu can be one such or another, but there are *only* situations, the *dramatis personae* are not so much negligible as nothings.

Love is not a human death game or erotic game of patience, it is not a soul, not a body, not a marriage, not an adventure — love is: a 'situation'; a constellation of objects, people, and times, one in which every object or time or even human component counts equally, irrespective of any ranking. Every Catholic child has been through that sweetly confusing age of twinges of conscience when budding sexual fantasies and equally budding religious notions chase each other around: we said our prayers with Greuze tears[8] in our eyes and felt that God would excuse us for the female portrait, the one carried around in one's pocketbook. Anyone who did not experience those partly uneasy, partly idyllic self-apologies knows little about love. Casanova's sincere sermon and sincere adolescent boy's eroticism fit alongside one another in his soul — that is what makes him childish. At this point moral insanity and Loyolan furor hover in balance — perhaps the finest sentimental and moral moment. One continually has the feeling that Casanova has a right to preach; something completely logical and completely free of hypocrisy is going on here. *God* wishes that the sermon should not be delivered by a bearded St. John in the wilderness but by a love-stricken Venetian young rascal in a periwig and without genuine faith: the whole religion is thereby cozier, more human, truer. After making his sermon, Casanova got a bagful of love-letters from female admirers; they straightaway smuggle into the sacristy.

Why should it be impossible and out of the question to label this as: frivolousness? How do we dare to say that the gondolaing *settecento* was religious, maybe because there is greater morality in this post-carnival ease? That it is all "I'll go to confession and have done with it!" because everything is in Pauline contrition-versus-ecstasy? Because man is somehow so incestuously warm, somehow in an intimately *fait accompli* position with God: that God seeks to fall into the gossip net of human life, and this is where it happened. A Calvinist holding God at arm's length and a baroque-Roman palling-up to God are probably equally bad extremes, but my theological heart mooches around the latter with unquenchable nostalgia.

The scene itself is unforgettable: a church next to the water like a swimming box of relics, the steps meeting the green paludial liquid like coins which have slipped just a nuance further out from an overturned stack of money; prows jammed together, gondolas lurch in one place around the gate like miff-necked black swans around an invisible morsel — the church is small, the whole thing no more than a boudoir, the women, in their balloon silks, thrown on each other — the lagoon's marsh reek, an oily fish smell billowing out from the eating-houses, many perfumes and stifling hard fumes of incense concentrated into a single Catholic dogma: that's Casanova's world. This is the image added to which I always imagine Miracoli.[9] When one first sees it: *from behind.* Thank goodness, we have such an entirely cost-free key to the reality-nature of reality: one must glimpse such magnificent edifices for the first time from the back, the 'bad' perspective. This is Santa Maria dei Miracoli: at one moment a powder-box at the edge of a green washbasin, the next moment (with its Byzantine artichoke cupolas) the new St. Mark's church, a celestial Constantinople.

In cupolated buildings like this the high, smooth walls almost outgrow the height of the cupolas, with the green Orthodox cones falling between the shoulders. They are always falling; the five or six cupolas hurriedly shrink as if Orthodoxy were doubling the perspective, were hastening them to double. Casanova's childhood sermon has grown together with this in my memory, and that too is symbolical: just like the miracle boudoir and Constantinople, so even Casanova's young days of the intensification of sweetest intimacy with the world right up till the fateful journey ("*ich muss... ich muss...*" [10]) to Byzantium.

12. Giulietta is twelve, girl X eleven, Y thirteen. All of them, however, are ripe for love; they are just as much cut out for dreams as for marriage. Nowhere are children of so mystical a hue as here. They are at once angelic and delicacies bred for voluptuaries, but they could not be otherwise for if they were just one thing, they would hardly be worth anything. Casanova perfectly unites voluptuousness with a completely sublime, divine naturalism — the shading of the one into the other gives charm & philosophical romanticism to his manner of making love. 'Youth' would by now be a pathetic blunder: children are what is needed. With Casanova, this too, as with anything else, stems from the most primitive logic of nature; it is not something random. There is undoubtedly something perverse in the cult of the child, but Casanova asserts that if we now live in a civilization, then a certain perversity is part of our underlying character: it has to be accepted like the air we breathe.

13. "*Geräusch von Ruderschlägen...*" [11] — this the first place that he makes a reference to water: Venetian waters overflow the whole world for the first time through this absurd little fragment of a

sentence. We are still too close to the Miracoli for us not to think of the water besides the church.

This water is heavy, oily, sluggish: it is impossible to distinguish the torpid slapping of fish on the steps, the weary sweep of the oars, and the greasy, faltering rise & fall of the waves. Stagnation here has become a mystery; the gondoliers prod the tortoise-dream waves and wavelets from in front of the prows of the gondolas almost like bricks. Nor does the gondola itself 'proceed' — the movement of the gondolas is more a form of vegetation of water and quagmire-reflex short of motion. The color: sometimes it has a grayness more neutral than the stone of the town, sometimes it is an unexpected green mirror, and on such occasions it draws the height of the houses into itself with infinite verticality, transparency, and magnetic suction force.

As if the palaces were trembling in the air in their own mirror ghosts — the water disappears entirely in the abstract frenzy of reflection. Here even the mooring posts stand in nothingness, like the eternal embers of sightlessness before the Creation. This too is an Italian game, a European precept, and Casanova soul: this darting to and fro from the slime into the mirror, from diluvial snoring into Gothic glassblowing. No longer water and not yet street: a secretive urbanity of this enigmatic Venetian element. Everything has to be related to this — *water* and Renaissance, *water* and periwig, *water* and ballet, *water* and *concerti grossi*, *water* and mass, *water* and love. Of how little concern, how much a nonentity is the water here to the inhabitants, yet there is nothing but water, and everything disappears in it. What is civilization in it, what myth-steam Atlantic?

Its fetidness and malarial breath, the typical decay of a town, or the Egyptian warmth of the mud pillows of sleeping crocodiles? Only we have such 'decadent' questions, not Casanova. Childhood happiness; the water carries one from one palace to the next: fine the first time, the next time no other way is possible.

14. He declares that he will serve woman. He is well aware that this is the sole form of love in society which will guarantee satisfaction: — with one party serving, the other being master. It would have been truly good if Casanova had written that scene in Mozart's *Don Giovanni* where Leporello in disguise sings that Don Giovanni is indeed the master, while he is just the servant. 'Spiritual harmony' and 'physical understanding' — nonsense. There is no love without the master and servant assignment. Either the man is master and the woman a submissive slave, or the woman is Semiramis, and the man a terrorized instrument.

The personal valet or the complicit maidservant: that is as far as it goes; the remaining division of social roles is rotten and misleading humbug. In love one has to give the orders, but ordering another is only sweet, and submission a delight, when in both the one and the other there is more purely legal than physical or mental motive. All idyllic poison of 'secretiveness' is sweeter here than anywhere else. If the mistress enthroned at the head of the table and the lackey who serves are in an illicit relationship, that is more thrilling than if she is in a liaison with one of the guests and is hiding it. Yet the small psychological perversion of a secret is an indispensable article of pleasure in civilization.

A liaison sweetly scrambles the thought of the slavery of Antiquity and of the Christian equality of man. But what is important everywhere is these indefinable 'scrambles' — and Casanova is the celestial apologist for this. In his time slavery still existed, and in the Levant one could still obtain a woman or child for money, and Venice was: the Levant, Venice was: Turkey. Is there anything more gratifying than to talk something over with the valet or chambermaid? What kind of mysterious thing is a valet? On the one hand, an automaton, a dumb machine, nothing more than an item of furniture — on the other, the repository of all the family secrets, a magical store of psychology and medical science.

It is not worth talking anything over with the parents or the gods — but it is with 'Tony' or 'Esther.' How sweetly social frameworks decay in valet-mistress or chambermaid-baronet relationships like this; and this bit of decay is more natural than nature. The finest novel must have been in the time when novels were still being written in which all that we know about a family's life is learned from midnight conversations in the servants' quarters, and where love, with Casanovan intolerance of faith, was equated solely with the master-servant relationship.

15. After trial runs with children and trial runs with servants, a fresh game and seriousness; what is conspicuous in the book is the vast number of occasions on which Casanova restrains his instincts: whether out of childhood cowardice or amorous respect or just plain common sense.

Those, roughly speaking, are the three reasons which figure, but he uses them time and time again. Without such radiant, restless, charming and tragic asceticism the world would be a torso. Asceticism is, of course, also a way for intensifying ecstasy, piquancy & deception, but in spite of that it remains a magnificent moral pirouette. Nowhere else is a greater urgency of gratification sensed, but equally nowhere is this the elegance, even grandeur, of boyish good manners, decorum, or rococo posing. The manner flashes here like a Syrian jewel; etiquette here, for all its charm, is often a grim dance of death — Casanova is in fact more than once on the verge of passing out. These long-continued periods of continence attended him for a goodly stretch of his life — though always leaving the coruscating paradox of: increasing sensuality, an increasing dance of death.

The fact is that a certain asceticism is just as decisive an element of the diary as freedom: it is precisely through their grandiose self-restraint that his greatest 'loves' roar over into Rousseau. Because Casanova is a Rousseau first and a Voltaire after.

16. "Nature first and foremost, not a gnawing, fiddling cerebral eunuch." One wavers for a while: is this the self-defensiveness of a banal epicure, or is it an 18th-century philosopher's *philosophical* anti-philosophy? The latter it soon emerges. There may be something in the nature of an unpleasant bluff about forcing a philosopher out of Casanova — but then there is no need for force: he is one without that. No one else is so splendid or could give such monumentality to the century's naturalism as he could. He gave style to a verity, and intellectualized a lifestyle once and for all.

Casanova is not an adventure so much as thought. Whenever he speaks of nature: one can sense these three layers — the comfort of the epicure, the childishly greedy naturalism of the philosophy of those days, and finally the lonely Learish, Leonardoesque death that is to be accomplished in nature. And this supreme poetic or mythical layer completely swallows up the other two.

It is irrefutably proclaimed to eternity that Park intimates more about the metaphysical figures of the gods than he did about the rainforest. We are now at the very essence of Casanova, his before-and-after-all-else *intellectual* character. This whole life (or, to be more exact: *book* about the life) could only be pulled off by having a thought functioning in it, not some dream or physical desire. A swindler could not have been so successful, only a philosopher. As I say, I take on a huge comic element when I seek to make a *"Versuch einer Mythologie"* with Casanova (insofar as I stylize him into a mythical figure of a philosophy-denying, nature-*philosophizing* mythical figure), but after briefly weighing the matter up I knew that it was worth accepting this. I sensed, with both mind and senses, that there was an ecstatic, maybe even tragic love of reality in Casanova's "nature before philosophy" type of pronouncements, and that philosophizing is annihilated into long-deserved nothingness — this is not a matter of playing games but of a trembling confession of faith from conviction. That life undoubtedly delimited reality's extreme bounds of irrationality; it was an enormous, almost supernatural ornamentation — it is fate's secret that in the end it was nevertheless fulfilled for us as a book, as art, as fiction, so as to excite us forevermore. So did literature make Casanova into a life, or did life force him into literature?

The dizzying victory of thought is to be found in Volume 2, when he converses with Mademoiselle Waisan in the hotel room at night. Casanova is delighted to see that the girl becomes quite philosophical.

It is clear that he is not greeting the snob or bluestocking or intellectual in her, but it is also clear that he does not drop in the word "philosopher" as a jest or out of conversational irony. Casanova means it in all earnest, the one thing that he takes seriously. He also sets to defining the essence of philosophy; that was more important to him than swift mating — but, on the other hand, the entire man was so destructively anti-paper that we have no need to fear that he will be seen as an impotent little teacher.

When the girl asks how a man becomes a philosopher he says with Elizabethan curtness: *"one thinks."*
Right through life, what is more, and one never finishes.
In other words, the distinction between thought and life
is lost: a life that is worth calling a life is thought, in any
case, and if a thought has some rational attraction, then
it was life from the very start, not some conceptual trim-
ming to percepts. This had not been heard so categorically, so irrefutably, from anyone's lips. What will be the
end of this unbroken "thinking with life"? Not a system,
but happiness. Of course, happiness retains its special
18th-century style, but human life's eternal goal & kernel
frets under this fine mask in its own eternal moon- or
sunlight: the universality of the primeval, offbeat search
for happiness. Where is such a logical, tragically determined and yet rococoishly free-and-easy relationship
to be found between eternal thinking and happiness?

We may slip too readily into a little 'Enlightenment'
cabaret for a moment when he considers that the pushing
aside of 'prejudices' is the most important precondition
for the procurement of happiness — this 'prejudice' is
an Enlightenment bogeyman, but then Casanova immediately draws her into his own absolutely secure intellectual splendor when he decides that prejudice is an obliga-
tion that we do not see as being firmly rooted in nature.

What Casanova means by nature here is whatever
can forever remain for European man from all religions of
nature, medical science, and petty philosophy; anything
of religion and philosophy about it being compromised

until now by Demeter & Diderot, has disappeared here; what is left is reality from a true humanistic point of view. That is precisely what is wonderful in it: this is the salvation of poetry, simplicity alien to religion, untrammeled by philosophy. If there is any reality for man, that is how I am able to imagine it, that is how I want it, and it is sure that we shall never find anything better than Casanova's demonic and rococo puritanism in our grubbing-up of *Untergang-fellahness.*[12] It was here that the European concept of nature attained its one and only classicism.

"Who, then, is an ideal philosopher?" — asks the mademoiselle. Casanova, who a long time before declared: *"Ich habe Platon gelesen,"*[13] responds, naturally enough: "Socrates." That name is more of decorative significance here (from which we are often obliged to suppose that it is a plus and not a minus) — it is important, of histori-comelodic importance, that Casanova, associated as he is with frivolity, should merge, once and for all time, with a philosopher's body — henceforth we are reading the Memoirs of Socrates; 'Casanova' is just a mask-grimace on Socrates' Venetian brow.

In this entire conversation, Casanova's tenor is so eerily secure, both stylistically and logically, that even his scorn for metaphysics (*"Metaphysik… daraus mache ich mir nichts…"*[14]) topples him from the symposium stage into the salon world of some kind of chattering petty rationalism. *"Alles ist Natur"* — one can almost hear Mozart's supreme aria for the Queen of the Night from the *Magic Flute* in a Casanovan marriage of curse and trill

— and whoever does not believe in this 'Natur' can only expect to be: *"verstossen sei auf ewig, verlassen sei auf ewig, zertrümmert sein auf ewig alle Bande der Natur, verstossen, verlassen und zertrümmert alle Bande der Natur…"* [15]

I shall have to point more than a few times to this deeper circulation (as if we were fern jellyfish of the lagoon under the residences of Grimani and Foscari) between Mozart and Casanova in the course of this catechism.

"Morality is just the metaphysics of physics": this statement, too, is at first merely the paper materialism of a Holbach or La Mettrie, but it is more than that after Casanova's whole youth, streaming forth from a Venice slaked in Paris — much more. We know that in Casanova there is a good deal more vulgar sniping at the clergy than is necessary — but not in this case. This statement might be a Keatsian metaphor, if you will: morality has the scent of nature, the mysterious, poetic aroma of existence, the shade of flowers in a May shower of rain, the opium fumes of poppies, the brain's free flights of fancy, lyrical holidays. Morality is the *'futur indéfini'* tense or *je ne sais quoi* of: very natural nature, something between convention and the Aldobrandini labyrinth.

At any rate, morality is, in essence and in aim: poetry. 'Metaphysics of physics' — that is a melismatic trick that I feel obliged to construe in a different way: here the particle 'meta' is distancing gobbledygook, the sure repose of old age in the eternally uncertain. 'Old age' — yes, for Casanova is twenty-four by now. Because this apologist for sensuality, like every truly great voluptuary: is well aware of the dreadful pleasures of the mind, of dreaming and illusion, every brutish refinement of "sleep & poetry." [16] "... *dann verschafft die Phantasie neue Freuden*" [17] — and elsewhere the Proustian dogma of: "*Wonnen der Erinnerung.*" [18] — What might the last commandment be for the missy before being bedded in the hotel? "*Denken sie*" — think. Casanova is not a connoisseur for nothing: so saying he administers the biggest aphrodisiacs to the girl.

17. Casanova spends the month of September at a country villa in Pasiano. He tosses in the crucial concepts with his usual nonchalance and dogmatism — anyone who wishes can concoct from it a way of life or perfume of myths. What are its ingredients, then? The first couple are: "*Trunkenheit und Furcht.*" Then, eerily simple: "September," and finally "*elf Nächte*," [19] or in other words counted & numbered nights. Here finitude whips itself up into joy, or joy into finitude, by healthily excluding any vulgarity of the "*Ewigkeit im nu*" kind.

What is needed is a villa in the country, in a specified village, on specified days of a specified month. These ingredients fit together, like a marvelous drawing, like charming aquatic plants, obedient to the magnetic eddies in the water: the Italian autumn and a tucked-away villa (the whole 'Casino' mood throughout the book up to the *non plus ultra* of Murano), the drunkenness and the number eleven, the fear and the specific word 'Pasiano.'

Love is the ultra-local flower of a single place and time: it exists only there, a millimeter further on it no longer exists. A few of the world's scattered elements for a moment, heaven knows why, coalesce: that's love. The woman is just a small punctuation in the matter, a pleasant, insignificant adornment. A chance stiffening of the world's heterogeneity: *that* is love. There is just one ideal constellation: a solitary little place in the Italian countryside, September and eleven successive nights.

Eleven successive nights and a city is no longer love but psychology or matrimony or lust or liaison, some dabbling mimicry, anyway. That is something that has to be learned from Casanova: that it is always necessary to want something quite specific in love, something quite practical or, if you will, quite *prosaic* in order that the latter should be liberated in all its myth-trumping run-wild magic. The root of every poetic type of joy is a matter of *prosaic* discussion and agreement: an exact contract with the cook, precise deals with the inn's proprietor, a practical, civilized harmony of armchairs, beds, window latches and discounted return fares. The moon's *raison d'être* is: a warm scarf; love's *raison d'être*: sheets of such and such quality, because cotton '*Fil d'Égypte*' is too coarse and the worsted fabric of 'Lanatex' too silky, and both irritate the skin: anyone not in possession of the totality of these *prosaic* facts, or in other words a sort of 'pure poet' — is always just a half-poet, and if he is simply half, then a fraud, liar, and dilettante.

The greatest mythic chance, poetry, ecstasy, happiness-nullity, is based on: technique, arrangement, and calculation; it is something that just has to be done; it has to be constructed. Casanova's finest lesson is to have dispatched this music-hall contradiction once and for all into the world of asinine shadow-play as "poetry" and "prose," "Orphic rapture" and "level-headed technical scheme." In place of these two non-existent entities there is a third — in Casanova everything in general just *is*, with no nebulous preludes and swaggering codas —, a glittering, natural working part.

With Casanova a lemon and slice of ham (at long last there is also true 'heroic play' in literature) are not 'nature' nor even a 'still life,' not a yellow seal to the anathematized South, not a flashy and saint-bugging naturalist program as with an impotent Rabelais epigone: no — in his eyes poetry, program, image and metaphor are more vulgar than death, a Casanova-less *ad-hominem* argument of *demos* — lemon and ham are precisely lemon and ham, pleasant, somewhat colored, somewhat tasty comestibles. What a huge triumphant value there is in an ordinary person saying of that 'ham' that it is 'nice' — as opposed to the muslin-winged neuron twanging of how a poet or a Greek god would declaim it, to say nothing of Dutch still-life painters. Should we put it into words quite bluntly? That: poetry must sometimes, to put it very simply, die? That it must be devilishly incurably compromised? It sounds disagreeable, but it is something along those lines: poetry and love exclude each other.

Love is pure worldliness, a purely practical question and function, a Baconian experiment *sans* empiricist poses: in love things never 'mean' anything because only 'non-existent' things have an awkward habit of 'meaning' something, and covering up their nude figure of non-existence fairly hopelessly in that semantic alibi; in love things are either good or bad, useless or favorable, always means to a possibly more satisfying joy, but they have no independent value, beauty or sense.

The Italian autumn is no mystery. As with autumn generally: it comes with the duality of ripening and withering. Ripening, therefore, was ostentatious classicism in an open-handed world — withering, yet another encore for anarchy among the other tried-and-tested. Is an Italian autumn, therefore, a sibling or enemy of the Florentine Renaissance? Did it, like death, undo senile Brunelleschi, or on the contrary, does autumn, turning brown, happen to be called Brunelleschi in Italian? How is 'ripeness is all' realized in this part of the world? What does it have to do with love and Toscanini, that form-shaping monkey? Does September sit well on Italy or is it a fancy dress? Now or never? And what about autumn to Venice? After all, Casanova is a pseudonym, his face a mask — it is always just a lagoon which is hallucinating in the book.

Italy and autumn, September & Renaissance. The mysterious relationship between a concert by Toscanini and crumbling leaf-mold was portrayed most splendidly in *The Death of Adonis*, a painting by Sebastiano del

Piombo. The picture's dream-rest plays out in three planes. In the foreground are three massive nude figures, especially one of the women, who with her spiral hair-lines immediately sets off the themes of Eros and autumn — her erotic softness, the languidity of a peach, is a bigger death than that of Adonis in the same way that, as a rule, it is the mourners who die, not those who are laid out in state.

In the second plane is the stretched-out figure of Adonis, like a temporal wave *interruptus*, the whole thing no more than a ripple, the froth of a dream: finally, in the background, but at the very front in terms of value, is Venice with a slightly stylized Doge's palace and Campanile below a sticky, taffeta-like sky garnished with sections of black leafy boughs. Is it not a fantastically daring idea to express the Tristan-rotting of love and autumn with the Doge's palace? To make leaf litter, a brown birth mark, a medlar tree transience, out of Gothic make-up plastered on a whore.

Was del Piombo not the only one who managed to unify into an irrational vision the Toscanini classicism of autumn and sickness, which tramples all into mud, marshy leaf-mould, and slimy moss? A mysterious reflection of identity between form and perishing. The nude itself, by being lovely and in love, is already autumn; if it's a woman, then she is undoubtedly September as well. What wonderful fellowship the big black sections of black leafy boughs and the Doge's palace have come into, and finally the leaves themselves, a horse chestnut

secret: the most important staging post in the chromaticism of Casanova's Venice.

In an autumn that is to be understood in this manner, Casanova spends *eleven* successive nights. He always
counts up the nights, the days, the hours spent in love:
love does not run all over the world but ferments in the
closed tumblers of numbered nights. We know that the
greatest pleasure in the second night is precisely the
fact that it is the second; the five in the fifth, the eleven
in the eleventh: the number is always a number. It is
one of the most accessible guarantees of unhappiness in
love if the possibility of a last assignation is utterly uncertain — it might be tomorrow, it might be in two years'
time —, that kind of thing is nothing. The game starts
where the whole thing unwinds within a predetermined
tight timescale.

A conscientious commentator can only touch the
duality of *"Trunkenheit und Furcht"* with great repug-
nance because it all resembles some sorts of mythological states of mind with ridiculous exactness — a Dionysian rapture and chthonic demons, whereas Casanova is
very consciously parodying these: he is plain drunk and
plain cheering it on without any of the Greek ringworm.
When just before I praised his counting of the nights
that, too, was salutary from an anti-Hellenic standpoint:
the number slightly cools possible *Night-Thoughts*:[20]
and these would be superfluous beastlinesses in what
was, in the end, a successful civilization.

18. *"Wahre Liebe macht immer zurückhaltend"*:[21] if Casanova were not occasionally nervous, if his psychology were not at times like his periwig, he could not have had the complete formula for love. When Casanova is in love, he is reticent, stammers, is afraid, is uneasy and commits clumsy blunders — and that does not simply make for piquant situations, but it is the rule. Casanova is fond of nobility of mind and the thousand tearful lies of sentimentality, high pathos, the little hypocrisies of manners and, above all, virtue.

Everything which makes him reticent and helpless, in other words. Only with him are things like ascetic gentlemanliness, golden-red choked lyricism, and groping under the table not strange: virtue, poetry, and perversion are self-explanatory identities. With him nothing is *separate*: 'separates' of this kind are the troubled world of art, lack of cultivation and art — with him a shoe heel is straight away *esprit*, the moral charm of virginity straightaway mutual narcissism, beauty straightaway *raison*, and the black paradoxes of the soul straight away figures in a minuet as well.

In connection with Casanova it is comical even to imagine anything like one of his women being beauty, a second, mundaneness, a third, lechery, a fourth, benevolence, a fifth, sentimentality, a sixth, domesticity and so forth: with him each one of them is whole, everything simultaneously; the sole difference is in the order, in the polyphonic treatment of the qualities.

19. Love is concealing oneself, secrets, lies, deception in civilization. From it a poet and moralist is able to coin for himself 'tragedy,' which is Greek for dotage. For Casanova, however, it is the animating force, the very lifeblood.

At night, when one's fate hangs on whether or not someone left the key in the lock or hung it up on a nail; when three candles are burning or just one on a balcony; when one has to flatten against the wall in the stairwell and leave the stolen cloak of a stranger on the coat hook; when one has to creep from one room to another along deserted soul passages: well, that is the world where there are two dominants — the lie & the object. Never did lamp, handkerchief, key, candlestick, stocking, sword, hat, seat or plate hold so splendid a triumph as in this trick atmosphere. Here too Casanova is 'absurd,' like everything which is in some way a thought: love is always the bond of a lie and an object: someone believes something which is pure eyewash, and a lamp is confoundedly precisely a lamp.

A woman again just provides a *"pastose Akkordik"* as I read in a book about Schubert, for the all-reducing topic of lie and object. Was it not this duo that our childhood memories held most parsimoniously? One always had to lie to one's parents, and fate always hinged upon a hat ribbon and flower. As well as on the arrangement of a dwelling, the relationship of the rooms to each other. *That* world, in the entire thrilling profundity of worldliness — that, all of a sudden, the bedroom could not be made use of because, after Granny's death, the big chest of drawers had been pushed right in front of it; that the mirror standing in the corner was crooked and it was possible to hug and kiss behind it; that the relatives, had they gone out to the theatre, would dine afterwards in a hostelry, but after a concert they would be back home, so that rendezvous could be set accordingly: in other words, love always faced some immeasurable ephemerality, some absolutely momentary fortuity and *not* God, a woman, or nature.

One is well acquainted with Europe's frolicking twins, one of whom is customarily nicknamed "this world," the other as "otherworld." By "this world" is understood Nature, stars, & flowers, the big *furor* of "*élan vital*" and the black tic of enthusiastic death, Paracelsian grand demonism of existence — and by "otherworld" religion, the great mythological review of gods and their moral shades, the despairing heavenly masks of eternity.

As one looks at the definition of "worldly," one knows that — Casanova cannot be familiar with such things, either separately in & of themselves and even less set in antithesis.

To him "this world" was not an animated grand nature, but a street two canals from the Chiesa di San Moisè, three camellias on the table instead of a lamp, exactly eleven thousand liras and exactly ten minutes to 11: not, not, not "existence," not "time," not "freedom." In just the same way, "otherworldly" was not an intolerable cargo of myths but at most a temporary shudder, a canalized Masonic hocus-pocus, a wee brooding horror, and that's all — after all, he had the fiery & transparent key of metaphysics in his hands: happiness. Happiness, which never knew, and never will know, the "worldly" and "otherworldly," Nature and God, laicism and theology — since only unhappiness makes distinctions, only a cripple "specifies": joy is unitary, and he found everything within himself. That is why he wrote such symbolically succulent sentences: "*Diese metaphysische Kurve erschien mir widernatürlich zu sein...*"[22]

20. The thing had a tiny wee charm about it in that Casanova, all at once, nevertheless constructed a theory out of his own non-theoretical realism — before he became a doctor of law at Padua he writes a dissertation in which he attempts to prove something along the lines that things about which man can have only an abstract conception cannot occur in reality. At first glance, it irritates us all to wonder to what end had Casanova despoiled his virginity so clumsily, but then one becomes reconciled to it as an adolescent may still be found without narcissus or woman, but never without a *thesis*. Unto Cæsar, the things which are Cæsar's.

21. But then he immediately refutes the matter — he opens in his diary the one true series of embraces, which is always preceded by a splendid banquet. Superb cheeses, salads, hams, roasted venison, Levantine or southern French wines. Here too one

would be courting complete failure if one were to perceive either just gourmandism or Renaissance naturalism. Casanova is anti-romantic; his bones are dry, his skin is parched and his blood, ascetic, his profile — Avilan, that is precisely why he can be passionate, truly shriveled of sentiment: pathos does not loosen but desiccates, like Syrian *karst* under the Syrian killer.

When as a prelude to love he gets ready wine from Cyprus and Italian cheese, he has not the slightest intention of flaunting some theatrical, anti-spiritual gesture — as Toscanini (an undying association in connection with Casanova from the viewpoint of self-torturing rigidity) said, just play exactly what is written in the score, or in other words he is not troubled by any myth of intellectual 'form,' so too Casanova only does exactly what is written in the notes of the body and nature, neither more, nor less. That mathematical 'point,' that algebraically split-off 'just,' is the sublime, the Italian, the classical in him: the Florence!

Eating soaked with good wine is a precondition for success in love, so let's eat and drink if we embark on physical capers; the body has to be brought into good shape, that's all. Here the Cyprus wine is also symbolic: Cyprus is crammed with Venus-underworld tree and boudoir-island associations; how fitting that there it is not a legend, or poetry, but *a drink*. "*Ciprus*": [23] for that word to have some point, murky associations may be enough, but for it to be the whole point it has to hit the stomach. Casanova is able to place myth, thought, and poetry in the composition-steeled orchestra of his world: there can be only association, only aroma — a thought is a volatile oil, a spice, the hint of a taste, whether a tang of lemon or marjoram: who would be so crazy as to eat a stew of cloves?

22. Thus to another essential point: the amorous trio of Angela, Nannetta, & Martina. If one were to examine the business superficially, one would say: it is the defense case for polygamy. Defense case?

Such a thing is inconceivable with Casanova. Here things may possibly transpire magnificently, with a truth shining out of them, "if they did not transpire that way, the whole thing would be worth nothing" — but this is an anti-theoretical light, never propaganda. Casanova falls in love first with Angela, then — *logically*! not on a whim — her sisters; these sisters yield to Casanova in the same manner, without jealousy and, indeed, even allowing themselves some sort of lesbian or quasi-lesbian second themes.

Three features are essential, then: it is an ancient human affair to fall in love with one's sibling, and if one does not have one, then to dream up a fictive sibling and love that like a musical variation; according to Casanova, an inclination to polygamy is just as much an ancient matter, & if that could not be achieved freely, love degrades irretrievably into psychologies and is perverted into morals; finally: every man desires some quiet lesbian waft around his love, because in that he sees an echo of his own notion of a woman, a woman who gazes at a woman like he, a man, does.

A requirement for a sibling, a requirement for polygamy, a lesbian requirement: in none of this was there any decadence, cheap poetic sponginess, let alone a principle. After all, when he travels to Constantinople and becomes acquainted with the life of a harem: one thousand things come to mind, but there is not even a hint of an apology for the institution of the harem, though in contrast he just as instinctively defends Christian morality as against the bourgeoisified *Tales of 1001 Nights*. Because in Casanova it is not odalisque-suppleness which is at work but a rigor which does not acknowledge *Arabia deserta* quibbling. If the bare truth is that a sister is also needed, and at least two or more women simultaneously, and those in such a way that the two women should be able blithely to know about the parallelism, indeed should both sleep together with the man: in that case for Casanova there are no words to be wasted on either morality or biology, it is something that must be done.

If a person should wish for the most attainable happiness. Here the emphasis is not on 'laws of nature' — such 'left-wing' twaddle is only said by Casanova out of abstractedness — here it is a matter of happiness! On earth this is the only way you can be happy with women — that afterwards you may incur eternal damnation or become a professor of physiology, even of psychoanalysis, those are insignificant matters, he did no more than assess the pure facts.

If one examines in oneself the two aspects, morality and poetry, which are not in Casanova, what does one find in them? In morality tragic obsessions, in poetry a peacock-plumed impotence. That, it goes without saying, is not at all to belittle either morality or the beauty of poetry: it is just that these aspects come a cropper from a *mathematical* standpoint of a happiness which excludes all else, whereas it is left to everyone's individual taste and ability whether or not one dares to illuminate life from the murderous focus of happiness with such *ascetic* harsh consequentiality as Casanova. Fidelity, gratitude, self-sacrifice — those are not worldly matters, whereas love itself is worldly, so that the sources of happiness can never be. Every Bacchic, Rubensian, and vitalist trait is lacking totally and forever from Casanova. For him the "worldly rough-and-tumble" is not *"Diesseitstaumel"* (the German affirmation, in contrast to the Italian, is already an otherworldly, sick swanking), but a bare fact, a *factum nudissimum*, yet with the greatest disgust towards every formulated *"Faktizität"* and *"Nudität."* He asserts, with facts, that one type of woman makes a man happy: that is the Nannetta and Martina type, or in other words, women who could just as little be called harlots as gentlewomen: instead of those two good-for-nothings an ideal third. Just as it is not corporeality nor even spirituality, but likewise a third, "exactly what is written in the score," not pure instrument-banter, nor even metaphysical profundity, but simply the music.

Thereby, out of the alternative of "adventure" and "grand passion" will be more: instead of that something better, the sole good, will reign. Anyone who finds merely corporeality in Casanova: is a fantasizer — Casanova seeks to be *happy*, pathetically, completely, tear-jerkingly, sobbingly, nervously, and also sentimentally happy, but for that physical technique and fortunate groups of women are needed.

Aretino's *Postures in Love*, and for those Casanova's so-called 'adventures' are the same as Brunelleschi's plans in architecture: a triumph of *mathesis*, a triumph of form, rigor, discipline, the victory of Mohammedan geometrical representation. If it is monotonous or tautologous, what do I care: one must continually emphasize that Casanova is the Brunelleschi of love, not its Rubens. If someone hit upon the essence, its deadly structure, he adheres to that: here Casanova hit upon desire for siblings, desire for polygamy, and desire for lesbianism in its trinity, and for that, in his eyes every soul, lyric, marriage and morality had to lose — fripperies, unhappinesses, prevarications.

There is a crystal-clear, pellucid, vernal Satanism in it all: the anti-romanticism of a skeleton. Because this is the love of a skeleton, not of the flesh: we are in the neighborhood of Africa. From this standpoint Casanova's health is also interesting: he says a hundred times if he says once that he was perfectly healthy, he was blessed with the greatest possible physical agility, etc. — a fitness that even in a layman's eyes seems more mechanical than physical, more abstract than something sensory:

it is no longer body, but the 'idea' of body decanted with Renaissance drawing-off, a cold, near-preternatural, deathly function.

But this is the heart of classicism, of classicisms, & hence of love, this death-like feeling for the essence and, doing penance there — with insane persistence romanticism stuck its indiscreet *proboscis* into graves & underworlds and gurgled out from them a slimy, barely-life: classicism, with Casanova, this Toledan 'sec'[24] madman at its head, sought life with its smoldering Arab rationalism, and in its place found unfeeling, untheatrical, ungodly, ordinary death. How natural it is when, in a later chapter, he thinks back on the nights shared with Nannetta & Martina, juxtaposes statements like: "...*bei meinen beiden Engeln*," and "...*meine erste Liebe*":[25] referring to *two* women in the singular, "my first *love*" and not "my first *loves*": as what is important is not that it is one woman or twenty-one but complete happiness. Men and especially women will gnaw away at their own monogamous suicide theories until the end of the world — that is their business; Casanova is not handing out tips.

This is an even more typical type of jealousy-free amorous co-existence, acted out with more than one woman, indeed more than one man, when a mature woman herself offers the immature and as yet chaste younger sister in the pavilion of a Tivoli orange grove: the woman is madly in love with Casanova, and, far from excluding, *logically* demands that her younger sister should make love with Casanova before her very eyes.

The copious psychology *one day* had to cease *this way*: not through mythicized corporeality nor even cynical sensuality, but this cheerfully, in a civilized manner, ceremoniously. Because this is the main point: that all this immorality is *not* a revolution but form, not the plunging-back of bodies into chaos, but a sonata. We know that this "Tivoli orangery"[26] may only have been possible juſt once, but Casanova, by his eerie consent, knows that love could only be good like that; in his view the reſt was clinical misery, a putrid proletarian sickness.

The ultimate intensification, of course, is the "Murano quadrille": the love quartet of Casanova, M.M., C.C., and de Bernis in the mirror-lined boudoir.[27] Here again one is ſtaggered by the Latin virtuosity, the Toscanini precision: everything possible from Arcadia's freedom and from civilization's shackles here plays out intertwined the counterpoint to its own *danse macabre.* "If for once the wife would not kill the lover but go with him into her husband's room — if the mother for once would not deny her daughter" on account of a boy but with him would show her daughter new embraces — these could be, and would be, the world's baseſt, moſt atrocious, moſt taſteless desires, but these desires are conſtant presences in everybody and moſtly unconfessed torturing secrets that are taken to the grave; Casanova shed light on them and (this is the main point) lived accordingly without any dithyrambic posing.

D. H. Lawrence's half-drunken Quaker buffoon, or Sigmund Freud's hypochondriac subworld founder of a religion: ludicrous residues of a bygone culture in which Casanova's *abstract* reason was the center. Casanova knows everything: either "Tivoli orangery" or "Murano quadrille" (I can almost see Toscanini's monkey head and conductor's stiletto), in which case you will know what the *one and only* possible amorous happiness is, or fate has denied you the chance and you will be a Lawrentian Pulcinello or Freudian Scaramouch.

It is very good if one reads this Casanova precisely when one is living in a monogamy which, from the standpoint of romance, has been phrased to ruin, when, in a kind of good, post-Casanovan, mongrel fashion, one is in love with: one grows together with a *single* face. Physically one will feel what an absurdity a love of this kind is, what a botch-work of lies; how the finest morals and most splendid body-constellations are mere neurasthenias besides those 'orangeries' & 'quadrilles.' Until a person has become aware of the uniformity of a *single* face and sickness he will not even suspect what nonsense is love, which is just a post-Romantic tradition of neurosis.

23. Just as the deepest sense does not arise from the orchestra where the conductor is a scholar, or has preached the angels' aesthetic, but where the maestro is familiar with all of the bassoonist's technical tricks of the trade and knows what timbre of gut strings can be obtained from which village's pigs: so too in love everything is a matter of *technique*, the rest is rubbish.

For exactly that reason we should not forget the possibilities of Casanovan trios and quartets, the first and last fundamental metaphysical fact: those immensely wide, mammoth beds in inns which were in general use in Italy in the 18th century. Without such places: Arcadia, Lesbos, and jealousy-free polygamy would have fizzled out. And the lighting: always a candle, one or two, or a big candelabra, but in all events candles.

How much follows from that — from the technique, the gesture, and the duration of lighting the candles and snuffing them out, from the instability of light, from the drops of wax and the odor. What a scale: when, for example, among five candles someone prepares to extinguish the last one. When the light is also fire, not just illumination; indeed, more fire than illumination. Imagine: a single *gigantic* sheet Sahara and a single sputtering candle; nothing more. Likewise a matter of technique, a mixture of bashfulness & total paralysis of shame: they blush gracefully but perform their ablutions in front of each other. To 'accustom' people to that would be: stupid beyond stupidity. It was a Casanovan moment in the history of civilization: there was no more — *historia* non *est magistra vitæ*, history is *not* life's tutor,[28] would people just take note of that at last. — And another technical aspect: let us speak about hotel layouts, not leaping fauns in Crete's barbarian woodlands, for at this time Italian innkeepers, with incomprehensible ease, pitched strangers into shared rooms: a trivial habit like that is always more important than any other amatory ornament.

24. Let me contradict myself — Casanova may indeed be the embodiment of every negation of amatory symbols and loathing of symbols, yet notwithstanding that let me note two words, which, like it or not, are amatory symbols: *"Das Päkchen enthielt ein Stück Wachs, mit dem Abdruck eines Schlüssels...":*[29] wax & key; may generous Giacomo excuse me for that.

25. I already broached the topic of candles shortly beforehand, but wide-branched candelabras, chandeliers, and forests of wax reflected four or five times over in mirrors deserve a separate section. These halos of light and fire sparkle, redden, and turn to ashes around Casanova's head like the red-hot crown of iron on the head of György Dózsa.[30] This was the pyre and sacrificial fire of his mundaneness — those candelabras sticking out their white tongues with a hiss in the corner of dark salons, the halos of elegance, royal luxury, carnivalesque self-assurance and Vicenzan aristocratism of that foliage of Venetian crystal floating in the air. Because a pomp belongs to those, too, as to every triumph of asceticism, a certain dizzying transfiguration, an ostentatious liturgy: this is the world of chandeliers, of 'Kronleuchter' (a wonderful word). What symphonies of sputtering & smell accompany Casanova all through his life: from short, tubby, trollop-tongued candle stumps to the dots of flame of Versailles glass fibres.

And besides the candles Venetian lampions (again, what a wonderful word!), sevenfold lamps of boarding school; lampions of the lagoons, from which light is cast on the water as if their yellow ribbons had loosened and the wavelets were rocking the lost thread; the greasy lamps of the monastery at Murano — all the lights, brands, candles, & lamps throughout a life: how splendid it would be to examine these one by one some day. The "*Nachtlampe mit Zifferblatt*"[31] is also symbolic: a marriage of solitary fire and couple-stingy time.

26. Casanova hates all kinds of homosexuality; however, he knows that a certain perversion is more normal than normality — after all, that is the inside-civilization in it. The classical exemplar of fashionable perversity is the episode at the ball when he and a woman exchange clothes in front of each other — the woman applies make-up on Casanova, putting on rouge and beauty spots, and they change shirts both with and without embarrassment *avec gêne* and *sans gêne* the too visible effect of her charms;[32] Casanova finally allows the "*Schlussakt meiner Aufregung*"[33] to occur monologically, in front of the woman, for which all he receives from her is resistance and rebuke.

In such a situation all that is ever of interest is: how many diverse things, which are already passionate peculiarities, become merely unconscious habits, tritenesses.

The background is enthralling: what is nowadays Art Nouveau was then dull convention — a historical game that one cannot have enough of. It is apparent that acts of undressing like that, while they may not have been self-evident at all events, were on a level, as nowadays, with a somewhat prolonged holding of hands between a man and woman, and Casanova's physical monologue was not much more brutal than, say, coughing in someone's face: warranting at most a 'Pardon me!' and not being seen as a matter for remorse. In other words, a 'law': (the word always being understood in a Casanovan sense and therefore *never* to be obeyed, hence never followable in an 18th-century manner!) there is no love without swapping clothes; it is necessary for the man to have rouge on his lips and a woman's shift to be on his body: the reversal of genders, comedy, masks are indispensable. Dressing and undressing is civilization's most typical contribution, and so is there to be: exploited.

To pass merrily, conventionally, and with a bit of moral *faux*-mumbling beyond such monologue failures or monologue successes. The best thing about the whole episode is its dreamlike childishness, the character of a childhood dream: on such occasions we ourselves change into women, no need for quarreling with peevish girls, our very body is already female and one only has to reach after it — and the solution is not embracing either but Narcissus' ceremony *without* any compulsion or love. Dream, perversion, infantile virginity, peruke civilization, etiquette and overworked psychology, again they shiver in a magicality beyond magic before our eyes: if we did not exchange clothes, if we did not exhibit the free body finale then — we are sick.

27. The topic of love is never 'a woman,' never 'one' and never 'woman,' but a *'scena'* — a situation, a dramatic constellation in a suitable entourage. It is not: 'I am in love with someone' — that is malaria; but 'I want such and such a configuration': and in that way it is Racinian and makes him happy. These "public consummations" are extremely important in the first volume of Casanova: it is youth personified, civilization personified. Youth: inasmuch as it is already much more than a letter by Narcissus but something less (not a bit emotionally, just *de facto* less) than a dialogue.

Civilization, although there is an animal spontaneity in it, the matter nevertheless occurs monologically because morality is in the air, the butterflies are guided by a decorum, a discipline. If ever the expression *'juste milieu'* made any sense, that is it. Who could say whether young Casanova at times like that is a dog doing its business on a street corner or a nervous, bashful, and dilettante ascetic?

28. It should never be forgotten that Casanova always has two sides: a large-scale sensual Puritanism and a small-scale naïf-enlightenment, fox-cub naturalism. As to whether those two really existed in his life is doubtful: here I am thinking primarily of the books, the mode of expression. In the monastery of Santa Maria della Salute he studied primarily *'Experimentalphysiks'*; it could be that in reality that was just as sublime an experience as the shifty smuttiness of the

'orangery' or the 'quadrille' — in the book, as in a novel, that kind of thing is undoubtedly a fall: the intellect slips to an intellectual standard. But that sort of compromise is an organic part of every dogmatism and prophetic life.

29. Is a greater change of fortune, expressionist metaphor, or change of faith conceivable than when, after gondolas, reception-room candles, and orangeries, he unexpectedly says, without any prelude: "*und wandelte im Wald herum, um meine Traurigkeit zu verwinden.*" [34] What's this? "*Wald*" in — *Arabia deserta*? "*Traurigkeit*" — in *Experimentalphysik*? And "*verwinden*" — in the midst of *fioriture* of shamelessness? Venice and wood — can those be accommodated within a singe skull? [35] "*Die Blume, die zu einem Gott mich machte*" [36] — he sings alone among the black foliage. That is nature: with its coolness, its smells, its loneliness, albeit beyond the sparrows' din of civilization but still this side of romanticism.

The *average* man's nostalgia for nature is worthy of the one and undivided creation. When a breeze cools — that is half hygiene, half mythology, yet neither of those, both more and less. It is half realistic observation, half intoxication in a whorish metaphor, yet neither of those, both more and less. When a somewhat inebriated woman or man goes out of a warm dance room onto a balcony or among the trees in a garden &, toppling onto a stone bench, says: "My! how great to get a breath of air," and meanwhile in his head the rims of glasses of champagne, the touch of women, the mendacious crescents of moons, amorous words, and sundry tobaccos, the grounds of some music and the words of an unexpected, strange sentence, practical plans for removing a liqueur stain, and a Buddha-lashing nirvana of caterwauling: when, with a head like that, one looks at the nocturnal foliage, then one is looking in exactly the manner God wished you to look — because from time immemorial just one man understands, in the language of oaks, birches, yew-trees and elm-trees, beeches and alders, the pantheists have been God's court jesters, poets and myth agents, the bonzes of angels: the slightly *average*, slightly tired, mundane Casanova.

30. Because what does he do af-terwards? "*... ging in den Garten zu der fröhlich lärmenden Gesellschaft*" [37] — back to the garden and the gossip. Be-cause this company is not a topic in sociology, neither a *civitas* of Christian brethren, nor a humanist group Plato-nizing & sporting in accordance with Renaissance ideals.

No. Anyone in whom the sociological, humanist, or Christian conception of 'mankind' has become en-trenched does not know what that garden gang is and whether they wish to mingle with it, and last of all they have to surrender any scientific, religious, or practical no-tion and in its place accept the *cross* of unbounded shal-lowness. Because one has to enter this society absolutely free of thoughts, of love, and of ideals — without yes-terday's memory & tomorrow's plan, cleanly, abstractly, chattering, in the insubstantial center of the moment of moments. The most radical eradication of all content: that is the essence of social life; of social life, of the absolute, absurd salon which is the sole majestic and intelligent response to the secrets of existence.

The world consists of itself and the thoughts pertaining to it: the world *per se* is a dumb block of irrationality, thought is an anarchic psychological luxury, blind ornamentation for its own sake — that is to say, man cannot need such a world and man cannot need such thinking. Society does not concern itself either with the world, or with thinking, because those are just two festive or drunken '*figurants*,' as the book writes about female ballet dancers: it turns its concern with strict workmanship only to 'proper studies,' or — in other words: clothes, dining services, marriage arrangements, travels, money.

The Casanovan lesson shines even across centuries — anyone unable to cast aside the humbugs of 'knowledge' & 'sentiment' and get used to that laughing, chattering society even from an *intellectual* point of view is of a thousand times higher order than a university chair or a Buddhist monastery and will remain a cowardly romantic of darkness. Our profoundly moralistic and profoundly rational nature, of course, hardly bears to avow the ascetic school of amorality and 'ignorance,' yet it must — because that is the maximum that man can act in his hideous loneliness. When Casanova crossed from wood into the garden, from solitariness to a clique, he bestrode *philosophics* and thereby won everything.

31. Casanova reaps most of his amorous triumphs in carriages — it should not be forgotten that springs in that era were probably highly imperfect: with the bulk of highways in the countryside being more uneven than the moon; that on women were a bunch of fantastic rags and whalebones which hindered movement; that at the back valets were able to peep and guffaw — despite all of which he would gain victory within minutes.

It is true women generally were more willing (at least in the book), perhaps more masculine in matters of the body, and it is true that sensuality has a sure touchstone: even in the most ludicrous poses it is able to surrender itself to the body's deeply serious joy — it calls for nothing, not even a particle of aesthetics.

To anyone who requires a so-called appropriate milieu: colors and scents, appropriate poses and morphologically codified foreplay and 'Abschaukelung,'[38] in a word, a 'mood' — he might have the prettiest, cleverest, and best woman, but if at all possible he entrusts the love to someone else. 'Mood' is: the most faded mask of impotence that he contrived for himself. One thing is true: to live for the body, even in the most exasperating burlesque posture, with the same pathos as Orpheus in the underworld for the lute.

32. There are sides which in an entirely naïve, schoolboy manner seek to portray nothing more than the colorfulness of life. That is needed

as Casanova himself is an abstraction, pure *mathesis*, a final air flower of Italian hysteria for form. For instance, a 'counter-poison' page like the following: he sells all his clothes to a Jew; he cohabits a house with a female dancer by the name of La Tintoretta; he has to wait six months for the bishop to direct his life; meanwhile between the Jewish rag-and-bone man and the Venetian ballet dancer he dreams about the papal tiara: "...*eine Laufbahn einzutreten, die mich vielleicht auf den päpstlichen Stuhl führen konnte.*"[39]

That is just as good a vulgar picturesqueness as sweet childhood. People naturally have such an immutably trivial image of Casanova that they can only imagine this dream of the papacy as a tawdry blasphemy, yet with a naïve Italian like him it is just a half-curse.

33. In love the body and clothes are decisive, nothing else. Is not a figure like that, for example, a blood-curdling spectacle? In a black periwig and scarlet cloak and with a sunburned face? What a scrappy hand of patience an *analysis* of the portrait, equally that of the mind and body, beside such theatrical colors. To renounce the parvenu pseudo-refinement of analysis — from the pick of the Casanova thesis at that.

To abandon oneself to the primary intimation of red, black, & yellow, then plop: throw round ourselves death's swishing domino and disappear into the godless grave. What is not without interest is the small fortuity that a good deal later Casanova wishes to have a garment made for him, and the tailor is called (he too is pleased at this): Morte.

34. For me Venice is so identi-
fied with water that when I hear it mentioned in connection with ballet or 'orchestra': I always think — how can
girls in garters and stockings dance in water, how come
the violins do not become clogged with water in the lagoons? Dance and violin are such dry-land, 'terracotta'
things, that: I cannot picture cellos on a gondola without
sardines wriggling into and out of the *f*-holes. And if al-
legedly the thing is not entirely so, a little lurking contradiction always flavors the maritime opera which belongs
very much to the Casanova staffage of accessory figures.

35. I was always a friend, in-
deed fierce apologist for *illegitimate* associations of the
kind that were experienced when I first read the name
of the "*Liu* family"[40] in Casanova. Liu? Hsien Liu and
Kwang Liu and Pu Liu, such handsome Chinese names,
yet equally Italian and 'Brunelleschian': the '*i*'-sound is
so sharp, that one syllable so classically compact. The
whole history, or if you like the whole life is for an "illegitimate association" — every truth is merely a truth,
but in exactly the same way as that for Liu there is Chinese. The German Reich is not a whit more 'Roman' than
this old Liu is Chinese; the absolute monarchy is just as
much an empty jest in Hobbes' head or absolute democracy in Rousseau's as my hanging vase, coolie, Buddha

or mandarin round the neck of that stalwart Liu from Venice. That is why a playful citation and swapping of ideas is always more than any 'historical philosophy.'

36. If Casanova can write down sentences like he was *"wie immer meinem sokratischen Dämon folgte"*[41] — one should be grateful. It has simultaneously a charming humor and involuntary truth about it. Humor, undoubted humor — "my Socratic demon" is too excessively a paper or mythical concept (it should not be forgotten that in modern-day European civilization those two can by now only ever be one) to be worthy of Casanova's true intelligence and passionateness, but humorous nonetheless because he uses it in a slightly parvenu manner with a naïve posture. Also truthful because for the clear line which life is under any circumstances one needs demonism, the pure demon of the cold outlines of dreary Latin landscapes. (St. Thomas Aquinas was born in Roccasecca, Sicily.) Only *thought* is demonic, never feeling — if that distinction is worth anything; feeling being nothing more than dramatized thought, active logic.

37. He notes about a woman that she was still living, ninety years old, healthy and in high spirits. Casanova's world is a world of that kind of ever-young — and we know that gaunt, tall, skinny people are hardier than the fat, than those fit as a 'proverbial fiddle': a person lives from his bones not his blood,

from desiccated manias not sprawling stillness. This is the world of perennial skeletons and ascetics: this world is not some sort of 'perpetual springtime,' not the 'flowering fullness of life' — that is the kind with which only the cowardly half-dead are acquainted — that senile 'lady' was simply tough: she goes and goes and is still going over time but without any trappings of time mystery and plenitude of life. At ninety years of age she is stirred by just the same snippets of salon gossip as when she was nineteen; she does not represent a Faustian totality of wisdom at all. The kind of actors in keeping with Casanova, alongside *abstract* hedonism: is that kind of 'tasteless,' prosaic sidestepping of death. Complete assurance of life: but without any frippery of optimism.

38. He cannot do other than evoke sympathy the way he speaks about the fit of seasickness which overcame him in a gondola. The only person capable of such childlike confidentiality, virtually a confession to his mother, and such amiable reasoning about nature, is one who was never acquainted with life's two most repugnant ordures: art-historical & scientific naturalism. When Casanova speaks about that he is not seeking an esthetic shock, nor is he even seeking to shatter an 'ideal' with a naïf-Luciferian gesture (the best about it all is that only naturalists imagine that non-naturalists have their 'ideals' morning, noon, & night): the muck of a literary program is not allowed to dirty his white cuffs.

39. We are in outright Keatsian climes when he speaks about his fair-faced friend from college. Even the young Milton is perhaps also hovering here, with his pallid young woman of Christ Church College. Is anything more touching than the desire of the first fair-faced, goodly, and smart boy? Can a woman be as fair-faced, goodly, and smart as such a meditative, blue schoolmate? The walks in the garden, the jealousies, the raptures over Ariosto.

Ariosto is Casanova's favorite poet, and justly so — Casanova is a *furioso* of *raison*, the Orlando of *logical* loves — a '*Doctor* Lunaticus' in the diary of tragic rationalism. Nobody can be so awed by the sight of beauty with such trembling reverence, with such sweet, well-bred youthfulness, as that 'pimp'; the *esprit* and cultivation impressed nobody with such adolescent faith as that chatterbox. (The fact that he is projecting it back from a tired old age and confabulating it with his youth is of no interest — here one is always speaking about the hero of the book, not truth.) If his entire being were not full of such childhood memories, with entirely brotherly fellow-feeling for such sallowly boyish lyricism, one would be unable to enter into such warm friendship with him over the course of the book, he would not be as intimate and charming. One should not forget the miracle, this stern, heroically nihilistic 'Brunelleschi' is also pleasant, warm, friendly, and inspires confidence — even in his rational-sadism he is as charming as a spoiled child. "...*flösste mir eine Freundschaft ein*":[42] and the word '*flösste*'

84

in the German version always puts me in mind of a flute, and in those garden evenings, hazy with infant-grade friendship, the Ariosto promenades, the midnight jumpings into each other's beds I continually hear the hesitant yet eternal fluting of an incomparable childhood.

40. That is precisely why this friendship-love composed of melancholic poetry and raven-plumed sensitivity becomes everlasting in Casanova; that is precisely why I am dedicating a separate chapter to the lantern which lit this friendship in the college — although I have already spoken about the 72-year carnival of the lamps in Casanova's life. That lamp hung between the two boys' opposite-facing beds as if it were the domestic moon o' youth, the enigmatically ripening Isis fruit of the secret — that lamp is solitary and holy among the Versailles candelabras, Venetian lampions, and Masonic torches. It is the gentle shuddering, dreamy phobias, and numbed rebellions of youth itself. Under this, amid its shadow palm trees, slept Casanova — pursuing his phantasms from Horace, Orlando, the doe-eyed dandy, the papacy and a completely, absolutely completely *womanless* world. A magic lantern.

41. To be pedantic — I can picture four major versions of love: one is an ancient-prehistoric state with no sex, where life has nothing in common with being male or female and a shared joy between them; the amatory adventures and fumblings of

boyhood among animals, objects, oneself and illnesses; the 'normal' affairs with women of a grown-up individual; and finally the conscious perversions. The first of those, unfortunately, is unattainable (cf. the nostalgic passages in this direction in D. H. Lawrence's novella *St. Mawr*), the last too romantic (it is only romantic *in theory*, because in practice it is only natural that one can become accustomed to it to the point of indifference), which leaves the childhood semi-darkness and the women. Women one can be bored with — whereas childhood is something that can never be, is only ever already past: it is clear that one wants nothing besides that.

Every stealthy agitation of the age is there in Casanova's nights in the college, in the tiny, amateurish, violet, and snowdrop perversions. Although childhood is an empire of the deadliest fears — both true joy and true corporeality were only there and never any more. A child's body is still homogeneous — a current of delight still runs uniformly throughout the whole: in the bodies of adults it is already encountering a thousand obstacles, toughened guts, hearts with distended valves, whistling lungs, mildewed and nauseating stomachs. It is one of God's greatest miracles that an adult body is at all capable of love: the whole business is so much merely the non-esthetic administration of heart, lungs, brain, and liver: above 25 years of age male nudity or female nudity is just a toll-house and internal medicine, but not love. When I see adults osculating I always feel that I am witness to a final act of beastliness. Thus the *ultima ratio: infans infantilis.*

42. The great thing about language; it can be anything: *"Der Docht schwimmt in Öl"* [43] — *Docht* and *Öl*: words more real than reality.

43. For a goodly while Casanova's life passed by in the Palazzo Grimani di San Luca around the Grimani family. As to what Grimani means for this book that can be read in the history of Monteverdi's Venetian fantasies. [44]

44. The moment when a good-looking Greek woman appears with Casanova is of great importance; she asks for official patronage and in gratitude yields herself by way of a reward. That Greek woman and Casanova's Greeks in general are tatters of a Balkan and Byzantine hodgepodge — it is a comforting historical delight to associate the name of Hellas with harlots with the clap and with wine merchants swindling on the allure of Byzantium. This is where Casanovan 'Balkan classicism' commences: that is slipshod, but nevertheless a classical something as it balances a big historical suggestion and shifty little dodges.

The clearest symbol here is perhaps Ragusa: half Byzantium, half Venice, half Balkan, half northern. The moral: it is a hundred times better to have mongrel rascals skulking in the shadow of 1001 Nights, Mount Olympus, and the Hagia Sophia than poets and myth-philologists. Scheherazade's tales have come to an end. Aphrodites and Demeters have become less than nothing, and even

Byzantium is just a carnival grave lamp: in other words, it is more a matter of vegetating parasites crawling over them than impotent 'interpreters' and 'resurrectionists.' Casanova sets out for the Archipelago — towards a new variant of the classicism of putrefaction. Like a young god into Europe's bud, into a cheapjack flea market of the *Untergang* in 18th-century style. All at once the Balkan silts of relativism attempt to loosen his strict rationalist outlines: after uniform Italian culture overturned history, the drunken alternations of West and East, the mysterious chasing of brutal barbarism and Hellenic 'spirit-rapping.'

In its filthy nakedness this history is: an identification of the highly exalted and sickeningly petty, the mysterious unanimity or meaninglessness of dying and birth: every value is nomadic irresponsibility. How much more sublime and thought-provoking Casanova in a Balkan Hellas puddle than Goethe in the philologists' Rome; Casanova in a caricaturistic epigone Muslimism than that same Goethe in the mendacious bubble of his *West-Östlicher Divan*.

Only the Balkan can truly 'loosen' — the pretty Greek woman with whom he meets, the most impossible phenomenon: she has no outline yet nevertheless is a positive: a Kotoran, Corfiote, and Cretan positive. Perfect harlot, perfect 'enlightened' Frenchman, perfect female harem-slave, perfect victim of a Celtic passion, perfect Levantine slave-girl, Mercury bedizened with all his graces: a mixture like that is the cultural achievement of the Balkans. Those who have not encountered the type: let them be pensioned off as stupid in the grave.

45. Midnight vengeance in Venice — that is just as organic a part of love as Keatsian children, Balkan slave-girls, or abstinence. Venetian pitch-darkness — that certain air darkness layered on a pedestal of dark-sea-blue; the darkness of narrow alleys, black even at noon in summertime.

Black gondolas and black oars, black mooring posts and the many blackened bronze gates: only the domes of St. Mark's Cathedral are bright like greenish whey, like half a dozen Muscovite new moons, like bud-colored dawn-time snow. Adventure, blood, a fight, vengeance: that is part of the female's body, a second embrace. The tiny bridge over the lagoon between two houses leaning towards each other in a white frame to red bricks like English bacon, the grills warped higgledy-piggledy like a poppy stem after a storm (I don't know myself what I should call out at a time like this? — that this is not a 'description,' or, that the world's only possible lifestyle is just a 'description'), Casanova stands at the street corner in a black domino amid window shutters, a crescent moon, viper-fanged stars and the columnar virginals of the Palazzo Contarini Minelli del Bovolo; the target of the vengeance is stepping unsuspectingly on the ringing cobblestones; first of all a dagger flashes then a big warm splash is heard from the water; a smell of the lagoon's stirred-up mud swirls in the air like the fumes of 'phosphorus' after a match is struck; then a tearing at windows, nightshirts, and candles, out of the dark lanterns suddenly spill into the night like coppers or pumpkin seeds from a hole in the pocket; Casanova dashes through empty, free, otherworldly piazzas and piazettas: jumps into a boat, the wind blows the patched belly of the sails, and above all this the Campanile midnight bell tolls: a gigantic "at exactly midnight" covers up the whole comedy like a bronze vault. *That* is love, *that* is classicism: to take romanticism upon himself in its own victorious extremes: Venice's colors and bloods.

Anyone who fears romanticism can never be a classicist; anyone who has not yet handled a lethal blade cannot be either in love or a person. Death: again it makes its appearance not with the trashy garnish of Thanatos swanking or any similar poetic interpretation but like a street murder, a *vulgar* criminal act: punctuated, *abstract* vileness.

The essence is precisely in the distribution: the milieu is more colorful than ever, Byzantine relics, cockleshells from the Lido, Turkish galleys, and the moon caught like Absalom in Murano, they participate with highly strung jostling in this truer wedding night of love: vengeance's murder, though the act itself is just a moral *formula*, perhaps rather more in the nature of a *formal* evil disavowing the devil before God. — We said that love is body & dress, nothing more. One ought to add: that vengeance, that murder. 'Passion' is just one of the hypocrisies of cowardice; insufficient; murder is also needed.

46. Then right after, immediately after: "*So fein war damals mein Zartgefühl.*"[45] What is the connection? The murder? No doubt he would claim for this, too, but since he regards that as being too self-evident he would rather link it to a little intermezzo of the amorous child. He strolls with a young slip of a girl and meanwhile it becomes evident how physically involved Giacomo is, and that causes pleasure, discomposure, *poesis,* and chaos; as a matter of etiquette they pirouette and blunder in ape freedom: in other words, again the complications of the main subject of civilization, the Neander Valley and finesse. Everyone knows that those people who are at all capable of tenderness and emotional benevolence are ethically much slimier in their sensual moments than otherwise: trembling self-sacrifice is a *bodily,* not a psychological secretion; the profoundly 'psychological' Charis-sweetness[46] is a certain type of tearful love: a particular chord or chord cluster of nerves tickled with the appropriate Aretino technique — whereby of course the love did not become a whit smaller nor the body larger. This dichotomy: the most charming expression of the relationship of the dependency of "*Zartgefühl*" and a little adventure.

47. Casanova is life, not literature (though his book, his book...), 'he is' and he is not fantasizing. Yet all the same: how does he himself express it? "*... die Wirklichkeit hängt stets von der Phantasie ab.*"[47] He is aware of the essence of love.

He comprises two parts: one is vegetative instinct, the second is curiosity about variants in female personality, curiosity about what kind of person lies behind each new portrait? These two together, culture and connoisseurship of characterization: the whole is love. Casanova is wise; he knows that there is neither religious nor intellectual mystery in love; the fact of love is the most unproblematic, most simplistic imaginable fact in the world — every grand lover came to that conclusion after the first kiss; only eunuchs still rattle on about the 'problems of love,' like beggars the fake farthings of a collecting tin. There is an endearing naïveté about the way people shudder at the thought of confessing that love is 'no more than' that and nothing more, a blind instinct and a curio portrait — believing that that is not much, is cynical, devilry.

They fail to notice that the more wildly someone is in love the more one is burned up by love even to the point of taking one's own life: and the more simplistically a person will view their being burned up by love: and the more primitive the structure someone finds in love the more furiously and destitutely will he be infatuated with and nuts about women. That perennial relationship is the so-called 'cynicism of love,' but at the same time — does it never bring anything to their minds between mortal burning loves for women?

Casanova professes the eternal one possibility of great intellect and great passion: he discovers the principle of all things (which on account of human nature, of course, at just about all times will be identical with the fact that we discover either some irrationality or nonsense, or if not that, then some utterly, likewise comically primitive structure), and when that mental gesture has occurred, with its own easy heroics, one yields to the desire body and fantasy (the two are the same): so that one may surrender oneself to the discovered nonsense with faith, somnambulism, death, illness, suicide or: to put it in a word, happiness. The intellect's sole criterion: to be able to perish for nonsense. As was said in the conciliar proposition of the Venetian night dogma: classicism is tearing into romanticism *without* hypochondria, like a lead bullet into a lake.

48. As a breather, a small, flecked picture again: the bishop arrives, on account of which Casanova sets off walking in the early daybreak. The peep of dawn is nature's most secretive secret, to say nothing of Venice's. How accustomed we have become to going somewhere meaning to do it at noon, or in the afternoon or evening, i.e., at 'visiting hours' — so how good it is that Giacomo sets off before sunrise to pay his visit; there is something ungrudgingly childish about it — with him being treated like a schoolboy; both ascetic, since he is on his way even before mass is said; and also romantic, as he sets off *"ins Blaue."*

Then comes mass, and after mass hot chocolate and, to end it all, three hours long of praying. Three hours long is a great deal of time — a whole lifetime, a whole century. Again the 'lax Catholicism' — a smart breakfast and three hours of prayer.

49. He sets out from Piazzetta on a voyage to Naples. Here it was 'merely' a matter of a conflict on which 'merely' one's life is turned upside down — a matter of a midnight vengeance, of the depths of Venice and of the lightness, the white openness, which is Piazzetta. To that Sun, to Venice, pertains an almost blasphemous declaration: "*So verliess ich denn meine Heimat mit freudigem Herzen und ohne das geringste Bedauern.*"[48] This is apostasy, schism, atheism: but the person who had chosen life and love had already done so earlier on. Let it not be forgotten that we have taken Casanova and Venice to be synonymous, indeed Venice to be the face and Casanova the mask — yet he is now quitting Venice like a shadow quits a tree when the sun suddenly pops out: cheerily, without a thought or feeling. That is alarmingly lofty, impossible to imagine, and at the same time one is aware that the only person who becomes acquainted with true love is one who has no homeland, no mother or home, no god or birthplace: who is without roots, geography, or history.

We are unable to be separated from a pressed flower, a glove, a calling card, or a scribble jotted in the margin of a newspaper article: in the Phrynesque[49] nakedness of Piazzetta Casanova discards himself from the abstraction which is Giacomo Casanova, discards the abstraction itself, too, as being a superfluous burden, in order to be left with a 'nothing,' not expressible even by a word or by algebra: the minimum of a minimum, which, on the other hand, he knows is the maximum of the maximum of amorous opportunities.

50. There is no person, only circumstances; is that not a magnificent justification for being sequestered by being quarantined at Ancona? The external fact that people were obliged to flourish and languish for forty days in one place. One can imagine the nearly interminable proliferation of dreams and ac-quaintances, the Narcissan living in misery and plans for a new life which blossomed over forty such days in a monastery. Admittedly, people in those days were not so (for simplicity's sake let us say) highly strung and sensi-tive as nowadays; thus, 40 days of slacking was roughly as much then as a single empty afternoon to us — and even a single empty afternoon is a lot, nothing less than a romantic infinity.

51. A few years later Casanova wrote a dissertation against premonitions. In that he only attacked the unpleasant ones because those are suggested by the crazy heart — not the bad ones, because those stem from the intellect. This is a typical high-culture at-mosphere, when sense and bad, ultimate knowledge and extreme pessimism are the same.

52. There are situations when *not* reacting, *not* observing betokens greater culture than

becoming acquainted and fitting in with analytical love. Casanova spends a few hours in Pola in order to inspect the Roman ruins; in Ancona he mentions Trajan's name.

Here a ruin is a simple, conventional item of furniture for Europe: not a triumphant symbol of some imperishable art, not some melancholy preacher of mortality, neither history nor lyric — just a ruin in the way a spoon is a spoon and a stocking a stocking. To make a cult out of past times: barbarian; a history professor is always grosser and more senseless than a Polynesian pirate or a *"Zartgefühl"*-gigolo.

53. The 'Balkan impromptu' has already taken place, now only the comfortably doled out details can come — indeed, are coming: a lovely Greek slave-girl. Is it not marvelous that slave-girls still existed in the 18th century? If a maid is heaven, then a slave-girl must be seventh heaven. A great lover can always be recognized from the fact that he has no sense of the individuality of women, of human liberty, of life having an end in itself: it is the kind of thing only cowardly idiots respect and only the dross of women is hoodwinked by 'loyalty' — the falsest word in the vocabulary of love. Great lovers handle women like beautiful flowers and beautiful books: they like putting the one in vases or planting them in the garden, having the other bound in leather or reading it in such and such a boat — what is truly great, exciting, and divine can only be an *object*; a human is so much an eternal singularity

that beside one human another is a logical and physiological impossibility; there can always only be one of a human being — and even that in itself is too much of something: it is a humanist utopia that women snap up to their own detriment. That is why the final goal is a slave-girl, who can be placed any which way like an object. Likewise the kitchen maid myth that men take unfair advantage of. Men often batter to death 'independent female individuals' yet with servile gratitude continually defend slave-girls against God and man. In Casanova's day for travelers to the Balkans that was not a pipe-dream but a tourist item. To be sure, it is still 'just about hanging on': but then it was the true 18th century — if one rolls back one's lace cuffs and blows the *esprit des lois* into spirits like into the silky *pappi* of a dandelion — then there were still alive not only the Middle Ages but the ancient world of the South Seas.

54. That is why Casanova writes to her without irony but with religious faith: "*Engel des Morgenlandes.*"[50]

The whole Orient makes its appearance: after the Renaissance asceticism of Italy the peeling, ghetto-like Balkans, and on top of those two stages, now, for the very first time, a third: Constantinople, Smyrna, Baghdad; Europe's adolescent dream — the enchanting East.

Just as in one of Ben Jonson's plays it is a logical necessity that the plot is reprised in the last act as a puppet show — a marionette being more than any human or

angel: it is with a similar inner necessity that Casanova
travels to Constantinople — it is necessary that the perfection should be strung out, go mad, become tinted as
an opium dream, become like a puppet operetta.

The nights of the quarantine period he spends on
the balcony — it would be clumsy to improvise a balcony
mythology, but... but: is not the balcony one of civilization's finest inventions? Part room, part open air, the
most symbolic location imaginable for man.

The grand, vast terraces to which far-extending
steps lead, twisting and crossing one another like fashion magazines decoratively scattered on the floor beside
a woman's divan: tiny little barely-saliences, Parisian bay
windows, in fact it is all a lace grille: a lot of hip-shaped
columns blackened crosswise by moonlight: each one is
like an old-fashioned lamp chimney, stuck together by
the two 'pedestals' (the balcony may be an enclosure of
that kind); verandas protected by glass or a pulpit-like
little balconette which has strayed onto a wall: Oh, what
a spectrum of balconies, those most consistent of its
chapels of civilization.

The commentator's life was also one such balcony;
he has not been alive since then. — By the way there are
two other trifles that I wish to note at this start of Oriental civilization: one is that when I read such words, tossed
higgledy-piggledy alongside each other, as *"Morgenland,"*
"Nacht," "Balkon" [51] — I am again beset by an elemental
force, that I first felt when I was being taught French, to
write a book with the title *Il y a* in which there would

be nothing other than a dry catalogue of the totality of the world's objects, feelings, varieties of events, and logic fables; and secondly (that was something I felt much later, of course), that I would derive the whole of Europe from Mozart's *Entführung aus dem Serail*,[52] rendering rococo opera as a single historical thought and life.

55. That *"qui mange du pape, s'en meurt"* is much more a literary, stylistic principle than a historical one.[53] Casanova's weakest point is the anticlerical and anti-monastic barrel organ.

In any case satire is a perversion beyond intelligence & art, even if we say of it "a good thing too" — but with Casanova satire is never good. The image of a drunken, illiterate begging monk is gray boredom personified — having merely the role of: reinforcing the Casanovan tenet — "Anyone incapable of cold-blooded blasphemy is also incapable of love." Casanova knows that a woman's appearance and simultaneously the annihilation of a most divine god are chemically inseparable phenomena.

Just as Venice has to disrobe from Venice, so too do the gods have to peel off into cynical damnation in order that the woman's experience should remain for the greater part female. And not an Isoldan passion, parching the sea and devouring the forest, but on account of the stopper of a perfume bottle or a song accompanied flatly by a crummy piano.

The rule here (there is no settlement or bargaining): in love one must immediately desert the greatest thing, a whole Olympus, a whole Rome, every god & church, for the most trivial, a shadow, a fib, a barely possible.

A man has to become so maximally insulated that there is no shadow, not a single memory, with which he would be able to cold-bloodedly disgrace his living parents and dead ancestors, because that is what love demands and it is unattainable at a lesser price. It is not the *hetæræ* who fixed Christ's rate but the meek, the crumbling, the mawkish and maudlin, the good, the pious, the Christ-like.

Who in adolescence did not feel the horror of the Antichrist when they slipped away from the living room for a first date? We knew that right then our parents had died, and with sweaty Judas hands we counted the thirty pieces of silver without which bashful, lyrical Verginella would not have admitted us into the premises, which were much more bordelloish than the bordello of "idyllic understanding." Casanova's blasphemies may be literary nullities, but they cannot be uncoupled from the erotic syllogism: blasphemy is a mode of existence.

56. At one point they are cast up in a peasant's dwelling, and while Casanova and his associate unsuspectingly seek to consign themselves to dreams two ghastly, diabolical crones fall on them and crave love from them. A great wrangle develops, they beat the host, a dog, and the crones to a pulp before taking to their heels. In the catechism of love the peasant & *demos* were given the sole possible position: infernal

humor or heavenly burlesque. What to a pious person
is moral value the peasant is to Casanova; he demonstrates the possibilities of an abominable caricature of
love, the inferno. There is no biology or democracy there,
however much of a 'biologist' & 'democrat' our literary
hero declares himself to be — here the people are precisely what the devil was in the Middle Ages.

An instinctive *anti*-humanism of quite superstitious
strength is the first flower of love — once *demos* is a fool
and hell only then can the girl approach. And that's not
bad for democracy in practice either: it was not Charis
souls who struggled for the great accomplishments for
slaves, serfs, and mole-peasants but haters and loathers
of the populace, hysterical pernickety types unable to
bear that there should be an entity like demos around
them. One thinks of Brueghel and the three Le Nain
brothers, but they are peripheral: what is important is
the 'completeness' of the purging — just as Venice became
nothing and the Church became nothing, so too must
the 'mundane-stricken poor' be a forever odious torso,
a Mephisto joke, otherwise the lie of 'affection' would
cloud the coruscating mirror of love which excludes that.

57. The autumnal theme for
a moment rings out once more in the work: he reaches
Rome for the first time in his life on September 1st, in
that eternal September, *Die Welt als September-Werdung*,
to flirt with the putative title of a German periodical.[54]
Here, though, that is just an escaped speck of mercury:

the big game flows around the morning *ignis fatuus.*

Fate may only be kissed for being in such high spirits: it happens to be Casanova's entry into Rome that
produces northern lights in the atmosphere, *Irrlichter*
and planetary fires — let the enlightened be a wee bit
jittery among the malevolent demons of the Tiber's
marshes. When a person is standing on the threshold
of something big, as Casanova standing before Rome,
Latinity against Latinity, with those fatally flashing eyes
and attacking zest, the way a person is accustomed to
facing his own essence — then the mystical light, the superstitious symmetry, the sign, astrological fortuity will
also always be there. Besides that is the other: he declares bluntly "superstitious nonsense" though *"garnichts…
machte Eindruck auf mich."*[55] In other words, the Roman
impromptu — demonic lights flash around his demon-
repudiating head; ancient Rome means nothing to him,
to him, the living embodiment of Rome. Is there not in
those two strokes of luck a link to the most cultured in
all cultures: the perpetual nightmare of irrationality, a
marsh-flame of ignited marsh gas — & healthy, blasé,
total indifference towards the triviality that he is culture.

58. "Worldly" or "money": it
matters not. "Spring"? imprecise —, "money"? precise.
"Moon"? a hypothesis — "ducat"? the solution. "Arabi-
an-golden Marie"? the finest dream —, "an unexpected
legacy"? the most erudite erudition about the earth: a
spring appreciated, a moon recognized, a girl who can be

deified. As with all absolutely worldly men, with Casanova women & love become ever less significant and more episodic, with only money remaining in its place: an abstraction of abstractions. But that growing abstraction in itself also runs through its own gradations: with Rome being composed of 'Caroline' and 'Pauline' dimensions.

By the time he is in Paris the whole thing has become mathematical. How wonderful it is that coins are also portraits — concrete images of mythological or historical figures. 'Caroline' — what magnificent Charleses there are: the Carolingian Charles, the mystic and cunning peasant; Charles Habsburg of black and yellow rotting baroque Spain; Charles Stuart in England, the man of the tragic game and Romantic etiquette: out of all those coins were minted, just as they were of the Virgin Mary and also of the ecstatically politicizing Pope Pauls — that is smarter and finer than a poem or history.

These historical-portrait coins are still only quasi naïve-epic preludes to subsequent fantastic stock-market manipulations: but they are there to serve as a reminder, the masks dropped: not to set to work on any woman without money, that is worse than a lingering suicide.

59. Casanova conjures up the entire Eastern Roman Empire with the names of wines — haggling for muscat wines from the Levantine,[56] Samos, Cerigo, Cephalonia.[57] How many things there were on the Peloponnese archipelago — Greek religion, the revelations of John the Divine, the mythical heraldry

of French knights, and finally wine, wine, wine, with jabbering Jews, scraps of Slavs, decadent Turks. In taste and bouquet these wines, from which in their burning mirror the most naïve, most honest, and most European figures of human history smile: the duchesses Plaisance of Cyprus,[58] Mélisande of Tripoli,[59] Catherine of Lesbos;[60] Theodora Tocco of Cephallonia and Zante[61] with the kings of Jerusalem and Princes of Athens, Dukes of Chios & Antioch, Counts of Tessos, Skyros, and Mykonos.

Even back in those days it was not just a matter of the relationships of Gothic aristocracy at dead Hellas costume soirées: the Balkans were already then the Balkans, the most poisonous historical symbolic poppy flowers. There gamboled Turks and Jews; out of senators would come Johannites and out of Jewish rabbis Moslem inquisitors. On the island of Naxos a Jew bore the title 'prince de Naxos,' which according to the Merovingian-style traditions of European feudalism was bestowed on him by Sultan Selim II.[62] Given names like Morea, Mistra, Kleopea, and Malatesta, it is not even a step to the wines — when Casanova drinks those he draws nourishment from the inebriating secretion of history.

If I could make a gift to Casanova, I would present him with the Byzantine goblet, excavated in Opatija some forty years ago, on which were portrayed busts of the tutelary goddesses of four sites: Constantinople, Cyprus, Rome, and Alexandria. Those four cities, grouped together like that and moreover together on a wine goblet, are on the level of a religion — even the one true religion: history. Constantinople: gateway to the Orient, mystery, with the erotic death of the Persians, the death-of-death of the Buddhists, with the crusader armies of eternal European nostalgias; *mâchés* and fiascos. Cyprus: the most ancient Mediterranean history and the most ancient Venus, a dreamier Ur-love by the mire.

Rome: the secret of the Renaissance, rigor rising out of Italian sloppiness, a form even stricter than death, Brunelleschi, Casanova — abstraction a magnetism more powerful than any eroticism. Finally Alexandria: that paradise of commentators, thinkers, relativists, the marvelous system of decadence on the grand scale, the most honest of modern-day Europe's legacies. What else is this Casanova margin of mine if not an absolute 'Alexandria'?

60. Somehow it is a very good assembly that alongside the muscatel goblet in question stand flasks of mercury: alongside the sweet amphorae of drunkenness the somnambulism of alchemy, midnight, the lie, the mysterious element of the Hermes ghost. Casanova is a mercurial fellow — abstract, white, venomous, flitting away and ever a blood relation to witches. *"Muskateller und Quecksilber"* — as it says in his passport.

61. "Torre del Greco" — one can read on one page.[63] Yet another unjustified association, a further clumsy play on words. Well, isn't the Tole-

dan painter a typically post-Roman imperial Balkan?
A wastrel Greek just as the wandering Jew is a wastrel
Jew. Is his brimstone mannerism not the mirror image
of the mannerism of the history of Balkan buffoonery?
"El Greco" — that name was not bestowed on a neo-
Classical, not a paper Olympian but a turfed-out Slav.
If it were not always like that history could not be one's
religion.

62. As a snob and as an en-
lightened man, he greets the parched earth of southern
Italy like: the empire of Pythagoras. So that is Magna
Græcia: that Sahara, that Gobi, Karst and Martorano.[64]
Or after four names why not a fifth? That's Casanova.
I hardly need say that Casanova is aghast at that desert
and flees from it, horror-stricken: the true greats haven't
the foggiest notion of what their essence is and even less
about the symbolism of their landscape.

Later, above all in Volume 3 of the memoirs, he
will find Paris magnificent, though that Paris is nothing
more than Martorano — just as much a manifestation
of Latin gauntness and fakirism as the Arab misery hole
of Calabria. Pythagoras was a numbers man, the Arabs
algebraists, the Semites gallop around in sometimes wild
rationalism (sadly they all wallow with the same naïve
leisure into the swampiest mysticism, yet all the same
numbers serve as their excuse). Casanova also does not
greet the numerologist mystic but the numerologist
ascetic in Pythagoras.

63. In the bare room of the Bishop of Martorano, sitting in an uncomfortable chair at a wretched table, in his ragged clothes, with his dry bread and his deaf-mute peasant flock: did Casanova not notice that the latter, that and forever the latter, were his spiritual and actual relatives? Not Rome, sickly in its Baroque cotton wool, but the clay-head fissured by the sun, the skin and bone Toscanini of peasant reason? I too had my *'Italienische Reise,'* and just one lesson has remained from it: starkness as deliverance. Does Casanova not notice that he is to love what the puritan of Martorano is to religion? Stripped, not to nudity but to the skeleton: oh, the Sicilian logic of shamelessness. Casanova, too, cast away soul, God, native land, nature, mood, morality, affection: he stood before women so scraggily in death throes as the Bishop of Martorano before his Christ. But the only ones who see this are those of us to whom 'Alexandria' is our ultimate prison — no more than a racy seaside outline game to the 18th century.

64. When the most Italian bishop seeks to define Casanova (who is still but a child of 18), he calls him a "sublime poet." In his youth Casanova was so universal that he even permits himself the compromising luxury of appearing as a poet in many places. That is important as this all-fired *'anti-literature'* has, after all, been preserved for us in its form as a book, a memoir. That is important because here poet means maker, a handyman, something Cellini-like, a matter for

a verse salon and periwigs, a Baroque fragrance next to the Baroque artificial flowers.

65. That, then, was what the Rome of the day was fit for. The cardinals and duchesses there were all passionate literati — but that was as yet a literature his side of esthetics and Romanticism, more of a social game, an impromptu & dry philological cultivation in general, thus befitting Casanova. Just as the Renaissance, like a true age of creating masterpieces, did not even conceive of the present-day notion of 'beauty' (which is merely a nervous nightmare of brute force, soul, nostalgic dream and human solitude); just as for Alberti, for example, architecture is not art but simply a thing, *'res,'* [65] beauty does not figure in the first rank but only somewhere in Book 6, & even there only as *"venustas,"* loveliness, attractiveness, with architecture not being expressed in stone but with fountains and water labyrinths: art is just a means for the convenience of lords and masters, nothing more, luxury.

Those two traits should never be forgotten about Casanova's literary pedigree, which even in the 18th century was enduringly & purely Renaissance: in part philological fakirism, a frightening aridity and hideboundness of grammaticizing dryness, in part a luxury for gentlemen, a salon game, witticism, *bon mot.* The favored poet Horace, 'worldly wise' (he was more of a Romantic nihilist than three Buddhas on the lotus throne of doubt!); the symbolic act: *"... so oft ich mit ihm in seiner Bibliothek die Morgenschocolade trinken wollte..."* [66]

66. Casanova was quartered in some good places. In Venice at the Palazzo Grimani, in Rome at the Palazzo di Spagna, from Southern Italy, out of Sicily, every culture untiringly dispatches its fiery rays: Arab, Greek, Norman — and the European synthesis of them all, Spain. If he could not bear Martorano rationalist stylized manner he was at least able to live in Rome in a Spanish palace.

This was a house of privileged madness in Rome — as it was the residence of the Spanish minister, who always looked on the Pope in much the same way as a Byzantine emperor might have looked on an archbishop of Rome; there this Spanish minister held sway over around ten thousand, and the Papal truth did not reach anyone, so that it all became barbarian murderers and lounging trollops.

In the palace the grand Spanish saints, fanatics, scholars with a thousand volumes to their name and vision-seeing nuns, Pope-devouring kings founding new churches and demagogic barefooted mendicants wrote their letters: in Rome it was nonetheless known as a bordello and voluntary house of detention for vagrants. That is where Casanova lodges — like an arrow among autumnal parasite boughs of foliage. It may be the essence, but it is precisely why he has nothing to do with it. (St. Thomas Aquinas writes: *essentia Socratis non est Socrates*.)

67. The fact that in that century eunuchs were still scampering around on Turkish

ships and as *castrati* in Italian operas has two implica-
tions. For a start magnificent voices, an absolute musical
purity, the particular mathematics that is alone capable
of having an effect on the senses; for a second thing, it
denotes uncertainty in love, confusion, hide-and-seek, a
depsychologized hermaphrodite mood which substitutes
with naïve and refined simplicity the moral conflicts of
French novels. One of Casanova's most passionate experiences, amounting to almost the dimensions of the
tragedy of the Princesse de Clèves, can be ascribed to the
fact that he did not know if Bellino was a boy or girl.[67]

That has a potential piquancy of the first rank,
Sodom and Gomorrah with all its subtle nuances, but
it is a much more first-rate mental battle, passion, dis-
consolateness, natural philosophy and asceticism, the
hermaphrodite game hardened Casanova into a hero,
a suffering man, a Lucretius rhetoricizing on the black
market. It seems that matters like that have some mysterious connection with *thinking* — for after all Salimbeni, the celebrated opera castrato, died as a *philosophe*.[68]
That kind of voice must be kept continually in one's ear
while reading Casanova; here there is nothing other than
Palestrina soprano weaving the Vatican as well on all
sides with secular *convolvulus* and a warm violin sound
lulling Venice. It is not even music but pure throat and
pure strings, two animal-heavenly effects, a sensual anti-
Romanticism of virtuosity, which scorns 'psyche' & 'experience.' That voice is one for which blood sacrifices are
made, for which a person is made to cast gender aside,

made to become one of the living dead, a caricature, sick: this is sadism in accordance with Brunelleschi's taste for the sake of the work, this is a disdain of individual human existence which, so it seems, only existed in humanist ages and which is the invigorating air for love and also for this embodiment of anti-humanism.

If I translate Casanova into music there are no instruments, just the classic vocal polyphony of Palestrinas, Ingegneris [69] and de Victorias, the pure materiality of the Italian voice. In the modern age of good-for-nothings 'deep experience' and 'superficial virtuosity' have come face to face in the assessment of musical performance: nothing else follows from that duality than that anyone who articulates a view has not the faintest notion of either experience or technique. Great art, the age of the ascetic clowns of the *castrati*, gives no cognizance to such a distinction; in that the starting-point is undoubtedly technique. The same for a rural charlatan and a sacred musician in the Vatican.

On the other hand, they acquire such an absolute technicality in technique, exploit the material possibilities with such infinite materiality and knowledge, that beside that our "experiences," "our poetic world" and "our flowering blue souls" are no more than a donkey grinding on a barrel organ.

The castrato singer is a symbolic shadow of Casanova: Casanova also sets off from his senses and returns there, but he does that so absolutely and absurdly that this drives him to even deeper emotion, more scalding tears and greater natural secrets than any sort of 'soul' alibi. Just as art can only live off perfect technique, love too is only divine and joyous as virtuosity.

68. Technique, therefore, does not compromise; it exalts. If love is a function of the body, then one should be acquainted with that means; we should read anatomists and not lyricists; go to a clinic and not the theatre. What do Casanova's pals discuss? Do they swap light-hearted jokes with one another, or do they deliberate on such topics as: do or don't the pleasure taken with a woman have an effect on the skin of the fetus?[70] If naturalism is a 'world view,' then it is more meaningless than an empty sheet of paper — if it is just initial training for love, then it is the only sagacity. But then it is just as thorny an issue as Antonio's pound of flesh: if so much as a drop of blood mingles with it, then Shylock will die, if this clinical sobriety and virtuosity is at the cost of a spot of intellectual posturing or a desire for knowledge from a so-called higher-standpoint: then sentimentality is a hundred times preferable.

69. In the homiletics on Casanova, times without number, the stereotype is trotted out that with him everything that for the world at large is two (if not a hundred) is always 'one.' It may be boring, but the truth is that this is not a matter of esthetics, or at most purely by chance. A "single" thing of that nature with Casanova is a "passing adventure" and a "grand

passion" — the two cannot be distinguished, he does not recognize them as being separate.

Most modern love tragicomedies take as their starting-point that the majority of women still insist on retaining the distinction out of misconceived self-interest and blind dogmatism. For them an adventure is always: 'only,' whereas a grand passion is always: a sacred institution. It is not worth the struggle as love always demands geniality of accommodation: reformation and pedagogy are ridiculous here; 'heroes' always tumble from the very start. When Casanova embarks on an adventure he is always madly in love: when he speaks of all-consuming flames, deranged nights, the devastating lethargy of regret and the *furioso* of joy one sees that he is not employing literary formulas but speaking from his kitsch Italian heart. An Italian who, when he declaimed Ariosto in front of Voltaire, started to blubber so much he had a job mopping up the dam-burst of his tears.

That is the way of it, a law of nature, and few women can live with it: anyone who genuinely loves them as they dreamed for themselves will, by nature, also love many other women, because his remarkable born-for-lovingness is inseparably identical to Don Juanism. Anyone who loves them with undying fidelity in comfortable monogamy is going to lack the raging fire that is love's sole sense, the carmine delirium. Just as one of Casanova's Janus-faces is Brunelleschi, the other is Ariosto, of whom he never could have enough and knows of by heart because he is more Romantic than any Romantic; it is just

that the body makes a fool of one, the 'spirit' (in the amatory sense) — an idiot. Most likely the reason Toscanini
was a good musician is that he had not the remotest idea
about what some people are in the habit of calling the
'content' of a work.

70. For a Don Juan type even
the thousandth woman is "the *first* true love," and so it
is with Casanova as well. Lucrezia is the woman of "the
mysteries of love,"[71] the others will all be that. A man like
that will find some greater verity with each and every
new woman — not the 'true' woman, which is simple-
mindedness; he never so much as 'seeks' that kind: his
most decisive feature is that he always *finds*, stumbles
over something; that is why he so quickly goes mad,
because he senses the encounter to be a divine miracle,
a mystic fortuity (how good simple etymology is here).
Without her having the remotest 'characteristic' allures,
the new woman, the eternally recurring: first always
brings him closer to the reality of the whole of nature
and the whole of society: when he parts from his new
lover he whistles back to the birds as a more intimate
acquaintance, looks with greater confidence into the eyes
of those seated opposite him in the carriage. That is why
he feels her to be 'first.' It is always touching if a simple
law also prevails on the greatest; this passage about Lucrezia is also charming in literary terms, with both of
them declaring that up till then they had not known
what love is. It is sweetly amusing that this illusion of

the "*whole* reality" and "nature itself" is always aroused by some ultra-individual little tic, which is such an individual little exception that, to all intents and purposes, it excludes her from reality and nature: in intonation, a flourish in shutting a handbag, the choice of a favorite flower, a flick of the eyelids or some ethical curiosity.

We always approach nature in two kinds of ways: with the mathematical generalizations of the laws of physics — and with the individual extremes and over-analytic impressionism of amatory interest (which includes the artistic, with which in this respect it is identical), that they are both huge intellectual pleasures, there is no question: but one feels inexorably that in point of fact they are private games having damn all in common with reality.

71. It is precisely this Lucrezia whom he finds besides him in the garden "*in der entzück-endsten Unordnung*"[72] — there was no other age in which so much amorous delight would have been found in the disorder of dress. This rococo notion of disorderliness is so saccharinely complicated that one hardly knows where to make a start. Typically, it is a fact that a 'balance of civilization' is: the virtuoso crossing of etiquette and chaos.

When he writes the word "*Unordnung*," even on a modern reader it acts with a blacker sensuality than a hundredweight of pornographic pictures: the way that in Mozart just one superbly placed bassoon staccato is able

to evoke death better than the thousand-stringed shrieking chromatics of a modern-day composer. There will be
other examples of a *big* demonianism of *slight* dishabille,
especially in the salon life of Rome. The musical analogue
is alarmingly malleable — one only needs to think that
music in the 18th century was able to make use of the
dissonance of a second: how satanic, how *'entzückend.'*
(To take just one example out of a million: in the first
movement of Mozart's *Piano Trio № 6 in G major*, K. 564,
the two chords of *d-e* in the bars after the stagnating
passage leading into the development.)

72. Just as perfectly as that sec-
ond relates to the effects of a raft of crummy fake music,
so does the little snake which glints its eyes at Casanova
in the park to the snakes of all mythologies and psy-
choanalyses, to the symbols of sex and devil, distorted
potency and occult alchemy. How far we are from the
world of ophites, snake heretics, Eve's snake, Moses &
Blake and the sign hung out by apothecaries! *"Sieh diesen
kleinen Dämon"* [73] — says the woman, since when have
I never believed that a bigger demon is the true one; I
believe only in these little ones, the Rococo.

Maybe this 'mythical idyll' in the park (here the
woman speaks of *"Geheimnis der Natur"* and *"Schutz-
geist,"* [74] so Casanova believes the woman is a little
touched) is the most stylish, most elegant, and poeti-
cally the most convincing compromise of every myth, of
course in the interest of a greater myth, not of sobriety.

The gods are only tolerable in forms like 'depths of nature': in the form of a bit of park décor, a fleeting excitement, a *kleiner* daemon, a female dream ("*ich bin überzeugt, es ist eine Gottheit...*"),[75] salon zoologizing. That the snake gods were a degenerate race one can see with one's own eyes; they had already become lousy even as poetry millennia before. That snake science, a Faustian knowledge of nature, is just a meaningless word which can only choose between a gesture and blind specialist positivism can likewise be experienced directly at first hand. So what is eternal? The semi-mystical idyll or Casanova and Lucrezia's half-game with the stray reptile. In this there is some internal massiveness, such a human possibility of fending off everything that it cannot help but be compromised. The form of the pirouette: a renunciation of myth and knowledge; this is the first and last, the rest is all a din of the funfair.

73. "*... und dann drangen wir in die Labyrinthe der Villa Aldobrandini ein.*"[76] The initial, elemental influences, the first associations push forward with insuperable impatience. "*Wir drangen ein*" — not entered or even gamboled in, there is no question of rhythm, etiquette, or poetry, just the rawness of conquest, a diabolical provocation — to rob, steal, humiliate whatever possible, life is so grandiosely useless that only irresponsible bestiality deserves the name 'style.' A garden labyrinth: the only real complication, the snake of objects, not of souls or thoughts.

The labyrinth of the parkland rounds: that is no-thing less than a counterbalancing of a simpering 18th century *Pastorale* Zipoli[77] and Minotaur monsters. Al-dobrandini: the magic of names, that is the sole aspect that is still rational and not mystical. It so happens that I have just been reading the *Poésies* of Paul Valéry and I was extraordinarily relieved that one of the many les-sons was that precisely the greatest rationalists, sheer intellects and Latins of *'pensée pure,'* find their ultimate solutions in the music of words, in rhythmic constella-tions, in spells of the *'Temple du Temps'*[78] variety. In a more adolescent era people considered the word magic to be Romantic gaudiness unworthy of the brain, but later on it was realized that where it had seen only sing-song gobbledygook was more, much more, than for instance a definition. With such a *mathesis* the word 'Aldobrandini' is also a colder-blooded precision. It is very much in keeping with that for one to speak in con-nection with Casanova, always a virtuoso eradicator of superfluous dualities and oppositions, of a fusion of word music and pure *raison*, of a long-suspected but now finally apprehended superfluity of a differentiation of intellect and emotion.

The names, then: Aldobrandini, Falconieri, Mon-dragone, Torlonia, Ruffinella. Casanova himself is well aware that a name "does not signify much," simply ev-erything — Voltaire, d'Alembert, Metastasio, Melanch-thon, Beauharnais and Bourbon: in his view these are not people, just names, not kings and reformers, which is just fiction & pedantic historicizing, but immortal melodies, each song defining one of life's aspects. Melanchthon's bones were consumed by the soil, his soul was purloined by pirate precept-angels; the one and only reality for which he had to live and die was: the music suggestion that flows forever from his grotesque name. It should be emphasized — that is how rationalists see it in their most exacting moments. Even if we were only superficially to scratch our historical sympathies a little we would immediately come across name-sonatas and nothing more: our most disquieting positivist data are declined by a soft twisting of the phoneme 'Cleo' and the sudden tiger-drasticity of the coda *'patra,'* as a result of which the taste, dogmatism, and revolution-furnishings of entire eras turn on vowels, labials, and unexpected aspirates. Only people imagine the intellect's intellectual nature so naïvely that they are afraid to admit that kind of thing, supposing it is already hysteria and a vulgar minor-poet's taste.

What sort of stories and engineering tricks are those villas in the environs of Rome? What is the essence of a baroque garden? Tivoli, the classical Tibur, where the magnificent 'quartet' had a say in Casanova's life, was reputedly already in existence four centuries before Rome's foundation — it is important that the villa, which is a fashionable, evanescent, frivolous affair, knows that it has something to do with the Etruscans, Pelasgians, or Siculi — a part-thrilling, part-burlesque Antiquity pertains to the spices.

The other such clove and nutmeg accessory — the ancient gods: a temple of the Tiburtine Sibyl, a water nymph, leading to the river bank; a temple of Hercules Victor leading to a black-market apothecary for the impotent, and from the end of the Lesbia galleries a belvedere overlooking the palm-grove of columns of a temple to Vesta. Antiquity and gods: a nation reveling in historicity or a voracious religion can do without that kind of thing, but never can a villa, a fluttering, red-and-white-striped linen awning or a wicker chair lighter than a flower in the corner of a terrace. Is not Hadrian a hellishly typical case, who in Tivoli constructed the finest palaces and luxury crypts in all of Hellas, Egypt, and Persia in order to admire the variegation of history, the good points of cultures?

This is a place consecrated to history: Clio can only be a prop, a spice, a suggestion for a lampion in the garden of a summer residence. Casanova was well aware that a sure road to the liberation of his love is this blasphemy of history — *"Entstehung des Historismus"*[79] or stammering love semipotencies are always unequivocal. Love seeks the present; indeed, it is the present itself, but with a tyrannical demand that the past can only ever be its eternal clown. Is it not typical that Horace also prowled about with the nihilism of Buddha here, in these skeptical villas, where gods and prehistoric ages practically belong to the cook's province? His *aurea mediocritas* is not at all resplendent and balanced: the whimpering of an animal under a colossus of disillusionment, of a person whom only a sickness of mind and poetry prevented (despite the historical atmosphere being similar) from being a Casanova. Horace and Casanova here were together in Tiburtine villa-cynicism much as Orpheus and Apollo in the last Act of the opera: the poet dawdling down below among the Thracian stones while the god (the non-poet *par excellence*) sports himself in his powdered show-off nakedness on a rooftop.

It has already been suggested that one of the greatest things in Casanova is that he is just as much good for Venice as for Rome — for an anonymous and eternal history-Carnival and for a very highly localized, late-Catholic (Catholicism always being autumnal; a woman rather than a girl) baroque. — From Casanova's Rome just two aspects will be touched on: the ruins of the empire and the late-baroque palaces, temples, and villas. Since both are symbols of decay, indeed are decay — in point of fact Casanova did not have a burning need for Balkan chaos as history, instead of just starting to penetrate in the form of as yet discreet smells: one is already irredeemably in pan-Balkan climes, and thereby neither will any good come of it for the Balkans nor bad for Rome. The Forum Romanum on the politely linking left arm of *death*-comus Casanova and the Mondragone villas just as politely linking the right arm of the *parvenu* comus. Love needs muck, and this is muck: history perished on evidence and, above that, a flashy derivativeness, decadence consuming itself in poses. Because compared with Rome we are still today absolute *parvenus*: our self-determination is *nulla*, every breath we take is secondary, parasitic in nature, an undeclared disease — to use medical jargon: Europe. It may be that we knew it, but the thought was not allowed into the deepest wells of the imagination — a city where every element, every fantastic dimension is uniformly and forever some dead or parasitic, some non-existing and some masked entity — where the sole cultural alternative is: non-being or falsehood. But that is already the last of the spume: behind its surf the birth of Venus is already glistening.

What is that baroque elegance like? Leaden, heavy, malleable: we are unable to reconcile that massiveness with the playful, aphorismic, and algebraic nature of to-day's elegance. The villas are also castes: insofar as the frivolous brain goes around in transparent *tulles* it has citadels around it backstage. The Villa d'Este at Tivoli is gloomier than the St. Rochus Hospital in Budapest, simpler than walls of Cyclopean masonry — maybe precisely that is the *négligée* in it. The Villa Farnese in Capravola is a hell of a weight in itself, in spite of all its snaking terraced flights of steps there is something majestic about its clumsiness. And the semicircular retaining walls with their large niches in the gardens of the Villa Aldobrandini and the Villa Torloni at Frascati? Stones which put one in mind not of a lute player making cliffs dance but of Sisyphus. Often the most fertile land is where a slight adjustment is made to the accustomed meaning of a word: behind the airiness of the word 'villa' lies the suffocating burden of baroque summer residences. Much as the villa itself is a funereal millstone, so the garden around it is a desperate throw which completely loses direction — having something to do with everything except never with nature. But then in Italy, as we know, there is no nature.

It is of vital importance with respect to Casanova's love that: there is no question of art in the construction of the villas, no question of nature in the gardens, 'beauty' and 'nature' are unknown, all that exists is the only true luxury. That is why they are the loveliest gardens which ever existed — a *'jungle calculé'* is more beautiful than a jungle or even a calculus. Just toss the elements down next to each other, not knowing in advance whether it will remain a catalogue or burst into an analysis — what is there in such a garden?

A row of cypresses, endless steps, stone terraces, terraced lawns, mute ponds, ponds with tiny fountains as navels, meandering balustrades, free-standing shrubs, potted shrubs, semicircular walls with niches, waterfalls with rounded and angular forms, lakes with ribbons of pathways which seem to float on the surface of the water hanging lakes, what were in point of fact gigantic wells with three or four levels of basins, unexpectedly densely leaved, cubist walls of evergreens, eerily clipped to angles, arches of triumph, entire peristyles cut out with shears, lakes phrased in similar fashion as if they were fretsawn glass fragments, a single fern species allowed to run freely for miles, then, in a footprint of space, a thousand varieties of floral curiosities, cut into little bits, colorless in their company. The Moorish gardens of Spain are like that; a *pessimistic* voraciousness of *abstract* plots of land.

I have three such favorites of redemptory force: the Villa di Gamberaia on the sides of Setignano outside Florence; the kaleidoscope of lakes of the Villa Lante near Viterbo; and finally the wonderful Piazzale dell'Isolotto of the Boboli Gardens in Florence. To begin with the latter, only briefly tossing the raw materials for reflection beside each other and leaving the decoration, for epigones or, on the contrary, those who relish a big challenge, the melismatic completion (the text or subtext here, like with old scores of music: only the essentials are given, the elaboration is entrusted to the performer).

The first marvel is that the huge citadel of foliage is broader higher up than at the bottom — which straight away sets into motion a refinement, a fiction, into the weed-rich world of a décor bloodier than martyrdom, the artificiality into monumental impudence, which is more than the truth. This forced yet uncapsizable floating is an elegant triumph of the lie. It is all wall-like, in the most bastion-style fashion, martially austere, reminiscent of the castles of Frederick II, yet nevertheless laminated, porous, and crumbling, in which the tiny devastations of light-caterpillars, flower-salves, dust and shadow, wind and noise can blithely play: the fusion into a single form and unequivocal mass of the autumnal sponge crumbling from the sound of the dungeons and thousand lights of the Hohenstaufen bridge castle at Capua; that is an excellent spiritual exercise. This whole court luxury wall and vegetation pie, in all its rococo and elegance: is funereal;

the clipped wall of foliage so dark, as midnight green as
the draperies of a royal burial — nowhere in nature is a
burdensome mourning of such weight assembled. When,
on arriving from one of the roads, one steps into the ring
around the catafalque, one nevertheless feels that one
has landed in an idyllic magic circle, a hellishly narcissistic self-centeredness where the emphasis is on dreams,
peace, and opium happiness. That notwithstanding this
should be tragic: the cosmetic secret of the late baroque.
— The inner experience of the ellipse would make for a
separate chapter in this garden-Loyolite meditation, that
of the inebriated circle which always remains a sick or
degenerate or lesbianized circle, a voluptuous distortion,
slipping and mis-reflectedness. The oval: half of the rococo depends on this, this circle is, after all, not a circle
in its light intoxication of self-contradiction. That ellip-
ticalness gives the impression of exquisite decadence, a
mild feverish dream to the Boboli area as well — at once
Greek trigonometry and ecstatic fault: as if luxury had
precipitated the anarchism and homesickness lurking
since forever at the bottom of geometry towards the elegant *nihil*-archings of parabolas and hyperboloids. And
indeed, this ellipse is worthy of Casanova: simultaneously a closed circle and a parabola slipping off into unreality. — This space is dreadfully simple — one feels the
same as he did at the age of around thirty in his relations
to women: fifteen years of self-torment, lies, psychological crippling and cowardice, the ridiculous dung heap of
complications were necessary so that he might finally

be able to say point-blank, calmly, in an equilibrium of prosaic honesty and a desire of cast-off mask, straight to a woman's face: "*I fancy you; I want you.*" How many pin-brained idiocies and brainless flourishes a person had to flounder through before reaching that simplicity, that black nakedness. How exciting and secretive a law of nature that simplicity only ever makes an appearance at the end of an excruciatingly protracted developmental path: the huge oval of foliage is also like a victorious re-signed finish after the useless complications of millennia. One senses that oval as the natural form of stillness: if silence is left to itself in an airless space, it will crystallize elliptically like that. Just as time is the redolence and vapor of objects, so silence is a chemical phenomenon identical with certain objects and forms — well, here we have located the scholastically eternal form: the lake-ellipse with a frame of clipped black foliage. — This space is *large*: large in an Egyptian or Palmyran sense, in an unsophisticated ancient sense, in the way it was imagined by the oldest peoples, who were still clever and they knew that formidably large dimensions were already an esthetic, indeed, *the* esthetic. This area is the primitive victory of an antediluvial Quantum after a great deal of later, ridiculous gushing about quality. Still, complexity does also have a share in the oasis of harmony — autumn plays out its part in wilting runs and flourishes; in the foliage, the water plants, it paints over and needles its way through the great phalanx of foliage, the flitting Proustian intricacies of the browns, yellows, reds and lilacs, the pyramid is also atomized: there is nothing lovelier than a garden paralyzed in a somnambulism of geometry, when autumn starts to grow tousled in color. Fallen leaves on the road — it is as if we were coming across fresh tears beside a mummy. — In between, lonely columns that do not hold roofs but through the radiating ports of their own mirror images, which they glue to themselves as if pulled to the tips of a horseshoe magnet.

The 'solitary column' is a special form of sentimental adventure in this garden: more pornographic than the Venuses of wells, more reclusive than Syrian hermits, more elegant than the kings dallying beneath them, and more melancholy than any autumnal chromaticism. Apart from which they were brought into being specifically in order to have a shadow or reflection — their stand-alone existence is naught beside that prolificity of visions. — A quite different function is possessed by solitary statues, which, if at all possible, are copies of originals that exist elsewhere. Adonises, Aphrodites, dolphins and Tritons; as gods: they were just impotent falsehoods — but as copies and backdrops: they are eternal powers. The white shade (slightly dirtied to grey) among green foliage and lakes of a different green tint: almost transparent stamps of the godless divine, non-erotic Eros: convention as the very first spell. Are those nudes naked? There is more autumn in them, in their sightless eyes, in the slipping-down folds of their togas, in the strange flexings of the knees, than in fallen tree leaves. — And the seashells? How do their folds and clusters relate to the pure giddy diadem of the ellipse? These marble ringlets and stone scrolls on the rims of wells or the pedestals of statues? Are these two circular scales not magnificent: the giant lunatic arch and this flower-like, vegetative folding of Archimedes' brain? — The fine texture of the iron lattice on the banks of the lake — a small hacksaw hypothesis beside a 'huge' body of water? The pleasure of shortening?

The three steps: the clean big design of the nearby lattice; by the turn the superposing of the inside and by now far-side design, the spot of chaos of the bend; and finally, after the turn, clean patterns afresh only now in horrific miniature. — Alongside this metal embroidery stone walls with their stout baroque calves as they float above the water — the Pandora's vases of the lead seals of silence. — But all that for the lake and from the lake, of the lake and by the lake.

The lake, which is a mirror, dark green, mute, shiny, heavy, marshy, autumnal and millennial. (Above all it casts these attributes from itself like dead fish.) On it the floating island — nothing is more enigmatic than a stone wall immediately on a water surface —, it's as though the floor of a room had been flooded with a fraction of an inch of water. — In the final analysis is this area open or closed? Have we ended up in the inmost part of life or shall we fly out of it straight into the heavens? Will we finally grow dizzy in the crippled whirl of the oval, or have we found its peace in the Promised Land of "sleep & poetry"? Has everything been solved or is this precisely the tension, hitherto unfelt, of anticipation?

If this Boboli pondweed of harmony will be the black rainbow of simplicity in my eternally barren life (because it is certain, quite certain, that anyone who reacts in the way I do to a spectacle and is narrowed down into this kind of stylistic constraint is: barren) — then the Garden of the Villa de Gamberaia is a symbol of complexity, Arabic Art Nouveau. Bush, flowerpot, fountain, gravel path, child's labyrinth, grey dead water and a beer tankard's froth of soap-bubble hue, cypress & elder, baroque foliage and Quasimodo fruit trees squeezed together on a small terrace, tossed between bleak surroundings and still bleaker firmament — that is the gardenia scherzo, the anthill. Last of all, the Villa Lante with its silver lake, silver villa, silver pinewood, silver hills on the horizon: an Oberon swamp, poetry as malaria.

When just before, in parenthesis, I characterized my fate as barren, from that it could be seen that the question of 'description' is a gripping, not to say fraught, issue in my life. Barren — although I did not apply the word to myself out of an immoral &, above all, useless adolescent whim of public self-humiliation; it certainly included a sober assessment. In relation to what do I feel description is barren? And with what am I able nevertheless to force it into a merit? — In leafing through Casanova, the first and the last is indubitably that set of social customs and ethically-related notions which makes the 18th century what it is. Thus, if I were really to comment, then under no circumstances should I produce garden descriptions; instead I ought to emphasize conventions, salon formalities, & the layout of institutions.

I thereby opened up one of the most savage battles of my life: the battle of the 'descriptive' versus the 'anecdotizing,' the Romantically luxuriant in statics versus the French moralizing style of a La Bruyère or La Rochefoucauld. I could give the opposition a thousand other names: one is the intellect, the other, gossip; one is neurotic compulsion, the other, unbounded aphorizing; one is poetry, the other, morality; one is nonsense concerned with the sole meaningful subjects, the other, complete sense concerned with the most meaningless subjects. So, what is it that attracts me to description all the same? First & foremost the fact that in an object, the oval of the lake of the Boboli Gardens, for instance, there are many more novelties, variations, elements, and shades than in any kind of so-called rational thinking. The most complex thoughts, poetic sensibilities, or philosophical sophistications are all stupefying platitudes, oafish homogenizing beside the infinity of nuancing of an *object*. Thinking, however, imposes a demand for nuance, a microscope madness; it goes where it can best satisfy that insatiability for atoms. That is always a material object, not some kind of human relationship, moral conflict, or anything else of that sort. Of course, description immediately runs aground on a dreadful self-contradiction: precisely because it is an object, the Boboli Gardens, an infinite tissue of infinite shades in comparison with the clumsiness and schematism of a thought: it is precisely on that account that I do not have suitable words to restore them: a description, whether poetic or surrealistic or photographic, is always an 'intellectual,' and therefore primitive, conventional something. The truly intellectual stimulus therefore either remains in the unproductive nervous state of such a stimulus or it really makes a start on 'description,' in which case it will in the monotony of conventional attributes. What an object is truly has no name and is utterly ungraspable. (St. Thomas Aquinas: *individuum ineffabile est.*)[80] Only a naïve and comic compulsion drives one into trying all the same. 'Style' is thus nothing more than an absurd undertaking; for after all it is impossible to think, thinking amounting to no more than lying, prevaricating, and castrating.

In front of me lies a picture postcard that I wrote to a friend when I was in the company of a French girl — the greeting from the Boboli Gardens runs as follows: "*l'inéxistence du* style, *l'inéxistence de la* pensée." I tried to specify more precisely the reason for this dual non-existence. This is what I came up with: the most stimulating for a brain is always the *momentary* encounter of a bunch of *strange* things in a *fortuitous* constellation; a composition of foliage, statue, water, my memories, my companion, my plans at a non-recurrent random point in time and space that never was: it is natural that this radically brand-new and wildly heterogeneous grouping has no name, and could not have one. Intellectual stimulation is therefore caused by a completely individual and new shade of a supposedly already familiar thing or a new, totally new, random constellation or system of hundreds of things. The former will be just as anonymous as the latter. Despite which the impression of a thought can only ever be awakened in me by a shade shaded to the point of absurdity or by that kind of constellation. Precisely that is the bloody crux of the thing — I do not sense the Boboli Gardens as a picture, not for a second as a 'colored vision' (I need that like I need a sore head) — but as a thought, a truth, for my intellect.

An inflexible rationalism might say that, out of cowardice, I am simply tipping onto a sentimentality for Romantically vegetating landscape mawkishness: the greater prestige of a mask of 'intellect' and thus seeking alibis for my descriptive barrenness. Maybe; until his dying day a person will never know for sure whether his truths stemmed from pleasure in attacking or defensive necessity; most likely mutually.

Yet can I justifiably call the Boboli Gardens a *thought* if, at one and the same time, it is inexpressible, if it can only be 'bad style'? Yes. Of course, I have to redefine 'thought' anew: a thought which seems relatively independent of self- and race-preservation causes a physiological stimulus, and that stimulus is always evoked either by an 'absolute nuance,' or by a fortuitous constellation of a thousand things, an aggregation of relationships which is unnamable from the outset but whips up passion in the brain. It is from here that my 'barren' mania of descriptions derives — I am always guided by a logical furor of discovery, an optimist despite its hopelessness.

I am convinced that the most monotonous fiasco of a landscape description lies closer to the natural history of logic, the truth, and intellectuality than all the philosophers from Plato to Kant. If an intellectual experience is tantamount to "a composition of the shades of reality," then — every structure, a landscape in nature, a Raffaello *Madonna* or an elementary geometrical figure is a thing a thousand times more intellectual than an out-and-out 'thought' — *only* décor is true logic.

A 'thought,' then, is *not* something cerebral, not human, — a 'thought' exists only in nature, in the objects of the outside world, and is identical with its composition. What is inside us is just passion — stimulation over and above this unintellectualizable intellect, a lyrical affirmation of this anonymity. 'Thought' of the old school is completely extinct, leaving the 'logic' of the million shades and constellations of the outside world: those are besieged with unremittingly hopeless love by 'description,' the only possible philosophy of the new times — all we have been left with is that passionate reaction of the *raison*-immanence that is merely felt and sensed but perhaps never to be expressed. To sum up — a 'thought' is both: an absolute *description* together with an absolute *stimulation*. In other words, exactly that has become the crown of intellectuality, whereas previously it had been a blemish: its slaves are copying and lyrical bias. If we realize that these two blemishes are two prime merits and two possibilities which exclude all else — that will be a Copernican revolution in the history of thinking as

Kant's was in his time. That is why it was worth becoming immersed, faithless to Casanova, in the dark shadows of the labyrinthine alleys of the Villa Aldobrandini.

And if the fate of thought in general is of no interest, this conclusion does interest me from the perspective of my own life: through it I am able to provide (the malicious of course will say "to mask") a rationale for the diary style of my entire *oeuvre*, my utter homesickness for an endlessly complete diary. That the roots of that might possibly be neurosis is utterly immaterial: miracles can be born of sickness, a hump from a wonder — just one thing is sure about apples, which is that they fall far from their tree.

Why, then, is a diary the ultimate ideal in place of the honest superstition of the old-fashioned 'objective opus'? Because once I sense the ever-new consequences of the millionfold shades of the world to be a *thought*, then, as I am first and last a *thinker*, not a living creature: precisely these constellations alone, just as they are, I note down the description, accepting the risk of an unstylistic self-contradiction. *Those* are thoughts. A true intellectual response to the world is not a myth, not a philosophy, not a novel or an essay: those are isolated fictions, irrational narcissifications, games, at best *"Les langueurs tendres"* as one of old Bach's sons said[81] — a truly *intellectual* response is only: a *complete life*, along with all its startling events, its endless chains of associations, the million varieties of mood. That this can also be disparaged as an 'illusion of Romantic totality' signifies less than nothing.

Metaphysics can at last find itself in this diary ideal: a complete intellect can only be a complete life, all landscapes, all loves, all books, all friends, all notions.

What was it that I wrote on the very first page of my diary? I may quote from it now that I see as plain as daylight that the separation of some form of fictive 'opus' and 'diary' would be an intellectual capital crime and damnation (assuming the inspiration of my life is truth rather than beauty): "... sentiment & image: those are realities, a thought is always just a plus floating around that, a vapor, something *par excellence* not wise and not an essay — the fact that all which exists right now, just the way it is — that, that is a thought, always the *tonality* of a total reality, constellated of millions of elements, not a theme or a song; it is not the thought which goes around with emotional accompanying elements but, quite the reverse, the sentiment-reality is attended by nightmare thoughts; the greater a thinker is, the more readily will he acknowledge the intellectual's diffuse, outward nature, more capricious than even hysteria..."

This is the melancholy difference between Casanova and the reader: he found love in the labyrinthine alleys of the Villa Aldobrandini — *"zwei volle Stunden entschwanden in den süssesten Entzückungen."* [82] The commentator? His weary apology for the curse of the intellectual.

74. He finally reaches the Pope, Benedict XIV. One has a hard time enumerating the number of perspectives from which this audience is

symbolic and important. The pope represents baroque Rome; the pope was already a baroque entity in Early Christian or good old Merovingian times — he is the eternal god of *history* above the ephemeral devil of abstract *truth*. Somehow the same kind of thing the nymph statues of the Boboli Gardens were after the total collapse of the Greek world. By chance he may also be the embodiment of eternal *truth*, whether out of amusement or *ex cathedra* strictness, but that is not his essence. His essence is to elevate the inconsistency of history to the grade of sanctity, as against the logical absolutism of naïve dogmatists inherited from huddling in the catacombs. He represents a much deeper, more human, more vegetative form of truth than any other variety of Christianity. Here relativism and God coincide at a single metaphysical point — does the heart have need of more? Those who, out of Protestant nakedness, demand 'pure truth' and 'implacable consistency,' with broad logical grimaces and gesticulations: have usually not even dreamed of the truth, which is always an inexpressibly complex situation, a curiosity of diplomatic balancing — all they know is elementary multiplication tables.

Even in serene hypocrisy this smiling pope is a bigger truth than any little revolutionizing based on the gorging of evidence. The truth is not evident, not logic, & not faithfulness to an eternal determinacy — neither Plato nor Christ dreamed about such philological impotence: truth is an ironic nightmare on the borders of our fate, at one moment a black demonism, at another a Brazilian

honeymoon butterfly, and smiling Benedict XIV represents that wisdom, for which reason he deserves a much
more mystical-Mannerist title than 'Holy Father.' In the
end, his truth can also be pathetic if Europe's stupidity by
any chance calls for 'pathétique' in its vulgar concerts, but
the essence is cheerfulness, confidence in uncertainty, in
compromise, which is not appeasement but an opalesc-
ing and seismographically fine completeness. The pope
is to logic what Casanova is to love: they were bound to
meet. His holiness is open, it is possible to gain admit-
tance to him unannounced, if by any chance that is what
entered one's head in the street on the way to the Vatican.
Imagine the many, many fully open doors, from the corner urinals and cherry vendors up to the innermost study
room of the Vatican — you may pass along that as on any
suburban street. And what does Giacomo ask for from
the pope? That he be permitted to read all the forbidden
books and to eat meat on fast days. Isn't that sweet? The
great libertine not only asks for permission in order to
say something to the pope: Casanova is Catholic, otherwise there would be no Europe, which always means, at
one and the same time, some exotic ideal and some just
as exotic compromise, decay in a spot of humanity. But
that is the most that can be achieved, that wild abstraction plus a spot of humanity — major humanity is always
fancy dress, a machine, black clown. Mention has already
been made of how even Casanova himself considered
it far from ridiculous to fantasize about the papal tiara.

75. More than one of Casanova's adventures (though the word 'adventure' may easily be misleading for with him it is always a matter of much more than that) is a dream of wish fulfillment come true without one tasting the sick, cowardly, or feverish flavors of the dream, the barren picturesqueness of a lonely man. Tivoli is an unnarcissistic, unpoetic, and unimaginative dream of that kind: candle, keyhole, midnight lantern, candelabra, evening undressing, interconnecting rooms, southern climate, orange trees clinking like coins, a virgin and a woman offering themselves alongside each other: all that, along with the full complement of staff — there is nothing more than that. Casanova was the only one able to portray the enchanting self-evidence of happiness, and thus he avoided the hospital vulgarity of craving & the repellent Nietzschean torso of an "apology for life." His happiness is replete with a most highly Thracian excess of sensuality (many a time he records that he only left off embracing because he had started bleeding!), despite which everything is charming, lyrical, sweet and self-evident: people had not yet realized what a stylistic wonder is concerned with in the literal sense. Dream and sensuality, retaining the whole anarchy of colors — the whole is nevertheless an anemone. The playful hide-&-seek of the word 'Tivoli' does a lot to define it.

76. Casanova is able to make magnificent use of small psychological *quid pro quos.* After all, the soul and psychology are luxuries, baroque

pomp, just as much a matter of decorum as togas more puffed than clouds on altar statuary. The 'soul' is no more than one of the social tricks of mannerism, a perfume, an aphrodisiac, and Casanova in decking himself out naturally daubs himself all over with that pomade. Instead of emotional confusion ("*Verwirrung der Gefühle*" as it was known to those who devoured perfume and 'soul' instead of bread): little artfulnesses. Cardinal S. C. and Marchesa G. write sonnets to each other, with the prelate asking Casanova, who is likewise in love with the marchioness, to write on the cardinal's behalf a couple of poems in response to her. Casanova has to write the stanzas in such a way as to be clumsy enough for her to suppose they are from the cardinal, but on the other hand they also had to express Casanova's own passion. A delightful situation — prelate and marchioness, heavenly and earthly aristocracy; the interweaving lines of roaming ardor, ecclesiastic restraint, and court etiquette; poetry as salon practice and Antique undressing; Casanova's hypocrisy and honesty: is not a situation like that a true world of love? The cardinal refines his 'divine' mythical awkwardness, the big humpbacks of loneliness of 'poeticality' is hidden by salon games; hiding, smoldering in the great freedom of opium, instead of a janitor day-dream of boundary-breaking passion. The cardinal is more than god, the swanky marchioness more than a 'profoundly human being,' the boudoir sonnets are more than specters of 'experience' — because they are in the service of happiness. Only that counts here. It is precisely on that account that the soul just feels comfortable in an atmosphere of mendacity deriving from just a bit of zigzagging of relationships.

77. How much more erotic, more sultry an atmosphere can be aroused by Casanova, with seemingly simple devices than all myth pornography taken together. He asserts about the marchioness that when he paid an unexpected visit on the cardinal during lunch she is wearing elegant *dishabille*. *Dishabille!*

To anyone who has envisioned with Casanova Venetian balls and *déjeuners* of the Roman baroque and Counter-Reformation, the marchioness' appearance *en déshabille* is a figure of more than ten Aretino embraces. That dishabille is in itself already the coming of the anti-Christ, decadence, a total lack of modesty. And she arrives unannounced — if Greta Garbo herself were to abandon her film role, descend from the screen, and lovingly kiss the lounging cloakroom attendant, that would not be so dramatic a turn as the marchioness' arrival without being announced by footmen. If for no other reason that is why it is worthwhile for a culture to hang on tooth and nail to the elaborate ceremonies of a mandarin elegance in order that such possibilities of revolution should endure. — Another such flower of decadence: the cardinal's dining table where the marchioness arrives is by his bed. Such a hotbed of 'chez lui' tenor, of near-infernal intimacy, such a sodomitic accent, is not felt anywhere.

78. The trio of Casanova, the cardinal, and the marchioness arrives at its most marvelous point — the poetic impromptus. When people began with nervous greed to put up a defensive shield round the baroque, which for a while had been scorned, then of course they had to notice, in music and verse alike, the supreme importance that was granted to ad-libbing in that culture.

In what brilliance worthy of Casanova this artistic habitude gleams; how impossible it is to picture anything else alongside Casanova. Inspiration is not born in solitude but beside the cardinal's bed, on the laid table, between the Marchesa who had strayed by in her *dishabille* & the Cardinal sipping his black coffee: freely, on the spur of the moment, feeling its way into reality, little more than a pretext for eyes and hands to be launched into a wilder St. Vitus' dance: "The proper study of mankind is man":[83] that is the quintessence, a living person's living hand and living eye, poetry serves the first happiness of gesture, not *vice versa*. A writing desk is more comical than a bidet in Walhalla; paper, text, the minimum. Mozart's finest variations did not arise through fate gripping the soul but a pleasant social ambience snatched him by the *hand* to — dance. *Geburt der Tragödie aus dem Geiste der* Plauderei.[84]

79. We don't want books, & we don't want gods; we never had any metaphysical excitements; we're uniformly uninterested in the past and

future of mankind; we never give a hoot about art and truth — all that have truly excited us to our dying day have been blissful situations: a dreamlike harmony of women, nature as a background, and health.

There are many such 'redeeming situations' (the sole realistic topic of desire, in contrast to the above moonshine) in Casanova: one of the finest is the continuation of the above-outlined scene. The cardinal falls asleep, thus Casanova and the marchioness can be alone. He 'falls asleep,' he does not fall captive or die; there is no need to hurt his feelings or hide away: both priest and Casanova feel most comfortable of all. A chance like that is rarer than a comet in a top hat — which is why for those real miracles, and just for them, we are indebted to fate. The marchioness goes out onto the terrace. Is there a happiness imbedded more deeply in demonic strata than after a delicious luncheon with wine to go out on a terrace, into the open air, a garden, which is nevertheless a room: there to rock between, precisely 'between,' the sultriness of the bed and the freedom of the forest? The woman perches on the balustrade — that is again an intimate easiness which is more dizzying than the erotic tricks of any apothecary. One of the woman's knees lightly brushes Casanova. The inebriated rhymes of the improvised verse, the cardinal's gentle puffing and blowing, the warm mass of food and drink in the body, the terrace frame of mind, the balustrade and the distant fountains, the *négligée* on the marchioness, the strange skin sliding by Casanova's skin — that lyricist rightly exclaims: "*Welche*

Stellung!"[85] He declares his love for the woman — a true, one and only possible declaration of love, this touch of sensuality trembling between the salon and nature, when the words of love are merely landscape painting: an expression of the fact that the garden is here, the terrace too, Rome is here, & here are we, and the wine was just fine.

Feeling good, the postprandial, disdained petty bourgeois 'middle class *bien-aise*': *this* is the sole interpretation of the *appassionata* that is not flat. It is the tow of melancholy in Watteau's parks, blacker in its wistful sugariness than all of Rembrandt's affectation of mourning. Digestion reveals more profound spleens and loves than anything else. As the Marchesa moves away to avoid Casanova's over-daring hands — in that one movement, in the bashful swish of the dress and the unabashed consenting look, the oh, so Lethe sweetness of love, its religious shadow and social drollery, are combined in a way that might, perhaps, never recur again. And with what ardor does Casanova enjoy the soft sentimentality produced by unvented sensuality and the wine — *"eine neue Wollust im Gehorsam."*[86] The entire amatory ethos: it is either a business 'ethos,' some form of legalistic kitsch, or else a sweet squeaking stemming from an aborted sensuality of that kind: Casanova will gladly squeak for an afternoon; there is no risk of his generalizing that digestive charisma and taking it as a fixed moral. *"Ich blieb bei ihnen bis zur Dämmerung. Dann ging ich."*[87] Startled, one is inclined to shout out after him — for God's sake, stay — nightfall, why do you chose that of all times to quit that park, the fountains, the moon-mirroring lakes, & the white terraces in the black shadows of the cypresses? Life does not consist of more nor less than this — is it possible to make such a fuss and say simply: *"Dann ging ich?"*[88] — If a reader has seen such a vision, he would close the door behind him on his lover, even if that happened not to be the Marchesa perching on the balustrade; he would never take a stroll again unless the roses of precisely this baroque villa, transparent as glass, were tangling the little couple's filaments of the rising moon; not for all the world would he go to lunch any longer with his best friend unless it were that cardinal, purring in his nightcap; above all, he would never, not to his dying, pray, read, or cogitate any more unless his god were a Roman step, his book, a well, and his thought *"diese Stellung."*[89]

80. Casanova is many things but specifically not a libertine, someone hungrily on the look-out for any cheap pleasure. When he takes pity on a pretty woman, it is without avail that he sees her naked and plunged deep in sleep for he himself is clothed when he lies down beside her. That he should lie down beside her rather than somewhere else is simply — a contemporary gesture, an 18th-century way of saying 'good night, sweet dreams.' Let it not be forgotten: the most fantastic things in Casanova, from an erotic point of view, are all gray conventions of the day: what makes Casanova Casanova in the eyes of a neophyte is precisely the anonymous age — one's own characteristics are located quite

differently. From the viewpoint of happy lessons, however, it is matter of the nth-rank, whether something is Casanova or the 18th century itself.

81. Casanova is inconceivable without opera, and opera is gibberish *galimathias* without the 18th century. 19th-century opera? — nonsense. There once was opera, here among us at that, but it will be no more.

What was this opera? First and foremost a social event, a huge salon where there were card tables in the corridors — Casanova lost and won millions in places like that where French and Italian scores predestined Mozart in fateful proximity. That is where procuresses strolled and ambassadors flirted: in those days the latter occupation was a frankly admitted occasion for strutting one's stuff just as the escaped Italian convict Casanova was but a hair's breadth away from becoming one of the French king's semi-official trustees of the first state for lottery: and the king of Portugal's representative at the Augsburg Congress. Opera of the time pertained to that glittering political nihilism or nonchalance. But alongside cardsharping and the politics of the salon there were also ballet & vocal virtuosity, pure dance and endless coloratura, the final, i.e., powder-compact-stage of Greek myth. Even monstrously "bull-in-a-china-shop" Beethoven wrote *ballet* music for Prometheus, not big-bass-drum and cymbal martyr's music for liberalism. Opera was an organic part of carnival, much as was the mask. The 19th

century knew separate ballets and separate myth-bison "*Musik-drama*" — singly the two are useless, the truth being that instead of pure ballet even a music-hall knees'-up has better musical and female material on show, and pulp fiction or raw philosophy of history is better than now mythical, now *verismo* "*Musik-drama*."

Opera's sole opportunity was the Mozartian variety: a marvelous balance of ballet-like stylization, puppet unreality, and the profoundest human tragedies — *Don Giovanni* is the musical sibling of Casanova's life, with which, willy-nilly, it has fused in our memories. Even the smaller operas of this period are like the black-dominoed figures of masked balls: at once death and a carnival somersault. Anyone who has not realized evenings at the opera filled half of Casanova's cerebrum. The Council of Trent is already opera, *Die Entführung aus dem Serail* blacker than *Antigone*.

82. And all those operas, after Villa Borgheses & Villa Negronis, with the naturalness of a bloom unfurling from a bud or the sole possible conclusion from logical predicates: "*... aber nach Konstantinopel muss ich gehen!*" [90] At the time Casanova was not yet twenty: a coincidence of old Europe's ever-naïve wish for the Orient and an adolescent's thirst for tales. This whole classicism of life-love-happiness that young Giacomo represents requires a mythical *fortissimo*, and that could not be anything other than Constantinople. This duality in Casanova is glorious — he is a Racinian-style

asceticism of happiness — an Arab formula, yet that succeeds so perfectly, his rigorousness is so dizzying, as to scatter ecstatic lights and legendary aromas around himself, his tempo that of a flying horse, his shadow the Persian underworld of Sindbad. The formula reaches its limits, the logical intensity reaches its ultimate degree of incandescence: it is necessary that the tale, a pure dream dance, should precipitate from it. Casanova is always the magical potency of the miracle — his abominable *"praktikum"* side is accompanied by an Oberon side as well, which attains expression in the trip to Constantinople that he had many a time felt to be an obsession.

As to what that 18th-century Constantinople is like, this is entirely explained by the first name that we read: Casanova's sealed letter of introduction is addressed to Monsieur Osman Bonneval, Pasha of Karamania. This is already decadent Turkey, but on exactly that account Giacomo can advert with all the more justification to words like *"Aberglaube"* and *"Schicksal"* [91] in relation to his irrevocable journey.

83. That Constantinople phantasmagoria is the counterpart of an amatory phantasm: he falls in love with Bellino, about whom he knows not whether he, she, or it is male, female, or an operatic castrato. He had the long weeks for which that uncertainty endured to thank for the greatest frenzy, the greatest moral loftiness, and the finest psychological shades of sophistication. The hermaphrodite chaos is

an extraordinarily vital lesson — it was necessary for us to see that love is: a luxury, madness, anarchy, life's *fioritura*, always a perversity from the very start, in the noblest, which is say, the only and most transcendental sense.

Not man and not woman, not delectation and not moral, but a frantic meander of happiness over the beingness of being — simply the character of life as an eternal crisis, boundless promise, and boundless deception, a pure Janus circus. That is why at this point Casanova ascends into rhetorical heights of the blackest passion and the blackest moralizing — this is where he confronts the essence of life itself, love as a murderous paradox, as a divine bluff. What the bumbling metaphysics of later times was only able to envisage with a Faustian *"die Mütter"* a higher artistic intellectuality managed to express with the *idée fixe* of Constantinople and this volatile hermaphrodite puzzle. Here humanity's big problem of 'reality & unreality' is not a problem, because even the unreal is reality: the type of personal device of an Emperor Charles V's *"plus oultre"* [92] is still from inside in the world — after all, it is possible to stroll in Constantinople, and that internal self-contradiction, however-interpretation, elementary indefinability, & aimlessness of a natural, organic, and vital thing which is the castrated or pseudo-castrated, disguised woman or man: is not a literary oddity but a well-known social figure. This Bellino is the first and last triumphant nymph of European metaphysics.

84. Bellino's associates, girls of twelve and eleven, likewise belong to this amatory category. The 'perversity' is never a moral and never a physiological notion: it is always well-founded, logical. These child whores proclaim the same as glass crabs, butterfly fish, seal-titmice, and caterpillar-frogs — vegetation is: a sophistication. Here value, purpose, and content are: *nulla*; the interminable joke holds sway. However, if intellectuals of the 20th century wish to experience this caprice of dogma in quite close proximity to reality — they should go to the zoo and inspect the branched rainbow gills of hydroid polyps on the walls of the aquarium or the marvelous counterpoint of lines between the skin shed by the colubrine serpent, the geminate Zamenis diadem snake, and its old body as both twine around a scrawny bush: the transparent empty sheath is a preserver of Olympian sterile rays and a reptile of the Greek islands which can leap in one's kisser. In this connection I must confess this is probably an extreme caricature of human dignity, the 'science,' let us say, the biology — when Casanova finds this, too, in a person, in these vagrant girl children, instead of such a circus of shame. Love here in reality, like the scores of baroque musicians — here only a bare skeleton part is thrown in and it depends on me whether I play it on an organ or sing it, play it on a harpsichord or violin: the amatory instinct is a bare skeleton like that, it is up to me whether immature children or a sixty-year-old will be my instruments. A child is super, of course, because in it both corporeality and dreamlike-

ness are excessively present: a mere 'morsel' (frog's legs, snail soup, woodcock excreta!) and a sheer *ultima* Thule, fable or stray star.

85. To an absolute, intricate degree, 18th-century women know, recognize, & accommodate to the fact that a passionate and lyrical man who is worth anything is always a *"homme de plaisir,"* never a *"homme d'amour,"* as the hero in a French novel puts it.

One of the least comprehensible wonders in the whole Casanova work: women who are passionately in love with him allow, indeed ask him, with the most supportive tenderness and mental elegance, to bestow his bodily favors on other women as well. People nowadays have got used to the idea that even pimps can be jealous and are capable of galloping into Proustiads — here the most madly infatuated Isoldan lovers only feel their nuptials are complete if Casanova immediately likewise honors a younger sister or three other relatives and four woman friends. It also turned out once more that this socially liberal sensuality articulates greater lyricism than a 'private flame' choking under the unseeing lamp glass of jealousy. The moment a woman dares to admit a man's endowment for pleasure rather than for love and has no fear of that she has thereby forever set the man free and lost him: she has immediately won for herself forever precisely what women really and truly want, which is not the body but admiring lyricism.

Casanova strolls with Bellino, the big love of his life, in the port of Ancona and they went on board the ships in turns, among others a Venetian and a Turkish ship. On the latter he meets up with a Greek slave girl whom he had known for a long time but, due to external circumstances, had never been his lover. The woman now exclaims: *"Der Augenblick des Glücks ist da"* [93] — and the business takes place more or less on the spot, there on the deck, in Bellino's presence. Bellino is struck motionless by surprise & shakes in terror, it is true, but that is not out of jealousy or, on Casanova's part, any thought that by doing so he would offend the greatest love of his life: not a word of it. Those are situations which give the greatest pleasure in studying this story, and, among all the lessons, the premier place is given to the story, the sort of situation which today is the most absurd of absurdities in every element and circumstance: but back in the 18th century, was the most natural of naturalnesses in every element and circumstance. If that scene is feasible, then one must see some absolute degree of 'otherness' in that words like 'man,' 'woman,' 'love,' 'lust,' and 'soul' are completely useless; it was not possible for there to be men, women, and psychologies if port-side intermezzos of this kind, along with unromantic discomfort — fitted into the frames of life. Modern man simplified 'love' and cut it to shreds with incredible niggling pedantry into a mythicized sensuality, mythicized psychology, and mythicized legal morality. Today in matters of love we jolt over from morals to the body, from body into the soul, like a slow train, between the two ends of which yawn huge distances, and for that reason it is constantly lurching dreadfully and almost coming to a halt. Here, in Casanova, there is not even the faintest foretaste of such a three-way division. The amatory situation does not run to such precise patterns (physical! psychological! ethical!), and does not have one possible definition (flirt! grand passion! friendship! convenience!): along with a thousand which are not savored as bookish complications but as unbroken charm. The old lesson cannot be reiterated often enough: only porters give definitions and horse-dealers give reasons. Casanova's demeanor is gentlemanly, which is to say, of the intellect.

86. The finest pages in Casanova are where he draws lessons about his optimism — here he is majestic like... But one cannot suggest a simile because he is more majestic than anything else. Here it becomes clear that he is not a gourmet but a second Elijah, no less fiery and hurtling round heaven in his chariot. The tone here is hard and solemn, like the eagle's cries of the Jesuit Bossuet over deceased kings; one can sense that Casanova is speaking *ex cathedra*. In the manner of a refrain, these big orations, spring-like in their black glee, continually keep on reappearing in the course of his diary — ever more resolutely, ever more *frantically* happy.

I have not the slightest intention of using cheap literary dodges to spoil things by tragedizing his delirium of happiness: 'black' & 'frantic' — I only use adjectives of that kind in connection with him in order to qualify the lost totality of optimism with vulgar sharpness. He disdains pessimism, and as always when he does or says anything, it is out of the highest intellectual excitement: in his opinion pessimists are just *"bettelhafte Philosophen,"* [94] only to be found among crippled rationality-lice: pessimism is a shoddy phantasm of bad nerves, having nothing to do with life or the mind. Life seeks happiness, that is the god, that is the body, that is the flower and of course, above all, that is also a *thought*: happiness is the one and only *fact* in life that has to be fixed, that is study, that is all — the Church never said anything different. Casanova sees the bumbling and *'bettelhaft'* seekers of happiness in the arts & sciences, the losers — and with justice, it goes without saying. The 'truth' is just a crazy periphery after each such happiness; beauty too is just a disguised cowardice of the nerves, an evanescing circus next to Casanovan happiness. Casanova knew that J.S. Bach was only needed by three types: himself, the demented, and snobs — and that is why he stands with an Italianately sweeping, but all the more religiously humanist, gesture alongside the non-genius, non-demented, and non-snobbish: on the part of at all costs *'primitív'* happiness, for women, good lunches, beers and wines, next to *"wohlgespickte Börse"* and health. He does not give it a name — he doesn't see 'Dionysos' in wine, nor does he see a 'petty bourgeois Sunday,' it has no associations — happiness is an anonymous primal experience, or, as he metaphorizes it: *"unermässlicher Horizont."* [95]

87. So, what is this happiness?
A sensual Acheron of a Bellino shadow. He poses the castrato the question: a *"Naturspiel"?* [96] There are few words
in a language which can so shake one to the root as that.
Should a person see destiny in nature or a game? Or a
game that is nevertheless destiny? A destiny which, in
spite of everything, remains just a game? Happiness? Is
this: the dizzying concreteness of bodily realities and the
colorful totality of doubts of interpretations which at-
tach around them — the two together. Romantic color
of interpretation lends the body plasticity, and the body
calls out for that as its ultimate demand, El Dorados
of doubt. Casanova stands before his roaming love for
Bellino as Abraham stood before Isaac in front of the
sacrificial altar — with one hand the father strokes his
hair (the reality!) and with the other hand he sets a knife
to his throat (that is the play of doubt of interpretation!): if one comes across ordinary women rather than
such Bellinos: then happiness will still be seen in that
vibration — in the undecided circling of destiny and play.

88. If one wrote shortly before-
hand about majestic optimism: what is set into dogma
after the joy of Bellino darkness is by then deification itself.
He writes: *"… wenn wir geniessen, dann stört uns niemals
der Gedanke, daß auf unsere Freude Leid folgen werde."* [97]
Are we familiar with that kind of pleasure? No. For pleasure: either we think it through & live it with Latinate
remorselessness or — the whole thing remains a rag.

The deliberation is as follows: the complete forgetting of pain, its total and, I might say, permanent elimination from memory, consciousness, and the world. Happiness recognizes no past and has nothing of a future — it removes and throws out anything which is not it, which is why the word 'deification' is not a good one because it is scholastically abstract, insubstantial, homogeneous. It is already a Platonic ideal of happiness, not a man in love, not a bed, not the 18th century, but a logical intensity and consistency that one can only illustrate with the blank pages left by Laurence Sterne. Or cry out with Shelley to an abstract skylark — "what ignorance of pain…"[98]

89. And thus onward to Curzola, Ragusa, and Corfu — into Dalmatia the most classical of European lands and seas, where Rome and Byzantium, the northern empire and the tropics are united in a marvelous greenhouse warmth; a true *"Land der Mitte."* As far as the vegetation is concerned: fresh clovers and asphalt-grey cacti, Alpine wild roses and Cypriot cypresses — is there a sweeter giddiness than a metallic evergreen and silky mayfly higgledy-piggledy like that? The same with Slavonic and Latin embraces in a hitherto unknown placidity of peace.

What in Sicily was a fiendish contrast of cultures is in Ragusa honeyed harmony. The sun's color, the fire in the air: the silver of Greek olive trees and the green mottling of Hungarian acacias avoid and weave around each other. That is a Casanovan idyll: floating above the strife of history and nature in golden-gentle harmony. Residences? Casanova speaks mainly about second-hand dealers and sorcerers — rather than heroes and gods: "*Griechen, Juden, Astrologen und Exorzisten.*"[99] In short: only Dalmatia is a possibility, Hellas is a fiction.

90. That is the reason for the natural attitude to it as opposed to what he says on disembarking at Cerigo: "*Neugierig das alte Cythere zu sehen*"[100] — curiosity, nothing more. Casanova can have nothing to do with Hellas, at most Watteau's Cythera. He strolls around in it but finds nothing to remark about it — the legends of the past are of interest only to the past-er than past dead, to the sufferers, whom Casanova has deleted from his memory.

91. When his ship approaches Byzantium, he is paralyzed by the marvelous spectacle; nothing in the world is lovelier — "*Dieser prachtvolle* Anblick *war auch der Grund des* Untergangs *des Römischen Reiches.*"[101] He formulated even more pointedly and puritanically the dreadful fact that the biggest turning-points of world history and theology, the fates of gods and empires — depended on impressionism: the priority of the existence or non-existence of Catholicism, Roman morality, or Oriental morality depended on something like a Manet sketch or a bar of Debussy's music. In place of all varieties of self-important historical genetics and

pragmatics, the *'prachtvoller' Anblick* as the sole decisive arbiter in both love and history alike. Let us finally realize the grandiose frivolity of *'sors,'* [102] the infinite Byzantium-generating and deicidal power: the ephemeral detail, the unbounded rule of the evanescent *vue* over the philosophemes and Chinese bastions of millennia.

One morning, the sea was an unaccustomed blue, the tiny white crests of the waves were especially parallel and toothpaste-fresh, the air had a sporting tang, the seagulls were a touch more melancholy, more like autumn leaves, and the distant Greek, Persian, and Russian yachts vibrated higher over the horizon than usual — and for this little picnic in May, springtime composition, which half a moment ago had not yet been similar to this, the very next moment had already long lost all that shivering May-day charm — that was why Rome had to perish, at the first Nicene Council Christ had to become a god rather than a man, the Turks had to enter Europe, and Russia turn topsy-turvy. "Great businesses turn on a little pin" — or to be more accurate: there is no difference between big and small things, a barker for axiology would swagger around for hours in vain.

For a radically just-an-observer and just-an-intellectual there is no difference between a gull's shadow and Muhammad's cultural crusade in Granada [103] — the moment is the only reality, and there the rustling of a Dardanelles agave in the wind is just as monumental and 'eternal' as a god. Fate, too, is just a private game, the nuance of nuances, an eternal destiny — that is the relativity which is expressed by Casanova when, in the enchanting outlines of Constantinople, in esthetic luxury, he senses a power more gigantic than huge empires.

I got out Gibbon's quarto volume on Byzantium[104] in order to read up on a few typically 'great' Byzantine events in such a way that meanwhile I was constantly able to float the sentences under the dilated pupils of Constantine the Great with which he first glimpsed that oriental city of birds.

My eyes alighted first on an elderly bishop of Seville by the name of Leandro, a veritable St. Peter and St. Paul and St. Augustine in one: a vast beard, crossed in an X the huge keys with which he opened and closed the armored gates for Seville's Romanesque god cauldron for the faithful and against heretics; under his elbow a mass of books with that heterogeneous European wine concocted (for our eternal mental death and our impossibility) from the tatters of Greek reason, Arab mathematics, Jewish Talmud morality, and Roman law: in his eyes Pauline fire, the desperate honesty of a convert and young goodness: his miter slightly tipped to one side of his head like the towering hats of Parisian women if they are jostled in the throng at a horse race: the whole figure is a majestic mask of 'value,' 'truth,' and 'worth it for all this,' in the theatrically green *plein-air* of destiny.

He sees that from Carthage to Paris Arianism seems finally to be swallowing everything; that is to say that Christ is not a god, which is tantamount to saying the entire world will remain forever Godless, the lizards of Seville and fountains of Toledo, the seasons, the sea, and the king's spud-sized signet ring are singular, the earth never gave rise to a god, even the most coquettish spring in Granada is going blind in anti-Christian pessimism — Europe is overrun by nihilism. If Christ were a god as thousands of diplomats, left-wing theologians, empresses, and Caucasian convocation plebs wish: then a virtually pantheistic tide of rapture will wash through Arius-black Europe, a more universal, more panic-stricken happiness than the Hellenic religion intensified a thousand times over. Everything in religion and philosophy hinges on that — 'Arianism' and 'Catholicism' are merely fleeting, small metaphors of local character around the two huge poles of mood: a nihilistic world and a world bursting with gods.

That green-bearded, semi-aulic, semi-jungle bishop senses that struggle with all its immense emotional purport, and he is fighting with every imaginable means that the 'god-world' cast of mind should be triumphant. That is why he embarks on a great journey: to Byzantium. For him Byzantium is: the birth or death of kings, Europe's existence or non-existence. How can there be a Byzantium at all on which this endless Arius or non-Arius problem depends — what is to be thanked for that? A weekending emperor at six o'clock at the crack of dawn was not breakfasting with head turned not to the foresail but towards the mizzenmast sail, and his mistress only woke up a quarter of an hour later in a tent wedged among ropes and life-belts, and thus the decadently es-

thetic emperor by chance noticed the Corot-fin tracery
of shores and bays.

The threatening proximity, indeed identity, of a rock-
hard dogmatism and an in-no-way-weakening Corot
quavers with rococo proportionality in Casanova's tragic
pronouncement. In view of the fact that it seems beauty
and decline are for ever more one, and the yellow stems
of the loveliest Japanese spring shrub can immediately be
associated with death, there is no need to compute the
odds separately. The rococo, it is by now quite certain,
was always more Spenglerian than even Schopenhauer.

All the same, this Leandro believes there are value
and purpose in history — it is for that the many councils
are required, for that a Merovingian marriage is necessary
for the Spanish heir to the throne. The big alternative
lurks in the figures, jewelry, and affected nasals of young,
fully child princesses as well as in the oak-tree sweeps of
the beard of senile Vandal 'sages' — as to whether god
is a world or zero? The problem of problems! — when
we know that with city-glimpsing Constantine and
Casanova, in point of fact, this kind of thing does not
exist as a 'problem.' The Spanish king was Arian: maybe
a pessimistic *Weltanschauung* sat better with a bunch of
his sort of crazy aristocrats than ultra-Hellenic, ultra-
Hindu orthodoxy, the persecuted dream of Orient and
demos, did with its gods. But the Frankish duchess was
orthodox — the child was: Catholic. She arrived at the
Spanish court and there won the young prince over to her
faith. Old Leandro sees in this romantic love a Council

more Nicene than Nicæa, a true budding of dogma. But would there have been any question of that if Byzantium and its tributary cities had not given such an insane emphasis to intellectual questions of dogma and faith? The queen mother tosses the Frankish princess into a fishpond; a white fish among the goldfish, almost the stuff of Tiberius' world in Capri, a superb ornamental picture. But it is not Constantine, Tiberius, and Casanova who are looking at this, not Debussy who would turn it into a goldfish impromptu, but Leandro, the denier of the moment, the truth bearer, the sackful of missions. One would like to find (after all, that was my reason for dipping off-chance into Gibbon) that definitive pictorial or dramatic formula which is capable of expressing the apparent contradiction and the true unity of the "frivolous and decorative moment" and "truth-freighted fate."

The parallelism of the marriage of convenience and the councils in passionate Leandro's ripening of dogma is wonderful: a willy-nilly cooperation of tiny little women and ancient *logos* fantasts. The matter succeeds as well, the drunkenly dancing miter-forest of Toledo and the Merovingian nightdresses are victorious — to such an extent that Leandro's Spaniards, when they exterminated Arianism, with the grand Don Quixote impetus, became more orthodox than even the orthodox, of course, and they permitted themselves a rationale of exaggerated escapade around the birth of the Holy Spirit.

All that, though, is Byzantine bravado, just as the whole of Europe is Byzantine bravado — a weekend of a single *"prachtvoller Anblick"* fading away into infinity. And they carry relics, bring in dogmas, swap abstraction for hairsplitting and giving raps on the knuckles: had it not been for Byzantium, could humanity ever have enjoyed such a ghastly materiality of materials as attains such triumphant expression in the sensuality of relics — or the logical and sophistic aerial acrobatics of the most abstract notions on display in Byzantine dogma-diplomatic salons and council-screwing academies.

Never was a thought such a deliriously and specifically self-consistent thought as here, material such an Eros-toxic thing as here, and, more important, never were its accessories, more natural than nature, so close to each other, as here. But these are all Leandro things; they are here to be destroyed in the moment. Casanova often writes that this is what love is: a portrait in a moment, a glimpse, but not more. All the same he is able to tack on a little life — the commentator is by now more out of balance, leaving the moment for a moment, running hell for leather from a 'Byzantium' that could potentially have been engendered.

92. But where is the Byzantium of councils from the 18ᵗʰ century! The Turks engage a French chef, the cardinals' friends are Muslim private philosophers, in love with drowsy indifference and elegant life they make a choice between harem, monogamy, and monotonous pederasty without any dogmatizing, moralizing, or esthetic garnish; the religious

disputes are simply salon condiments — everything merely in the service of comfort.

The whole of Turkey is a *'pavilon'* world, a jabot for a turban, a *négligée* for fate, a Marivaux for Mohammed. Casanova's first Turkish friend is stoic; in the weary alleys of his garden he strolls between Christian optimism and Turkish pessimism with an aristocratic calm of tolerance and doubt such as Europe never knew; with us Europeans even the wildest impatience is still always more stylish than patience — that rococo Turk was able to give style to even tolerance. Among the flowers: because the seashore there was full of flowers. As if this gentle doubt and *pavilon* fatalism were hovering, even in the trimness (one is tempted to use the almost sickly word *'soigné'*) of the flowers. In these exhausted Dardanelles and Golden Horn gardens we breathe a somewhat more soothing and drowsier atmosphere of compromises than in European ones. One will never sense the lazily fluty spleen of an *après-midi d'un faune* as one does here. This is no longer a compromise but a golden glittering marsh: a complete stagnation of love and religion.

93. On the other hand, this is where Casanova, nineteen years of age, will truly become a theologian, because the most splendid picnic *fête champêtre* steaming in the peaceful noonday sun is not the quiver of odalisques among dancing bushes but a religious dispute, or rather religious buzzing under the smoke rings of the *nargileh*. In the 17th century the

ever-hot-headed Portuguese Jesuits and wild Muslims clashed with each other in the agitated Mughal court — here instead of Jesuits there was a child-adventurer; instead of scholastic dervishes, lethargic pederast intellectuals. For a while this was considered to be a decline. Since the time of Casanova we know it was the sole apotheosis that was at all able to overhaul history and thought.

Casanova's role as ephebe theologian was fairly odd if it comes to that: on the one hand, very Christian, on the other, he was a great apologist for sensuality, which although in principle they do not, in style and manner, usually excluded each other. In Casanova Christianity and enlightenment coincided, in the face of Turkish fatalists and harem chompers: that was perhaps the most piquant and profound result of the Byzantine excursion. Turks were excessively spiritualist and excessively sensual: whereas in the adolescent Casanova, representing the whole of Europe, 'soul' was the equivalent of nervously fresh, hunting-dog-unerringness of thinking and sobriety; while the "body" was simply "clear contact with the world," the basis of reason and the fine mechanism of joy, Aretino engineering.

At Ismail Effendi's it was different. There 'soul' was mystery, destiny, obscurity, nauseating fate, curse and stupor; the 'body' was likewise something dark, a sick numbness, mythical spittle & opium, compared with which "holy matrimony" and "Aretino-ness" were negligible differences.

The end of the big nostalgia for the Orient, therefore, is: *vis-à-vis* the Turks, Casanova raises the enlightenment to the rank of theology. If there is any romantic aspect (ridiculously minimal!) to the entire oriental trip, that was not accidental: it remains a permanent warning that for Casanova Constantinople was not a harem exploit, but intellectual in the highest degree; nowhere else in his diary-novel do such prolonged philosophical dialogues occur as they do here.

As measured against medieval theology, this can be rococo patience (*"alles was Jussuff mir über das Wesen Gottes gesagt hatte..."*),[105] but besides later epigones of love it is nevertheless sublime: for him it is more natural to talk about God, confession, and morality than about women! Casanova is only able to be a true Aretino because his metaphysics are even truer; his entire life is driven by a single *thought* in just the same way as Kant's.

94. *"Dann ergriff ich selbst eine Violine"* [106] — the fact that Casanova plays a fiddle in *Tales of 1001 Nights* is just as weighty symbolically as the fact that he theologizes. Giacomo is not particularly fond of music, much more so of society, the ball, & opera, but then one would not get anywhere without gigues, chaconnes, counterdances, and *furlana*.[107] What would that century be worth if one omitted music? Or J. S. Bach, about whom no one will be able to tell whether he stood closer to St. Thomas or Paganini? Casanova *had* to play the violin in just the same way as he had to go to Byzan-

tium: it was demanded equally by the Italian, the amorous, the intellectual, the 18th century, and his being Casanova. One should also not forget the miraculous synthetic beauty of music between virtuosity and lyric, thought-out fugue and salon-smelling dance. When were Italian folksong and German private madness, metaphysics, and chanson in such magical balance? When were Florence's incisive classicism, street queasiness, and vulgar sugariness together in a single violin air?

In these musics, fused with the most pliant naturalness, were: the aristocratic and the vulgar, Lutheran loneliness and Italian peasant community, abstraction and sentimentality — it was necessary for Casanova finally to pick up a violin and to play it, play it with Venetian frenzy until daybreak: this marvelous late-Baroque music which brings everything into balance is the most fraternal expression of his life — as these commentaries should be, first and foremost, Casanova partitas, sonatas, or suites. Alongside the music are theatrical circumstances: he hands the violin over to a professional whom of course he could not have from anywhere else than the Venetian embassy (Venice in Byzantium: that is almost as colorful a tautology as Venice in Venice); a woman with a black velvet mask enters, Casanova later calls her a "nymph" (no hackneyed convention exists which could blunt the heavenly-beauty of that word), and a violent national dance commences, one movement of which, for all its barbarity and Venetianness, is nevertheless a 'ronde du ballet.' Mask, nymph brilliance, popular dance, salon rondos, & all this European zigzagging in a Turkish luxury villa: around a 19-year-old Voltairean, orthodox defender of the faith: that is now starting to look like mendacious, studied picturesqueness, but in the diary it is natural, like the trace of its flight which a swallow leaves behind in the sky. This where young Casanova is united, and completely at that, with young Mozart, the composer of *Die Entführung*.

95. But to crown two unexpected roles, those of theologian and violin virtuoso, with a third surprise — there in Byzantium (nowhere before or after) he experiences a form of love that later centuries felt was just their own: the nostalgically poetic, an utterly dream-like, narcissistic solitude: in other words, the most cerulean romance.

It happens one summer evening, when, by a moonlit pool, he sees in the dark garden of Ismail's harem three odalisques bathing among fish, marble steps, waves, shadows, and fallen leaves. The way to this "moonlight party" is superbly arranged. First he breaks the seal on a letter in a secluded nook in the labyrinth of the grounds. A seal, which is red, heraldic, meltable, and mysterious, is an eternal symbol of love: in it run a kiss, rite, secret, vegetation, innocence, & form at once. No art or blind philosophy hit upon such a perfect analysis of and monument to love than whoever it was who, as the Hungarian colloquialism has it, "discovered sealing wax," the lighting of a candlestick, the seething, the initial flame & smoke, the smell of incense, the dripping, the scorching paper, spreading the blob of wax, the signet ring, the negative of the crest on the seal and its positive impression, the frozen figure, the edges outside the seal: that is all myth, Proust & Paracelsus simultaneously.

A second such object prelude to the vulgar-divine (is that tautologous?) game of bathing moonlight: green window shutters which glare out of the Mohammedan white walls of the villa. Who would not be thrown into a fever by the light wooden sound of window shutters, the dry rattle of the thin, oil-paint slats, cracked by rain and sun, the creaking, the beating of the iron cramps on the wall, the uncertain friction when searching for the small ring on which the cramp needs to be hung — together in it, every morning, a permanent '*villégia-ture*,' the chirping vacation. The lattices, which could be expanded and shrunk, may lie horizontally, in which case the palm of the hand might be laid between them ("Take care, they're all covered with dust" — "Oh, never mind"), or they may sit close like the tiles on a roof, and then in the hotel room the transparent, thin darkness with its whiff of *plein-air* arises, finer than any night; a window shutter is enigmatic, more closed than the doors of a strongbox, more evocative than bedrooms or anything else — is there anything more soothing than a grey-walled château with all its shutters shut? The secret of secrets. Is not the whole pastoral game, the encounter of salon and rural dwelling, present in the black-&-white zebra stripes traced by the shadow of a shutter on the wall, the sole fine wallpaper and fabric pattern which merits the name?

The topic of the third prelude: the fish. Casanova goes on a fishing trip with Ismail; they land a few fish with hook and line, and in a summerhouse had them grilled & seasoned with oil, eating them thus *à la rustique*. The fish, *betta splendens*, floating shards of mirror, jelly-stars and ice-blooded flowers, those are perhaps even greater symbols of love than are seals and boudoir window shutters.

The fourth? The fact that the home-owner who is acting as host has homosexual inclinations — salon perversity is a near-indispensable prelude to a romantic vision; of course, Casanova stands just as far from such hosts as from dreaming; with him a philosophizing estheticism in connection with women, a dream culture for the dream, those too are already present to the degree of perversion, so he has no need of homosexuality. The most conspicuous aspect of the whole odalisque spying episode is that it is such an outlier among all the other Casanova 'adventures' combined — the fact is that this concerns an image, a sight, a dream-like vision, which is so foreign to the whole work that one can believe it was not Casanova who wrote it.

This is where one wakes up to the yawning gap that lies between love as a 'poetic dream' and love as a deed, as an *actus purus* of dramatic swiftness — here he realizes the autumnal intellect and even more ancient heart of 'Alexandria,' how much dreaming of love, sophist *rêverie*, alongside senselessly forced mythic symbolism & nostalgic poetry, had made him forget deeds of love. Deed and thought, history & philosophy, the contrast of fugitive estheticism and fine life in the field of love: it is no surprise that increased nervousness would be the response to Casanova of the Alexandrian commentator, for whom the essence, as to any citizen of 'Alexandria,' that is precisely the point — the dilemma of blind creation & overly percipient comment, the tragedy of the epigone.

What is love? To spy on those forbidden nymphs, or in other words to flee from life, flee from children, from procreative embraces, from a wife, from liaisons, dialogue — and to live solely for those meanders of romantic notions, radically independent of women, that are evoked by naked figures gliding for a moment before the moon? Or else, not acquainted with the moon, never sensing any fragrance, not even suspecting the nipple of gods or the music of lines of verse (that is to say, untouched by the remotest shadow of analysis, myth, and beauty) should we step into relations with women, the dreadful anti-emotional and anti-intellectual puritanism of dialogue and liaisons in place of the Narcissus tautology? A facile answer is easy: life does not make such a marked distinction between a prosaic liaison and Novalisian theomania, spying on Susannah and possessing Susannah, myth, & practice.

But anyone who speaks like that is as yet unaware of the curse of Alexandria, which inevitably consists in being unable to find a transition between the two: once a woman has been seen in a dream-like milieu, she will for ever remain in the doorless myth cage of unreality — and the women with whom he has been brought together by mundane games or acrobatic-inclined corporeality will never be able to swing over into the golden gloom of Hölderlinian opium metaphysics. For 'Alexandria' love has split in two, and the trick does not exist which will ever again hammer the myth part and the brain part into one. It goes without saying one cannot 'believe' in either or enjoy either. The 'Alexandrian' lover ended up between thought and life: the dream's aimless and barren enrichment is revolted by thought and amorous myth ecstasy, the agonizing identity of every baroque and every lie — the mute irrationality, blindness, and self-centeredness of this life jostles him from life, from ever-active lovemaking.

The commentator had already seen Rousseau, had seen pure action love and pure poetry love: he was a long way past both, both in time and mood — and by now he could only be a dilettante, he could only stumble with ghastly and, above all, woman-frightening awkwardness among the myth litter and deed litter, & he would go to the grave as a buffoon escorted by the snickers of nymphs, in a coffin sticky from the spittle of unsatisfied women.

This was a theatrical danger signal when Casanova watches these moon trout in the Cypriot evening as if for a moment he would transform into Lucifer who with black *Schadenfreude* signals the amorous decadence of coming centuries, starting with the excessive sight of women, a pretty picture.

It is impossible in this connection to surrender two abiding impressions of my younger days — one of which is Petrus Abælardus' copy of *Sophismata Erotica*, found not long ago in the Roscelin library,[108] the other was Tintoretto's *Susanna and the Elders*, an accusatory symbol of every amorous look and *non*-possession. Abelard's *Problemata Haeloissae* ('Héloïse's Problems') has long been familiar to us; the *Sophismata* constituting a completely subjective introduction to it, the sole topic of which is the deadly clash of "love as a vision" and "love as possession." He returns to his very first acquaintance with Héloïse: the spirit of the giddiness of the first glimpse is the same as with Casanova in the harem.

"... I saw Héloïse twice. Once was before the cathedral on a stage, when she played repentant Mary Magdalene in a passion by one of my brother-canons, the second time was in the chapter's library, when she pulled out for me the complete works of Roscelin. Those were two Héloïses, that's for sure, with one having nothing to do with the other, or at most that I love both exceedingly. I knew about these two independent pictures, foreign to each other, indeed perhaps even mutually exclusive, that, for one thing, they do not exist so much as they are unending optical illusions of subjectivity of which every proof of reality is laughably lacking (and yet reality is surely the perverse object of the perverse desire of a sapient person); for another thing, I knew that images do not have causes, nor can they have consequences (in the field of neither deeds nor thoughts) but are solitary & closed in the eyes, even to imagine their continuation is absurd (» *imagines solivagae oculi nostri et clausae per aeternum contra syllogismum absurdum* « — as he says with graceful Latinity). Apart from the fact that there were two of them, then, since they were *images*; I knew that they were beyond thought & deed, and not only were they not approachable for either divine or secular thought, but for no thinking of any kind. This is where your love is ! — I spoke aloud, chuckling like the swan in the legend scoffs at the fish with its screeching (» *voce cygni ridente* «): there is not *one* person to capture, for you already have two independent images, and afterwards there will no doubt be a hundred, infinitely many — and possession, which by contrast is one-way, cannot influence the infinite, which can only ever be an object of contemplation ... But God be with you for ever, sweet contemplation too, because an *image* is your object, and an image is an indefinite irrationality; beside a thought, with its anonymous colors, it is like evil beside good, *quasi* Satanas ..."

Did anyone better express the romantic barrenness of the woman-image than this intrepid scholar with this subordinate clause of *"imago quasi Satanas"*? Or the tormenting secret that the experience of love, at the very first moment of its inception (when it is an absolute *image*): is beyond the reach of thought and deed alike? Because with an image one cannot make two: possess it and turn it into thought; it is not possible to copulate with it and one cannot assimilate it as a truth, and for the time being there is no third technique to hand. A woman, however, is at root and in the end an *image* in the view of Abelard's *Sophismata Erotica*.

But then there is only an image! How does he carry on with the foreword?

"... I insisted nonetheless that I should at least make my attraction towards the captivating apparition intelligible as appearance (*simulacrum desideravi sensus*), seeking what might nevertheless be the cause of my love? That is when I found that precisely what ought to have frightened me away, like a finicky vulture from plague-ridden innards, was what I adored, what ought to have killed me, like the head of Medusa did the Greek soldiers: you. That in point of fact Héloïse in every inch of her body was *not*-I, was the born enemy of Abaelard in her soul, her life and clothes, her aims and gods (*et numina in visceribus eis exultantes in* non *esse Abaelardus*).

In other words, only the most quintessentially not-I can attract — but if such a quintessentially not-I (in his private baroque: »*substantialiter contra me*«), then I can never have a relationship with her. I therefore cheerily accepted love, because I saw that I had found the absolute of the most foreign material for the philosopher, the proton paradox, which, for workers of truth, is much like the philosophers' stone to alchemists: it is more important that we recognize the biggest and clearest imaginable anti-rationalism and *irrationality* earlier than the greatest reason, because for a moment the former is earlier than an incipient thought (»*nonsens semper primordialis et quasi radix arboris veritatis*«). You may suppose that

I wish merely to point out the luxury of deliberation (» *luxuriam pseudomeditationis* «) instead of recognizing the well-known natural causes of love for myself, yet that is not so: I sensed no Héloïse in my bones, I do not wish to enjoy her physically, I find no intellectual sense in that — so what is taking place inside me is: » *modulationes naturales irrationalitatis.* «

At that point I was overcome by great sorrow, because philosophy had never yet consoled the philosopher: because do I want with all my strength something that, with little pedantry, I might also express as: I do not want it at all in point of fact? Why many instead of one, why an image instead of sense, why not-I and anti-I instead of my warm shadow and my brother?

Since morality never harmed thinking, since one and the same mystical force elaborated them (» *eodem gemitu noctis nati sunt...* «), I tried to work out this amusing wonder, this secular apparition, from my morals. Were self-denial or self-torture to drive me towards Héloïse? And if one virtue comes to mind, even if that individual is not moral, just brainy, a sin will also immediately occur to him: what if the headless-tailless snake of vanity were to entangle him with its mandrake *alruna*-green rings? [109] Or both at once? Do I wish to win over for Abelard the born anti-Abelard? And if that is so, I ask you, should I feel I am a hero or an egotist, or maybe just loony? Hearsay has it that the philosopher does not give much, but since, to my knowledge, love was played better more than a few times beyond library walls, I took into account the speech according to which a sense of happiness, so-called joy, supposedly ought also contribute to love and the woman's desire: however, I had no experience at all of either the budding or the shadow of this hypothetical divine flower, of neither its fragrance nor its famous golden hue (»*aurum floris defluxit*«).

»*Sum maniacus?*« — I asked just now, suddenly scared, and all of a sudden I felt that the two fine images were going completely pale, becoming more or less nothing, & it was only in my heart that there remained, like a second heart and unbidden beating: the thought of woman.

For a moment I looked out on the garden of the chapter's library, and when I saw the sparrows hopping from springy branches to springy branch, I saw the moon, which that day was so impatient that it was already unfurling its single white corolla by day — that was when I knew that the happiness *semper alienum corpus*, I knew that superstition is wisdom here, and if love did not make its way ahead with a movement like the branches, the sparrows and the impatient moon (*miracula laica*), then it was something very different, at most just a *variatio Abaelardica thematis ignoti*.

Where have I ended up? Among *images* to which are linked *idées fixes, moonstruck obsessions*! My friends, I don't know if you are familiar with that feeling, one of the ghastliest: when you see right through yourself, and you experience that there is not yet even a rudiment of spontaneity within one. That what I want is a pure No, and the way I want it is pure fixation?

Who among you (my galling suspicion is that a lot of you are like this) wants something which suits you according to the conforming figurations of nature, and the way you wish, that happy sunflower rotation around their sun, not the slumping of a dead body to a hostile, cold, and repulsive ground. When I realized that my love was not natural (though I remain indebted to you and even more to myself for the natural and non-natural philosophical illumination and thus in my foregoing talk I feel drawn more to superstition than to purity) — then that thought carried along in me everything else, in accordance with the well-known drunkenness of analogies — not just my love for Héloïse, but *all* my deeds and I began to feel my secret quivering even before myself as being unnatural: my eating, sleeping, philosophizing and faith all at once seemed forced, arbitrary, artificial — as if Abaelardus had never been necessary; I had become nothing more than a whim of my mother's womb that was to be strangled.

Why is Abelard famed for his huge desire and for always yearning? Because in point of fact he never had a single desire and yearning in life; all he did was spy on the outside world, from grasses to philosophers, and he saw that the grasses want air and the philosophers, precepts, and since Abaelardus never ever wanted either air or precepts, he was ashamed of that, because he saw that there were more grasses and philosophers than Abelards, whereat he commenced *deliberately*, dryly, arbitrarily, in Arabic fashion and ascetically *acting out* the desires: he pretended that he was wishing for things, fearful that if he did not dissemble desire he would not be considered a person, he would be like the dead who modestly mutter horizontally (*horizontaliter iocos ascetarum murmurant*). And thus while watchers beside me in the cathedral square believed that a lust (?) had blossomed within me for the saintly actress: like a lesson I adopted the external signs of desire a thousand times better and a thousand times more laboriously among the spectators than Héloïse on the boards of the stage — thereby excluding for ever from fulfillment of desire, if only because acting out the desire so wearied him that afterwards all I could do is pray or sleep. I felt like someone preparing to commit suicide. *That* is the black peak of perversity: out of intellectual considerations, acting out natural desires (not copulating with animals or corpses, which in comparison is innocent mannerism).

Héloïse lives among books; I need not have been ashamed that I am only able to see the purpose and essence of my life in a book, and yet: Peter did not deny Christ, like I did my character as poet & philosopher in front of Héloïse, at that moment I saw her in the library of the chapter. Oh, woe is me! we always see women that way, without premises, they never evolve from nothing (*mulieres non sunt conclusiones*). Why do they excite one nonetheless? Because it is the philosopher's only fitting subject while the world lasts, nothing else: like *non*-philosophy and the *non*-philosopher, the unconscious world; at the university not the rector or the dean, not the *systema mundi* or *scala scientiarum*, but the doorman and the scullion. There was no other teacher at the university who took so seriously as I did the reality of the outside world, the average man, animals and superstitions, illiterate peasants, drunken soldiers and women making love, who always watched the baleful magic of these with such faith. From boyhood on I knew that Abaelardus was just an interlude and the game mobilized for the Héloïses: I stripped from myself every Narcissus rag of wisdom and artistry in order to do penance before the greater reality without being able to become that — I was only able to act reality and spontaneity for a short time — but when things came to a head I would flee: grotesquely & uncharacteristically.

But comedy has no bounds: inside myself I tore to shreds on the altar of Héloïse precisely what she wanted from me: poetry and intellect. How many times did I cry out to what, with raw unphilosophicalness, I adored and cursed as reality as to what you would give in place of the intellect and poetry that have been denied on your account? I plucked from myself the very last scales of logic and sleep; here I stand, begging for admission in front of the average man: let us see what I get? Need I say, something less than nothing? And that shiftily, like a scalded cat, I crept back among my fellow canons, having not found any more tastes in either reality or philosophy? But if on Maundy Thursday I believe that a philosopher's sole aim is complete self-abasement and submission before *reality* — then on Good Friday I nevertheless find that, to put it like that, it is perhaps a sin: if every wrinkle of my soul and every line of my hand is for all that the brain's and the winged metaphor's; is not it just as much a blasphemy to deny these for women (Héloïse!) and for lifeless objects, as denying God is blasphemy?

I can see the insatiable shaming of my intellect (that Héloïse has awakened in me) in three different ways: as scientific heroism, as a Gomorrhan sin against nature, and finally as comedy and ridiculousness, because one cannot withstand it without a smile if the creator of miracle plays squats before the actress like ungainly phantasmal lions under the soles of the feet in cathedral statues, or the author of books seeks to learn from the deaconesses in the library the scholarly answer to big scriptural questions of the like of whether the demons who were in the world before Jesus were in real or merely jesting, playful power. Because you have not seen Abelard *flee* from the mind — a sleepwalker does not dance so madly above the housetops; a unicorn does not flee in such wild panic from roving hunters; a hetaera does not curse empty-pocketed lovers as I do the mind.

I feel the hunt that my mind and inner beauty set off in the service of thoughtless and ignorant reality was downright obsessive. The bewitching symbol of this is Héloïse: not human, not a fellow being, just a glittering object (*splendens ahumanum et luminosum*); I shall never hold a dialogue with her; and she has not come even into my dreams, nor will she ever, in order that I should take into consideration her feelings and thoughts, or in order that I should so much as alter my obsessions about her; in order that I may quite simply completely misunderstand; — only I am, because everything started off from spectacle, and the *image* of her is just my own, she cannot see herself in this way, so that the woman in my love does not enter even fleetingly into consideration.

But what are her other enemies that so-called naturalness should bloom between us? One of them is: the infinite softening and sorrowfulness of my heart before what she likes, what is simple, what is like a grass or a lamb's tongue, what is the opposite of my sophism-riddled life.

Emotion; celestial gratitude; daydreams carrying one away; the distant stars; God's goodness, for after all it was He who showed me Héloïse, and in the paralyzed intoxication that goodness (the original text uses the phrase *theologica bonitast* twice); and sensing in a single glance the combined goodness of my mother and Christ: all these intoxicate my soul into such seraphic giddiness, such a weeping and wailing meditation, that there is no awakening from the opium of these poppies (*papaver in somnio angelico permanet*) — a soul sunk in this *stupor poeticus* barely gets as far as either deed, or bed, or marriage, or even just conversation."

Is it not strange that it is precisely the turning of the infinite greatness of emotion, grateful wonder and thus colorful spectacle into some kind of morality which, in the end, one imagined to be the essence and *sine qua non* of love should become the killer of love, the unornamentable, diabolical root of passivity, the *diabolicus fons reconditus*, as he says, giving the Augustinian wisecrack: *"amor amorem semper occidit, cor cordis vitam eripit..."* [110]

That was perhaps the thought uppermost in my head when I produced Abelard alongside Casanova admiring the bathing odalisques; *that* is where the millennium-old tragicomic thought was first expressed that sentimental clingingness makes a love life impossible; that esthetic delectation, a softening of the moralizing *agnus Dei*; and thanks to fate that set the magnificent woman before us: all that *'occidit,'* kills, takes us *away* from the woman, while it was able to take Casanova, and this is his biggest secret, behind the curtains of four-poster beds — it leads him *there*.

But what is the second *"inimica soror"* of the possibility of love in Abelard's soul (which one would remark, just by the bye, with his usual affectation: *"arboris umbra arborior"* [111] as he calls it in one place)?

"... what I always think about a woman, whether I am approaching her, beside her, or after her, is in its whole and in its parts incommunicable to the woman. My admiration may be infinite, but some law wishes that the brain should be occupied with something else. Namely, with three.

One of them is the metaphors, poems, and music, the indescribable Oriental gardens of dreams, words, and statues arising from the woman's beauty that the sobriety of dialogue is unable to support; before her I could only be a rhetoricizing buffoon even if I were to declaim God's works. Therefore the principal joy that we get from a woman, which is this *aegyptici et persici flores* of our imagination: they wither there on the spot and decay into nothing. Black swans hissing among the soothing reeds of death (*cygni paludis mortis mihi susurrant*), but of course I have to ask: is she not feeling cold, and I have to answer that, before too long, the vespertine bell will ring and it will only be possible to get home by the path leading to the right by taking a big detour, etc.

Another incommunicable thing next to these unborn swans: all kinds of fantasies of physical desire; not that things of that sort arise naturally from my begotten fatigued blood, they don't; all they do is break out into leaf logically, one after the other, like the columns of numbers of a mathematician — the embrace, abstract varieties of obscene positions from which I myself blush: how could I communicate those to her? Although they are closer to communication than metaphors and they alarm girls less than exiled Greek swans (*hellenici cygni* — though God knows why?), I must nevertheless seal them for ever.

The third incommunicability, after poetry and pornography: the endless fabric of elementary observations (here Abelard employs the name of a textile which, on the whole, may correspond to *petit-point* tapestries), which, most captivating and flattering as they may be, for a clever female gift for nosing things out are always fabrics of profoundly critical character. To say nothing of the critics!

Apart from those three things, when I am with and for the woman, do I or can I think any differently? No. Therefore I keep my mouth shut and my triple silence excludes me for ever from love and happiness. I therefore said that the boundless tenderness (when, between the nails of candle flame, I spotted the little statuette I bought for her on Holy Wednesday!) and the three types of in-communicable thought render my joy in love impossible. But I promised yet one more. *Ecce: mors.*

For a while I believed that the thought of death would only keep my mind occupied as an intellectual and moral problem, to which I would with my usual facility give the *solutio prima, secunda et cetera Abaelardi*: but not long ago I came to the realization that this was a trite error — death is present in all my sensory organs, in my breath and in the beat of my blood circulation, I am nothing but death, *secunda primiorque identitas mortis Abaelardus*. There are some who write *danses macabres*, some whom agonize for years on end in a terminal disease, some who end up in a madhouse due to a fear of death, but I am jovial; I drink a lot, I often cavort with princes, and every now and again a woman halts beside me, perhaps with pleasure — yet all the same my every moment pulls me deeper into an agate tomb like a willow tree burdened by rain sheds its leaves into a lake. Because the main thing is that I think of death at every moment separately, afresh, and right from the beginning as a discovery — not just a grey undercoat to my life, it has nothing to do with spleen & gently muttering melancholy, not at all; from moment to moment the destruction is reborn anew within me (*renascit et rerenascit mors originalis in me*).

Imagine: there is not a single heartbeat of mine that I do not hear, of which I would not keep a record, not count, whose strength or weakness I would not keep an eye on like a wind-hungry sailor on the swelling or slackening of his sails — is it possible to live in uttermost *hypochondriasis* & along with that to love? No. A body which does not feel itself as being sick in some way but as being *the* sickness excludes a happy love. I tried combing through my memories as to whether I always felt so absolutely the impossibility of love — had I not perchance in my youth, with dogmatic fervor, over-formulated such differently directed desires as those which bind my limbs now when I ought to tread towards Héloïse as she appeals to me? *Quia placet.*

I am well aware of what I wanted in my youth, and it may be that I want that today as well, but that is so hypothetical, it is not accompanied by even a single movement; it's all much more of a mental shadow (*cumuli cerebrales*) than a wish. I wanted three.

For one thing a playful, evanescent, passionate yet nevertheless spark-like physical relationship with women: the lips as an onward-buzzing fly, an elbow span, a momentary bending of the back, possibly a bed as well, but even that ironically, as if one were only quoting and not ourselves composing something — midnight balls, flowers scattered in the wind, shooting stars are like that.

In these, nonetheless, the deepeſt, at leaſt for me
the deepeſt, pathos & once upon a time sorrowful cynicism, became fused with theological irony. Because we
are comprised, on the one hand, of biology and, on the
other, of ratiocination. However we know that, on the
one hand, the *bios* is irrational and has knowledge of no
more than the dead; equally we know that *ratiocination* is
juſt an ornamental discharge, a cheaper decoration than
the cheapeſt decorations. What is left? A flying kiss and
flying semi-love: a mundane geſture — inſtead of the
lameness of «life» & «thought» (*scintillatio mundana*).
Yes, indeed, but if women do not need something then it
is this serpentine mucking around; they are unacquaint-
ed with the black barrenness of «life» & «thought»
and suppose that they want the whole body and all
the thinking devoted to them, and anyone in whom love
is juſt the fineſt fragrance but not the prettieſt fruit:
they avoid and deſpise like an invalid.

What was I after besides this ever only brushing
but never graſping rococo? The conqueſt of some ex-
otically and royally unusual ornamental woman — a
princely morsel for my princely vanity. Let her be beautiful, rich, divine, and single so that she might satisfy
my insatiable vanity, coldly and with indifference, I let
the moſt gorgeous women go beside me because they
were not the moſt gorgeous of all; I saw them as hunch-
backed gnomes, mirror-skinned & mirror-eyed hermi-
tess-nymphs, because in my logical lunacy they did not
resemble boundlessly wealthy, boundlessly ariſtocratic,

boundlessly theatrical and boundlessly lovely women. Needless to say, had I found that I would have been unable even to wave to my love: a figure like that leaves my senses (*s'ils existent*) completely cold. But who is the madman who dared to talk about sex in love instead of: the obsessions of *vanity*?

The third wish of *Abaelardus semper pubes*? A finitely metaphysical solution (*ultima metaphysica in prima physica*) of losing my individuality through the body, much the same the sort of dream that I deem from the tales of Crusaders' that the Far East dreams.

But those three things: mundane joining in the carnival — lonely beauty-automat — and Orphic dreaming of permanent incorporation into a poetic body — were totally foreign and, from the very outset, mutually exclusive, as if they had not arisen in one person but in three, born thrice somewhere else. That not one of them leads to Héloïse is sure.

Sequitur imago Haeloissae: she is getting on for thirty-five years old, already a woman but like a young girl, fragile, slender, scrawny to the point of abstraction. Alongside her, how empty the sentence that albeit she is a woman in her twilight years, she is like a girl. How independent her womanliness is from any womanliness, and how different her girlhood, too. Although elementally and in her juices a woman, there is nothing in her of the mendacious baroque of a mature woman before the climacteric; though more childlike than a child, in her there is nothing of the April virgin-sourness or jejune grace (*arida gratia*) of young girls. The maturity of thought and feeling of the femininity within her, the resigned and autumnally golden composition of her soul, it is not maternity, not proliferating lard, not sensual loam. Nor is her girlishness spanking freshness but some abstract readiness for childlike brightness, entirely private, poetic, celestial and clever brightness as if it were not her body smiling in its youth but a cherished truth of God. How much I would like it if this were not an adventurer's philosophizing, not the parroted meaninglessness of affection, but a portrait now that I have allowed myself the curse of vision. Imagine, instead of the luxuriance of spring, a single leaf of woodbine among stormy March clouds — a *point*, a single flash of vitality, then you are familiar with her youthfulness, which I call abstracted because sages have long known that this is the *cacumen sensus*.[112] If you wish to gain for a second a notion of the woman's side of her Janus body, then do not rummage among the tatters of wintry locks but on the Mount of Olives peek at the midnight silver of leaves or the shadows or the logicizing soul of the Lord in stage-managing Easter week — the deliberate senility of the *intellect*: that is her cosmetic womanliness. Thin, thin, thin: dances of death, skeletons, miscarried reeds and barren fig trees come to mind; barren even if wound round by a child's chaplet (*si pluraliter madonna, nunquam érit donna*); women may play out their prattling parlor games about whether she is slim or thin, sylphlike dream or consumptive hack — here I am not concerned with either mundane or physiological points of view, *sum theologus*: that is the magic of the Gothic, at once skeleton and fresh blade of grass, thought's narrowness of precision and asceticism's sensual teſt doll.

This reaps its ultimate triumph, of course, in the length of the fingers, the lancet arches of the fingernails extended like snake's tongues: with hands like that, the never frankly usable and never, in honeſty, fully deliberated, ſtupid contrariety (*ſtupida contrarietas et insipiens*) of withered self-denial and sensuality — one resigns and wishes: *caſtratus et sodomitus fit in eodem tempore.*

It is intereſting that the ankles are not at all as thin as that — as if nature wished quite consiſtently to play through to the end the game that fat women are sustained on needles, seraphic birches on ſturdier roots. The shoulder blades scarcely cover the lungs underneath, juſt as the sharp-edged carapaces of sheaf-winged, coleopteran beetles their theatrical little sails. Should one seek to graſp the twig-thin wriſt and find there a loose silver hoop: that is only natural — for in the end it is a bare and free bone tucked under a parchment skin. The neck is likewise thick, and it has furnished for itself some utterly self-serving oldness, and like a broad bolt of lighting with swelling-out and vanishing woodbine veins, one after another, like the x-es of cording on the sides of old drums; even the color is ſtrange compared with the reſt of her skin: brown, yellow, dirty leaf-litter. Above that rises the »*corona ambigua*« of her head, a marvelous combination of mummy-parchedness and the color of stained glass, of sadistic worminess of reason and an unbounded bower of goodness. What can the world need, one asks, if not these two? A mind more ruthless than executioner's or hangman's assistants, hunting with the poisoned arrow of thought for every shade of reality which is inclined to flee — and besides that goodness, my mother's warmth and blessing, in my ears the melodic southerly breeze of love and protection. Anything apart from these two is nothing.

Let us start on the head by the hair: it is parted in the center, the whole hairstyle is a bare minimum; around the nape of the neck a pageboy peruke (I am able to perceive of even real hair, there's no knowing why, only as a periwig) is screwed on. Its color runs the gamut from the most insipid dirtiness to every chameleon glimmer of gold as if she had had it tinted at some stage, which would be no surprise, since she returned home from Archbishop Guillaume[113] in Byzantium and she scattered a few noble passions of that sort. Mostly it is divided to the left and right of the parting, above the brow, with the bangs of hair (curved) in one place convexly, in the other concavely — and only if she prepares more formally for herself is she accustomed to twirling it uniformly far on both sides, combing it slightly apart in contrast to the flatness of everyday.

At times like that the imagined models of the painters of decadent Pompeii spring to mind, the pastel chignons of *fin de siècle* impressionists (*comae fumantes saeculi ad nolle volantis*). That was how she was most recently, when she brought me the questions of her fellow nuns, rolled up in a single scroll: like a young branch in the wind, in a long, black gown, skinny and yet stately on account of the black mourning dress. With broad, pointed spike-shoulders, her elbows thrown back — the skinny arms, the swing, the many colors of Byzantium on the face under the black coif: she was an incomprehensible rainbow of the old women of Brittany in their Sunday best, a harbinger of death, a young demon, an individual with airs of affectation, and a sizzling flower. If there is an aristocracy, poetry, and death, then that holy trinity made its appearance there for the first and last time.

The brow is low, very faint freckle algae float on it as if they were very deep, already somewhere in the pages of the soul, which is why they are so muted. Her skin is thin, which admits all the hardness and bumps of the bones, the whole not much more than a cuticle. Already in life she has just a skull, not a head; she applies make-up to bones, omitting the skin. Sacral fads — until Guillaume traveled to Byzantium make-up was sinful, now anyone not as mottled as the portraits in mosaics is guilty of sin. The ridges of bone running from her temples under the eyes are dreadfully apparent; her face is hollow as if the cheeks were also eye sockets, and on the upper ledges of these rifts is flaunted make-up touched up by a dusting of powder. The nose is very long, with broad lilac and broad wrinkles; reaching below her chin one can feel an upward dent like on the bottom of wine bottles. The horseshoe-shaped jawbone could be sawn. The mouth is very small, with very sharp, fairly distinct, nicely parallel fluting of the lips — strange how that sharpness could be possible (*quomodo agitur*) when the skin around the mouth is so soft, are these petals budding from the bone? Alongside that contrast another: she has a very long row of big false teeth — how is that small mouth nevertheless able to cover those disproportionate ivory bricks?

For the last, or maybe not at all, I have left the eyes, with the complexity of which, I believe, neither thought nor non-thought could wrestle. They are enormous — but straight away I sense that you will understand something quite different than what is actually there. By big most people understand a roundness, largeness, globular darkness, bulging depth, Eastern lassitude; but this is something different. What is decisive is the horizontalness and length of the slits of the two eyes — so long as if the eyebrows and the small lashes on the lower eyelids did not form arches but were simply two parallel lines. As a result a lot of the whites of the eyes can be seen, and it is not necessary to roll the pupils much to the side for them immediately to give the impression of flashing, a paradoxical and indefinable playful cross-eyedness: it is not the brown ring so much as the longish whiteness and the many lilac purples on the cheekbones which play the leading role here. Such fullness of life in this November rosette of bones is entirely unexpected.

Finest of all when she sits next to you, and she holds her head right to the side, practically bowing it over onto your shoulder, & she thereby collects her life, her womb and her god, her love and her cleverness, her sensuality and her goodness all together (here the listing is not just a matter of seeking for a sound effect as a precise taking stock of character), and meanwhile directing her pupils on you with fixed doggedness, commandingly and beseeching, meticulously and sleep-dilatedly. If *everything* really is life, not just metaphorically but with clinical pedantry, which can accumulate in the eyes, quite startlingly: it is here that I learned for good and all: just as those jungle plants whose harum-scarum roots, ruffled litter of leaves and bleak branches are just suitable for, in an implausible elbow crook, a *single* flower of paradise to go crazy in the air with its scent and shape. Where the eyes are able to glow with such Holy-Ghost obstinacy as the Janus mirrors of hell and Elysium (here these two extremities are again not ornaments but a strict thesis, deliberated with logical scruples) — it is no wonder if the body is macabresque: the bones just vestigial cinders on the bonfire, hungry for perfection, of these eyes. And the other looks! When she cocks one of the eyes high and triangularly on her brow so that the eyebrow is poised above the cross-eyed and ironical blaze of the eyeball like the conical fool's cap on a clown. Or the thousand parallel hairsbreadth wrinkles of gentle, idyllic joy lengthways on the eyelids? And on to that the continual restless movement of the face, like the wriggling of quite primitive animals on the sea bottom. In fact it is always a matter of a sweet counterpoint of both movements: one of nervousness, the other of habitual stylization — as if the twitches of a ruined cocaine addict and the coyness of a swinging baby had been combined. If you speak to her, she starts, bends, stands back, and coils up like the fine lace of horsetails does to the continual calling of raiding waves and breezes. I have not encountered bigger rhythmic secrets than those in the last works of senile Gregorian cantors: the nervous wriggling of brushwood and meanwhile the calm of the dead seas of the Pan eyes.

Who is that, what is that? — I ask myself, and perhaps I shall never get an answer because reality falls outside the university playground of question and answer. — Who is that? At one moment a ghostly notability, an embodiment of all Paris' elegance, a degenerate flower of feudal luxury — each is a Vogue salon metaphor dress of hers — every glove, and the next moment a fugitive hermitess, a sentimental Narcissus in whose provocative make-up and azure buttons sink solitude, black lyricism, and the sonorous elegy of the heart sobbing in *St. Matthew Passions*: precisely these are the objects and gestures which a short time ago were haughty aristocracy and are now symptoms of bouts of Orphic homesickness (*symptomata orphica*). Then once more she is again the scholar, a Jewish rationalist among Paracletan nuns, tight-fisted, unimaginative deliberator of causes and effects, honest to the point of self-torture — only in the very next moment for her to melt into the downy lukewarmness of an immoral kiss.

These opalescences of character lurk in her caress (a woman like that will never in her life say of being together that it is good, that she wants another or she sticks to just one: someone like that expresses everything merely by her presence and her look); the look is nothing but wool and down, the fingers like an anteater's snout or the arms of a pair of compasses — the will may be caressing, but the touch is prickly, like an acacia which gets entangled in our eyes. Meanwhile she is fearful, experiments, and shakes nervously as if shivering with cold; she may also play around like a child with a new toy: all that play and unbridled self-sacrifice flitters in the fingering caress by her fingertips and not the palm of the hand. That is what Haeloissa is like.

Anyone who *sees* a woman as much as I do will, in the end, be her belonging and will no longer look at another woman if he wishes his love, too, to live (*si amorem quasi vitam putet…*)."

So much, then, for the caricature of the Casanovan type of one and only reality. The tragic aspect of life is that such a complicated mind and complicated heart as Abelard can only be a caricature — if those two supposedly absolute values as mind and heart radically perceive themselves as themselves, and — there being no other way — move in counterpoint within a person: those values are lost in burlesque, nervous compulsions for analysis, and baroque pursuits of color. In the final analysis, that is why the commentator cited Abelard's sick scholasticism at such length in order to give a feel for the eternal comedy of the love — or pseudo-love, constructed on visions, sentiment, and meditation, but now, at the end, it nevertheless becomes fluctuating: at one moment he is minded, if not to defend, then at least to take pity on such Abelard types (Abelard would call this an *epilogus apologeticus*).

Will it always be so in the world? Anyone who burns up his brain and heart on the natural-stone altar of truth with such huge energies as Abelard does will leave behind only a mannered, baroque sophistry: like a ballerina leaving a tattered powder puff on the dressing room table — so does that mean a great work about the great truth will only be left behind by someone who has not squandered his heart and brain during his life? Apparently, yes.

Who are those fortunate elect of God, who may be deeply immersed in His red Acheron of intellect and passion but do not immerse themselves as deeply as did Abelard: and both in the underworld carnival of experiences and in the works which ensued from them find the middle way of redemption between the helplessness of chaos and the tightfistedness of sobriety? This Abelard, when once he was left alone in the bishop's vestry and with greedy fingers (the way that Héloïse reaches towards his lips) pawed the pearls and golden embroidery of the miters, the statuettes of the bishop's crosier, and the glittering pectoral crucifixes — then he was not merely a neurasthenic adolescent, a sick esthetician and a Narcissus ambitious in his cross-eyedness: he experienced at that moment a giant ghost of every power and beauty, the Pontifical Tartarean paradox, the mysterious poles of Reich and Jewish fisherman, every strength of beauty and truth — is it not horrible that from this intense intelligence only ephemeral baroque rhetoric can derive — while from a Casanova: a world-trampling triumphant classicism? These pages are Casanova's praise and disparagement of all Abelards — but very much against my heart; for the style of my marginalia is sufficient precisely for you to: see whether my heart is in truth with Casanova or with bohemian-scholar Abelards like this?

Those who want the papacy as young Abelard did in that store for *infulae* opening onto the garden: you will never achieve that — just as he could never be happy with Héloïse because she rejoiced in him so ecstatically and with childlike sobbing for joy. Thoughts and emotions do not lead anywhere out of themselves, they remain thoughts and emotions: two neurotic galley slaves ripe for elimination. Did anyone wavering between a secular and the priestly life experience with such tormenting sweetness, such logical force and sensual freedom: the contrast between laicism and ecclesiasticism as did he that particular spring in Soissons, when at noon he poured wine for princesses of Laon[114] and at night sang psalms with priests? What became of him? Neither a secular nor an ecclesiastical lord; in his works for a scholar, a poet, for poets, a barren sophist, before princes, a sleepwalking intellectual, in councils, a stray knight flirting with the military: will that forever be the fate of he who mercilessly lives through every possibility? — will striving for totality always be a burlesque? In society an outlaw, in art and science a jumble? At such times one has most need of God and the otherworld when I think of those unfortunate torsos — it is necessary that God up above creates from Abelard a whole priest, a whole poet, a whole theologian, and a whole falconer margrave — he felt the quintessence of these roles so *completely* as the minutest affectations that he could not truly have become that down here; but up in heaven most assuredly.

Heaven, the otherworldly existence, is not fitted for anything other than the vast ready knowledge of classicism and instinct for classicality, which evolves in and is cast by such a baroque neurotic in order to some day nevertheless be able to fully enjoy himself. Because I looked this Abelard straight in the eyes and I know him well: he suffered a lot behind his tangled life and tangled style. Fair enough! Real earthly life rightly could not care less about these unproductive sufferings, it only sees a disorderly career and an opus moldering into fragments: but God's purpose is to produce unproductive sufferings in our stead, so that what is neurasthenia in us, as mirrored in Him, will be: classicality, intellectual and emotional harmony.

For his boundless love for Héloïse what did this Abelard receive? He lost her, he had an illegitimate child buried, he had himself castrated, he was spat on at the council, and in the end he drove himself into intellectual anarchy and thereby earned himself the judgment of history: a highly-strung charlatan. Who else would be so anachronistically crazy as to write a plea for the defense of nervous disorder? No one. But I want to defend precisely that immense health, harmony, classicality, and sense for reality which accumulates in such a figure despite the chaotic life, or precisely due to that: however much distaste separates me from any Graeco-Germano-Jewish notion of 'Geist,' here, since of course I am speaking for him, I must nevertheless resort to him: above the *Sophismata Erotica* there unmistakably hovers, like a more important whole smell in the case of a portion of a flower, very much not a sophism, but reality, simplicity, health in a work and in life as a whole — which, let's be honest, is more than Casanova's.

I know what a puzzling curse it is to be a chirping sibling of sparrows and afterwards communicate that to a fictive world in such a language as to convince them we were wedded only to books, not to living birds: I know what a pest it is to feel in one's soul a natural, April love, simpler than a daffodil, and when one divulges that to the woman and demonstrates it she believes one has acquainted her with dry mathematical deductions; to collapse completely, on Good Friday, before Christ's grave in plenitude of virility and moral hardness — and the first deed which ensues is uncertain, sentimental, loquacious, and merely decorative, as if one had not been born in the monumentality of God's grave, but a matchbox padded with cotton wool. Why did this Abelard, this caricature, this brother, live in such baroque slavery? If someone experiences in his heart the full reality of a reality and complete saturation of the problems in his brain — then he got close to reality but lost touch with the past. If someone leaves behind harmonious creations that indubitably engenders in us great satisfaction and happiness, but against that the acuteness of intensity and of the problem will forever be lacking.

The two together are impossible for evermore: the sensual wholeness and problematicalness of a solitary poplar or a smiling Héloïse cannot be brought together with a rational and Cartesian work under one hat — Abelard lives and proclaims the essence, which is why he remains a clown; Casanova, by contrast, lives a brilliant life and writes a masterpiece, but in the end what in reality is truly exciting to our sensory organs and brain is left out. One may choose. So as not to slip too far out of the keynote of my commentaries, out of politeness I shall make my stand beside Casanova.

As a result I must also reprehend the symbol of the second illusion and *non*-deed, Tintoretto's *Susanna and the Elders*, and along with that pass sentence on my whole youth, indeed, probably on my entire life till the day I die. An eternal symbol of the legend of Susanna will be at once — a marvelous crown of poetry and the rawest caricature of a life of vision-chasing impotence. The elders *watch* and Susanna is *naked* — but true love (let us for a moment be non-relativist enough to dare to say 'true') does *not* watch and could not care less about nudity; it always steps into a relationship, a woman's body and spirit are purely momentary, almost abstract sparks of excitation, merely a negligible point that the man should act together with the woman (behavior!), i.e., flee to another level of abstraction.

A nude figure does not portray a woman, just adolescent fantasies — women have no body, above all never a naked one —, that is exclusively an anatomically verifiable area of a sick boy's cerebrum. It is of no consequence whether Narcissus sees himself or the nude figure of a female stranger in the lake: the two are totally unambiguous and equivalent — the nude of the female image does not represent so much as a fraction of an inch of stepping outside the chalk circle of narcissism.

A Lenten banquet of the cadavers of elders and adolescents: the image. I rejoiced in this childhood pictorial madness with distressing, calamitous pedantry — if I examine my conscience it is only alarmingly late that I shall find a thought in it, after a harvest of images luxuriating from end to end. The picture was the essence of my youth, coupled with the certain knowledge that it was also the surest sign of my lostness: I always sensed its moral and intellectual sterility. At the same time, of course, I insisted on translating this identity of images of my entire life to logic, constructing simple theories whereby I fancied I was able to vindicate a greater rationality and wealth of logical precision than in thinking devoid of images. It does not matter whether I was right or wrong — I spent my entire youth dying for images, and I have a hunch that even today it is only in images that I find the realistic third thing after the barren falsehoods of 'reason' &

'unreason.' As to whether life is order or chaos it is naïve to decide that within literature — an *image* is needed, a Tintoretto, in order that the conflict should be made redundant by a third, independent reality.

What attaches one most tightly to a host of phenomena of life is that at one and the same time one keeps in mind a bad conception of something alongside the real, corrected impression. Almost no one, I suppose, for whom the essence of the doge's palace in Venice does not amount to him picturing a strong pink, virtually red color, and in reality had learned that it is practically white. The essence of that whiteness is that behind it the illusory ruddiness ineradicably shines on.

That is how I always was with *Susanna and the Elders*: on the basis of reproductions and a hazy childhood impression I imaged the whole picture in dark, depths-of-the-forest gold, and black-green: midnight shades, sunlight breaking through and salad-yellow bobbles of bud in the familiar paradisiacal trinity. These colors are also closely related to the permanent golden brown of dreams — and by the way the colors of dreams can be distinguished from reality very precisely as the former are not, in point of fact, colors, just some sort of indicators of the general condition of impotent private mythologies. Suffice it to say that is precisely what the actual painting by Tintoretto is not like: it has a silvery cold, all open, grey, watery-foggy atmosphere. The frame is also not a heavy Venetian sautée of gold but a cool fish decoration. That was enormously important — from a moral standpoint: somehow the whole Narcissus wallpaper was rescued into the outside world, the burden of dreams was vaporized and aired into being non-erotic.

For the sake of unity of Casanovan style, I say, I shall judge the whole world of Tintoretto, but in reality the case around this nervousness of nuance has not yet been decided: in any case I also do not know for sure whether these chemistries of impression between real and imagined colors are genuinely exclusively the weeds and poisons of vital and intellectual impotence or maybe, after all, the sole decisive virile backbone of the most divine of gods, the most intellectual intellects, of life?

I do not know that this antithesis of 'black-gold' and 'rain-silver,' which on being written down is perhaps merely adjectival slovenliness on the part of old-maid esthetes: whether this is a getting lost in subjectivist tinkering or, just the opposite, objectivity, a positive dawning of true knowledge of the world? Or if nothing else a long-needed, natural eradication of the puerile opposition of 'subjectivity' and 'objectivity.'

Tintoretto's *Susanna* is bathing in a fairytale setting, a land of dreams; this is the sole setting for which we yearn — or if one prefers: the sole thing for which we yearn is always just a setting, nothing more; a setting which it is not, which it is incomparably 'not,' is the ultimate 'naught.' Setting and more stringent unreality — again that encompasses a whole adolescence, a whole world of enquiry of Narcissus eroticism and romance and romance in its not even attempted management or non-management of itself. Even to recall the infantile cockfight of pre-romantic and contra-romantic hypotheses is nauseating.

Only one thing was of interest to me in the bound-less radicalism of my subjectivity: some unreality was the essence of my life, the thing which drove my dreams, my belly, and my blood could only be that *Susanna* image, never anything else, irreplaceable — but that would never be anywhere, because it did not exist. Thus 'raison d'être' and 'unreality' were for ever, inseparably, the same thing for me. The *élan vital*, i.e., a basic and central instinct, which lets my heart live: that does not construct practi-cal images, but fantasies and myths of that kind, and the whole of reality is a *"Sturm und Drang nach Irrealität"* [115] — or rather (as with umpteen thousand other opposi-tions): reality and unreality are useless pseudo-notions which express nothing.

Simultaneously I knew that Tintoretto painted that picture when he was about 40-45 years old: the Susanna which was an adolescent synthesis of my adolescence thereby changed into a symbol of harmonic creative man-hood, maturity, mastery refined into suggestion, a lyric of classicism. An adolescent admired it, a man painted it, portrayed elders — that constant awareness of the *whole* of life is likewise a perennial romanticism. I some-how sensed that I could never be a classic man, either because I would die young (who does not die young?) or because I would remain infantile even in my fifties. That is why for me Tintoretto's 42 years was a separate, closed fairyland: Susanna's plumpness, the luxuriant foliage of the trees, the darkness of the mirror, and the aristocratic elegance of the distant park was the very definition of 'settled' manhood. There is nothing more moving than an adolescent's stubborn abandonment, with all the honesty of resignation, of the possibility of a creative manhood.

Just as the illusion through gold and disillusionment through silver was a duality in my dreams — so too there arose a duality between recollections of it in Vienna and seeing it again in Venice.[116] In Vienna I always saw it in the morning, in rainy grayness, after a rest in a large middle-class hotel after strange milk, diluted coffees, prickly bread rolls, parchment serviettes, and flashy white washbasins — the whole picture froze in some disenchantingly cold morning ambience, Lenten.

When I entered the room I always had to turn back, it hung on some such wall. The lighting in the room followed the whey-flavored hotel morning, a real '*Kunsthistorisches' Museum*-room lighting just as the seminarians calculated somewhere: "*optimale Beleuchtung*": death. In Venice? In one of the small side rooms of the Ca' Pesaro, human figures, and not in the alarmingly naïve roof lighting before readily creased velvet curtains one afternoon in summer or autumn, but always afternoon, and in the doubly marsh lukewarmness of lagoon-green air and a sun glowing gold through the yellowish curtains: in my legs the quiet shuddering of the boat and the huge stumbles of balcony thresholds, in my mouth the noontime, human tastes of lunch rather than the morning clinical tests appropriate for an X-ray investigation; oils, fish, the half humdrum, half market crowdedness of the little Cavalletto restaurant, in my veins a half-gratifying, half-disgusting little postprandial fever; whereas in Vienna I was at home, here the deadly metaphysics of foreignness spied on me, there I broke away from everything because being a German was a game for me, whereas being an Italian was a phobia-riven martyrdom: everything was so elementally alien, hostile, and deadly fantastic that I was amazed my memories and old thoughts were not all destroyed in a trice.

One always arrives at Venice at noon after a sleepless night, at the end of a bleak, colorless forenoon — and suddenly comes the baroque Ca' Pesaro afternoon: an afternoon without a day. Without a night, like a timeless, eternal afternoon, the most afternoonish afternoon one can imagine. Only the evenings are real: daybreak, especially that of train windows, the morning, noon, afternoon, the twilight are none of them times but nightmares of general mood, completely unreliable, merely conditional and neurasthenic entities, but most of all the crazy Yugoslavian night in the rail-carriage, the Miramare[117] misprint morning, the stultifying Piave morning, and after all that the Venetian afternoon, swooping down on one, perhaps that is the most unreal of all. Venice starts in the afternoon, at a time that is the epitome of continuation, the vegetating 'Abschaukelung.'[118] What sort of *Susanna* was it after the Viennese, together with all the rest of the Tintorettos; it was as if there were an invited company there, not a museum.

I then saw that in the painting it is not a matter of peeping, of guile: the elders and Susanna have long understood one another, they have coalesced in the summer and September sunshine, in their Renaissance dream community. With regard to the picture, it is naturally insignificant whether what is going on is peeping or a peaceful idyll: it was only important from the point of view of my mood, and if once, before I die, I would decide whether the ambience is god or some sick whim then it would be in front of Susanna.

The game between 'content' & 'form': if the picture is one of peaceful understanding and not evil-minded gloating, then the subject, just an abstract-sensual ornamentation of blotches of color, the non-content having a more profound content than the content, or in other words, again the ever-present romantic temptation — a purely alogical matter like, e.g., the style of a painting signifies a more profound intellectual knowledge becoming, so to say, logical in the same sense as, e.g., a picture's content.

I therefore felt that I was deep in Paradise, and the female figure was Eve. That is the chasm: when a figure may be Eve, Aphrodite, or Susanna or me. Interpretation-chaos? Metaphor-immorality? Is the picture anything or nothing? — Or do I hang on with pedagogic tenacity to the idea that, here, "Susanna is being spied on by the elders"? — thus, to a fixed and therefore sterile content; or do I surrender myself to the picture's "polyphony of moods"; in which case I reach a second sterility of "anything" & "just an intensity of some kind."

It also always appealed to me that Susanna had found a way from an apocryphal writing to the center of art — she retained a heretical, secretive, perverse character from that for ever, and this underground, accursed quality of hers is indispensable for romance. I would still be unable to be faithful to her even to the present day had that painting not forever rendered the difference between the Renaissance (geometrically Florentine) and the baroque (relaxedly Venetian) mode of composition insignificant.

What does the composition have to do with geometry and dynamics, symmetry and asymmetry? A composition is always a new, unprecedented, & inimitable unit of a tenor which can just as well lead to Florentine order as it can be born in Venetian disorder: it is always an 'undefined perfume,' never structure. Is that baroque? Renaissance? Nonsense. There is just as much geometrical refinement as impressionist dissolution: that is exactly what is so marvelous in it — perhaps what I like most of all is the nonchalance with which it unifies and destroys Botticelli and Turner. This was successful only in that single painting. — What is that foliage cum-folding screen? Compositional virtuosity? Certainly. But how much more natural are the baroque rigmarole and pose than they are in, for example, a wall set up in a similar position in one of the frescoes in the basilica of Santa Maria Novella in Florence or in Ghirlandaio's *Visitation* (the meeting of Mary and St. Elizabeth) in the Louvre. The 'flourishing geometry' or 'Euclidean rose' is maybe a worthless play of opposites, but what is one to do if the sole ambition of all nature and the greatest works of art (not the mediocre ones!) is a worthless play of styles like that: the foliage wall in Tintoretto's *Susanna* as well.

Just as Renaissance asceticism and baroque profligacy were here able to become interchangeable (let it not be forgotten that such a synthesis was the sole aim of any worthwhile human cooperation and never anything else!), so too did the two poles of nature in this garden setting — springtime lightness, the bud, the first bird to whistle, the suicidal pain of a mother in labor, death, the eternal fall, the devilishness of roots. Because there is no doubt that the embrace of love is nature and also the trills of the blackbird at dawn — but it is equally undoubted that these two naturalnesses oppose and embrace each other as Christ did Satan, the sky does earth: love is lethal, barren, something sick, whereas the morning blackbird is clean, lifelike, equitable & redeeming.

These are not epithets or casts of mind, let alone myths & 'Weltwahrwehrdung,'[119] but natural and definite human experiences. Man is thrilled by such antithetical colorations: irreconcilable poles of vegetative mortality and vegetative merriment. And the two coincided in that Tintoretto world: there spring and autumn are finally identical, the sickening death throes of jungle eroticism and the meadow health of fresh grasses became one.

How naïvely and clumsily the mirror is posed in front of the woman, the 'modern' and the kitchen frame in entrancing sorcery. I am more fond of that maid's mirror than I am of lakes — the prosaicism of the object expresses the tragicomedy of Narcissism much better than does the wishy-washy showing-off of wells and swan-basins.

After the gold, that silver tone is important, and after Vienna the melting into Venice; but it was just as important when, in my childhood, I discovered for the first time the impressionist, broken brushwork. That signified an evolution in my childish heart as if I had learned that Baudelaire wrote the Holy Scriptures. My father, like any father, (thanks, eternal thanks to them for that) taught me without the least emotional fervor that there was such a thing as an "old school of great painting," after which came villainous madmen. Since then I have found little that needs retouching in that sketch of the evolution of art history. The painters of old, so I supposed, had 'precisely worked out' everything. If I had not had that naive belief, then I would not later have been sensitive to a thousand nuances: it was a sole and indispensable intellectual precondition to my whole intellectual life that a childhood superstition grew into an error as part of us, very much a part — and it was only in relation to this that every hidden wrinkle of reality became clear. Through *Susanna* I sensed the first perverse intoxication of thinking: the essence of things is something quite different from what appears to be the case — if there can be 'Impressionists' at the end of the Renaissance (this was a childhood, & therefore the sole philosophical deduction): anything can be anywhere.

Was that not how one experienced it in reality? Liberalism in Byzantium, Hellenic *cosmoi* in French Gothic, Jewishness in Christ, classicism in Freud, Buddhism in Portugal, and the same game in time: history became & remained a flea market of dimensions. Ever since when, of course, the game has become a dispassionate intellectual routine, a boring and tedious technique — here, before Tintoretto's painting, however, it is still always intriguing: I still feel an elementary sodomy of sacrilege, blasphemy, and art in the loosely dabbed leaves & clouds.

Just as the discovery of 'impressionism' meant an orgiastic nihilism, so too was spotting certain rudimentarinesses of sketching and brushwork: I am horrified to this day by the teeth on two sides of the comb — that is so naïve, both in itself and also so primitively dabbed on in that position, like those scrawls by nursery school children (evidently indispensable to gaining a knowledge of the depths of the psyche) that psychologists all and sundry are accustomed to append to the end of their books, labeled Fig. 1 and Fig. 2. Does a certain infantility belong so organically to great art? Let us try to reconstruct that dizzy happiness when a child living in admiration and horror of adults notices that there are puerile traits in the most ideal adult, in an absolute artist, and more than that at a vital, conspicuous point. That comb resulted in my feeling that art and culture these days are not the mystical ballyhoo of snobs but just as much primitive fidgeting as yawning or scratching oneself. Too right!

But historical relativism caricatured to the point of absurdity (it is worse being *semi*-relativist than absolutist) and "art is equally as primitive as an amoeba reflex" was still not yet enough of a lesson from that dream, from contra-Casanova. Here I discovered the greatest character sketches in art, those 'flesh and blood' ones that a decent burgher (under the cloud of a thousand rights and justifications!) will never renounce, those humanist prehistoric images of humanity: not if it comes to that, but those did not in any way stem from humane observation of man, quite the contrary: from stylistic tricks, from mannerism, from ornamental, all too-inhuman obsessive ideas.

This Susanna is supposedly a person, a 'typical' woman; she has a mind, intelligence, sentiment — unlike what *faute de mieux* pass as 'motifs' of stylized human beings in modern-day art and applied art (they come to the same thing). (This is the difference: Tintoretto merely sought '*décor pur*,' despite which he gave rise to a living, breathing person; modern artists seek to express the essence of man but only get as far as movie wallpapering.) Take for example three crucial 'features' of Susanna's face: the big eyes, the pointed nose, and the protruding lips. These are fingerprints or mannerisms of Tintoretto like the way a bus conductor draws the crossline of a T sign ten feet in the air or a woman draws her stockings to her knees before the petticoat to her shoulders. Whether it is a reflex movement or a contrived mannerist trick, or both at once: in any event it is not a psychological sketch or character study, not an insight into human nature or any other *fin de siècle* tommyrot. The black shading of the eyelids: the flourish of a signature; the pointed nose: a permanent graphological retribution; the pouting lips: a routinized decorative stunt. Only out of this mannerism is so-called humanity, a living portrait, a vivacious personality born. Is that not enough big lessons choked into one picture for an absolutely thoughtless, indeed anti-intellectual adolescent?

When I mused on that kind of thing willy-nilly I had to come to the realization that never in my life would it be a matter of Tintoretto but only of me. In all the years since then, down to the present day, two eras are constantly alternating: in one I struggle desperately with choking subjectivity — in the other, with just as desperate a logical force and yet honestly I strive to explain that my Narcissized destiny is the source of greater objectivity than that of objective people, if not so lyrical-hysterical temperaments, whose objectivity I attempt to reduce into sham-objectivity. Now, for instance (and also for the sake of the aforementioned antithesis to Casanova), I touch on the apologizing version: I convinced myself with religious reasoning of the greater objectivity of the completely individual lyric.

God created man, His supreme goal was the individual existence of individual souls — as we are familiar with God from the Bible, from medieval philosophy, and in the greatest quietness of the heart (I believe that we have just those three sources), it seems that never in His

life was God interested in 'truth' and 'objective contents':
He did not create 'ideas,' though one can somehow imagine that such physiological relativities as Adam and flowers, despite Eve's inclination being almost at right angles
to His symmetrizing trend of thought, He dashed Eve off,
not by a special act, but as a postscript to Adam, signaling
that He does not seek order and cosmos but something
significantly different, which of course is not necessarily
'chaos' as a comfortable contrast. God is a humanist, the
most savage, the most anti-theoretical thirster after only-
man-and-nothing-else and thereby of individuality, the
self-servingness of individuality, the private frenzy of an
anti-objectivity of spirit.

This is the eternal, animal romance of Christianity: the world is always a single soul, and that single soul
dances in front of God; everything else is just wing flats
on the stage. Plainly love for one's fellow-men and collec-
tive work are possible only where people are clear about
the individual's unending self-servingness, his inorganic
solitude: only he who is able to appreciate the divine
secret and treasure, like the one which inheres in the
unending one-sidedness of subjectivity, will respect and
love his fellow-men.

Christianity is an individualistic furor — a religion
can be nothing else. Why did God create Tintoretto —
instead of the naïve trinkets of all kinds of 'eternal valid-
ity' and 'absolute value'? So that he should see the world
and God in the rich and drunk, parrot-like relativism of
his own individuality, and I should see him as best I can,

in Venice and Vienna, after coffee and sardines, with a
woman and boy, in sleep and with a painterly X-ray: not
Tintoretto but myself decked out in various Tintoretto
fripperies.

God demands elementary irreverence with regard to art and truths — since the Creation the angels
chuckle over every absolute & objective —, the aim of
the Elysian fields is relativity, the individual variation,
the higher scholasticism of the optical illusion. I die:
only I was reality, God wanted me, He resurrects my
body, He is fond of my most relative parts, and even in
His salutation He will not take it to a holiday camp for
Platonic philosophy students who are free of subjectivity but will give back my body; or in other words, my
Tintoretto distortions, my Tintoretto mendacities; philosophical absolutism was merely naïve barbarity, a fashion, an interlude: theology quickly tumble to it; it did.

This Tintoretto commentary is merely the sole example of what this book claims to be in its entirety: the
whole of nature and the whole of his story are always
just a single person's decoration; God always confronts
one person, reality is always just a dialogue of these two
souls; metaphysics: a ghastly and glorious 'tea-for-two'
in whose place we shall never be able to put anything
more sensible.

This is what the Venetian morning gave expression
to when, while my friend bathed in the Lido, I dashed off
in the summer heat to the Madonna dell'Ortó in order
to pray at the tomb of aged Tintoretto. The fact that al-

ready as a young boy I was conceiving of artists not as pictures and books but as fellow humans was likewise something for which I could thank my religious upbringing as I knew that the creator of a body of work dies — and it was always a duty to pray for the dead, so that many Hail Marys rolled over Verhaeren's baloney and facsimiles of Rubens;[120] those obligatory prayers picked out the person from the dreadful lies of a 'memorial.'

It was noonday, but a pleasant Italian pimp was always prepared to guide me along the way; the church, need I say, was locked; by knocking on the neighboring door, of course, I got in; the place was in upheaval, under restoration, as everything always is everywhere when one travels, & a really tiny tot in an altar boy's costume led me to the grave; I still carry in my head Tintoretto's self-portrait at around 70 years of age and the bambino stumbling ahead of me; he insouciantly opens a small door beside the burial vault; in a whining voice he points at the marble tablet: "ecco," and on that note left me on my own. I was happy that, although the great Mostra was going on nearby,[121] at that moment I was the one person among the world's population of two billion and however many who was in proximity to Jacopo's body; I knelt down; an 'Our Father' and a 'Hail Mary' for happiness in the otherworld; a few words in confused Vulgar Latin for the fate of art; checking of wristwatch, did I need a hotel or train, the way that tends to be so in connection with the West's marvels; I blew a kiss at the stone, tried to mop up the tears from my face; could not find the exit and strayed for quarter of an hour in the stink of lime and brick dust; finally one of the workmen lays hands on a key to the main gate and I am once more out in the open air and hurry towards the rotting deck of the jetty for the canal-boat service, for a *vaporetto*. I am dogmatic with the endless soppiness of an adolescent's sniveling; just that, that was something, and I cursed art history. A line of the Apostles' Creed comes to mind: "I believe in the communion of saints" — it is clear that this, my sepulchral complicity with Jacopo, *this* is heaven's plan, not art history, that filthiest of disgraces.

The whole Tintoretto spell was puerile: Tintoretto's mannerism was childish, the senile self-portrait — childish, it was a child who led me to the tomb, I myself am eternally puerile, there was even a warm childishness in my friend's attraction to Jacopo; the whole congealed, late-afternoon Venice united into a dream of five- to six-years-old boys. After all, van Gogh and Rembrandt are also mannered, El Greco and Leonardo, too, but nowhere did I feel such a warming naivety of puerile flamboyance in mannerism as I did with Tintoretto.

None of this is 'truth' and "it does not offer any genuine specific plus" to the picture of Tintoretto, that's for sure, but I live for myself and thus for God: and eternity does not seek 'concrete pluses' but that I should wholeheartedly relive an indefinable, superfluous, frivolous and insubstantial shade, and from the middle of that '*moment stéril*' squint gratefully (competing with Schubert) at the sky.

I never felt intimacy to such a degree as I did with Tintoretto: odd that it was him in particular, whom many people found to be baroque rhetoric, theatrical, and Jesuitically posy — but for me he was my childish brother, a foolish member of the congregation of the Order of the Immaculate Conception of Our Lady, a dreamy old gent. Catholic child superstitions, Catholic feudal spleen, Catholic impressionism: that was my childhood and I had no other. I like Tintoretto in the way that, for the odd moment, I like women: I have seen his miraculous alien fire and nevertheless the proximity of lamblike amiability (that Abelard's love for Héloïse as well, nothing else, precisely that, he said); I am in human, loving connection with all his figures and technical tricks; every special quality is a sentimental delight and pain, like the chance discovery of a long-forgotten object after the burial of a dead body.

It was quite curious when I caught on to the simple fact that one man had painted the *Bacchus with Ariadne Crowned by Venus, Minerva Sending Away Mars,* and the *Three Graces* in the Doge's Palace — in other words those unsurpassable fusions of wavering court classicism & myths of love, along with *The Annunciation* now in Berlin: that impressionist rabidity and expressionist feverish dream, a most egoistic daubery of color deliriousness: the appropriation within myself of the ambiguity of two styles (albeit evident even to a blind man) had the eerie quality of a family link, like my grandfather being resurrected, or locating a sibling, or Héloïse's pupils to Abelard.

More than likely this is the banal situation of every art *vis-à-vis* other arts, but I sometimes shudder at the infinitude of the egoism with which I halt by that hysterical link and, what's more, one colored with glosses of dogma. It was then that I learned there is not a shred of intellect in my life — everything is emotion, sentimentality, a tyranny of moods, but in such an inundation that any program of romanticism is Jansenist self-torture and rationalism by contrast.

Before Tintoretto I accepted that Pan sentimentality and declared it to be divine, and I promised that I would elevate it to the dignity of reason. That was no mean thing even as an experiment: what would happen to an 'absolute sentiment' if it were not as dilettante and compromised as romances were a century ago; if it were not consistent in a manner for which there was no precedent? Needless to say, perhaps, that this too would require asceticism.

Here you have two anti-Casanova 'examples' — although as it happens this style of apologetics of both the swaggering or the more modest defense case for an anti-Casanova state is sufficient: to take up a stand by Casanova and to suppose that his midnight spying on the odalisques was just a comic exception and to proceed further on towards more sincere matters: like faro, roulette, *trente-et-quarante* and blackjack.

96. As to showing that money and love are the same, that is something one learned once

and for all from Casanova; love is a question not of people but of circumstances. But this money is only 'logically' clean in relation to love as long as the sweat of work and morals does not stick to it.

One cannot appreciate sufficiently the fateful fact that Casanova's loves take place amid sessions of roulette and faro, card-sharking and lottery hyenas: this money is the most abstract in the world, free, transparent, frivolous, insane and ideal. Anyone whose fate lacks such a life and death connection between women and games of chance should not look at women, because he will run aground on the mudflats of psychologies and morals. Only the internal nonsense of games of chance: the crude marriage of *materia* and hysterical luck is worthy of the internal nonsense of love. Airy, atmospheric money; clean, completely virginal and metaphysical money. Money earned by 'holy work' is immoral as the religious character of the ceremony of work is not worthy of the material; money won at cards is the height of a sacramentally cynical attitude *vis-à-vis* material: the frivolousness and uncertainty is the one thing which is logically and morally worthy of materiality, the *"tiefste Weltlichkeit."* [122] An adventurer here is more pious than a pietist: he is in an airier relation to material; there is something in cards of a sport worthy of angels.

Just as a true embrace is not the tension of all muscles, not the clinging of the flesh-material of the whole body to another (which is merely a movement expressing sentimental impotence), but the sudden interplay of a single glance and single nerve fiber: the muscles of the body are all inactive, it is just a few filaments which flex, and those, too, do so totally independently of will and force (the fact that the embracing is a sufficiently lifelike thing can best be determined from this hundred per cent *freedom* from any dynamic), so the essence of an encounter with money is also precisely not force, dynamic work, or morals but a mathematical caprice of fate, a game, chance.

The analogy is wholly eerie, on one side is the whizzing roulette wheel and healthy embrace, on the other side a sweaty banker's 'heroism' and the anguish of a woman working tooth and nail. The former (to use a pair of Casanovan terms from the vocabulary of alchemy): is a 'philosophical' handling of materials, the latter just impotently 'mechanical.'

97. Classicism and virtuosity are unambiguous concepts; Casanova as well. The kind of virtuosity that just as he is in his element by his operas or by the private card tables of courtesans, he is as happy if he can be a Robinson Crusoe — which is what he would be on an island in Dalmatia.

Until his dying day, Casanova retained from childhood what was the most valuable: the profound and absolute infantilism with which the Casanova superstition that never reads Casanova is unfamiliar but which separates him from any mere adventurers and, in his fortieth year of life, made him a blood relative of Hamlet in the literal sense of the word. Robinsonades are

just as much decorations of love life as empty money
won at cards. This setting up quarters in the small empire on that Dalmatian island was a rather cunning
compromise of the family householding instincts and
Valéry-grade Narcissus parlandos. Casanova wants to
get married a thousand times over in this life — in his
case the lover relationship is always for want of anything better: he sees the world as a Catholic burghers'
garden of potential wives: he is constantly wishing to
stay with all of them for ever more. When he avoids
marriage that is done against the dictates of his heart
out of honesty with regard to them or due to other external circumstances. That kitchen-centered, stocking-
darning, and aspidistra-watering world is one side of
the Robinsonade; the other, of course, is adventure, an
adolescent undertaking, a Red Indian romance. Here,
as is often the case in Casanova, women are incidental.
After all, this is a matter of love.

98. Now another sentence of
almost Biblical rawness from the 18th century. A woman is
asking Casanova to recount one of his adventures to her;
with the sole proviso: "... *nennen Sie nicht die Dinge bei
ihren richtigen Namen; das ist das Wesentliche.*"[123] Women
were significantly different from nowadays — adopting
a position close to Aretino was just as much in their
blood as Buddhist bluster-virginity. If a maiden: then
she was an absurd virgin to etiquette: if a woman,
then an omnibus of the carnal.

The two roles, the two deliberate types of virgins playing woman and women cowering in a trauma of deterioration do not get mixed up into a gray 'human' muddle. *"Erzählen Sie"* — this near-masculine, challenging tone belongs just as much to Casanova being able to be Casanova as just one half of Toscanini belonged to music: the other was his magnificent orchestra. One can sense in that female's partner the pure voice of an *'altera pars'* of the same rank as Casanova. *"Die Dinge"*: that German gem comes to mind the way that Rilke was in the habit of uttering the word; the whole of German existence in history hung on the essence and aura of that word. The wild, indeed lush realism of the rococo is felt in it: the woman asks for the essence, the *Ding der Dinge*, and that is what she gets — first from Casanova then, a few minutes later, from Mozart. The reality that the rococo shows to women who prompt the telling of tales can be elementary, brutal, and precise, because it does not name things by their proper name — for proper names have the major fault that in point of fact they completely cover things up, like a violin case does a violin.

Either I want reality, in which case I have to name 'play names' (in Mozart-speak: if I want to toss my blood into the faces of the concert-going public, then I must write minuets, not *Eroicas*), or I use 'proper names,' in which cases God speed! Adieu, *Ding der Dinge*. This alternative is fittingly confirmed by the 18th-century lady: *"Das ist das Wesentliche."* [124]

99. Theaters in that era were three things: musical virtuosity, or in other words an 'Orpheum' or 'music hall' worthy of the name of Orpheus; a gambling den; and lastly (this is what raises the point) a row of theater boxes, or in other words, floating salons for passing through where, of course, anything was possible in the dark.

Casanova spent every evening in theater boxes: not in theaters but in boxes. This is once again a characteristically 18th-century unification of the mythical caves of Venus and the modern salon, just as important as ballrooms or eternal Venice.

The easier possibility of being late or leaving early was inherent in the arrogance of the upper classes *vis-à-vis* the inferiority of the arts and theater; the seats were free but nevertheless there was scope for adjusting the number up or down, according to the size of the company; the fourfold optics of the lighting in the foyer, the darkness of the box, the gloom of the stalls, and the brilliance of the stage; the reshuffling of the family after each act; in the eyes the conductor sawing the air and on lighted music stands scores reminiscent of dress shirts; on the legs a calf and ankle stolen from a neighboring woman; open bags of bonbons, liqueur flavor, opera glasses, a fan, a crumpled program, one sheet of which is already on the floor, the remaining tatters of which can only be read in the direction of the lights ("Is that Vestris?... No chance, that is Campioni...[125] no, that one is slimmer than Vestris... maybe, but he's so... let's have a look..."):

all this is starting material, love itself. The stages of the seat: armchair forward, by the balustrade (with the heavenly luxury of leaning on the balustrade itself); smaller chairs in the internal space; low stools without armrests — small taborets — at the back, by the door. And what sort of love is born on the one or the other!

100. No one could leave off embracing with such naïve insouciance as Casanova. Never so much as a neurotic moan or fit of pique — that, too, he does like a virtuoso playing a Paganini étude. Here, too, the accent is on two, which the fact of breaking does not affect — the one is love, lyrical frenzy, and Italianately sobbing *"Liebeserguss"*; the other is a refined game, etiquette turned deadly serious. The halfway or pseudo-gratification is a completely equal-ranking counterpart of the whole-hearted kind; not a torso beside the real, but a variation.

101. Two pages further on, of course, we get a fully Sophoclean-style apologia for complete gratification — with the poles of *"Tod"* & *"Zärtlichkeit"* in a way that was only possible in the heyday of the 18th century. How great the puritanical manliness, the poetic perspectives, the decorative salon mythicizations and childish rhetoric of supplication with which he attempts to persuade the woman to surrender completely — the very woman who happens to be a believer in *"alle möglichen Tändeleien,"* and *"Vorgenuß,"* [126] such a one of

whom Casanova, too, on other occasions, was an obliging
master. What classically poised speeches this sentimental and sensual Italian makes; what a Florentine Seneca
he still was even in moments of desire. It is a secondary matter whether he really declaimed it at the time or
just in his diary-novel: in its natural chaos of egoism that
style is no longer artistic but an ethical triumph. All in all
the dialogues would be worthy of a separate essay were
the essay not so readily liable to turn into a punishment.

He recollects the refined legalistic symmetrizations
of the most trifling chatter and diplomatic exchanges
of correspondence. Might that be 'bon ton'? That is only
possible because he knows with the manic perspicacity
of a Paracelsus and Hercules what the essence of nature
is, and he seeks that with faithful brain and childish out-
pourings of the heart: is not the defense of embracing
noble because it is articulated with a tragic humanism
of a mature, Goethean view of nature which refutes any
imputation of lechery. Is it not one of humanity's most
splendid utterances that he makes via one of his female
characters, Signora F.: *"Verrate nicht Liebe und Wah-
rheit!"* [127] Love is truth.

102. When he feels great love
he is sickened by courtesans — he recounts his innocent exploit with Melulla, a courtesan from Zante, [128]
like a maidenly member of the Order of the Immaculate Conception of Our Lady would her first confession.
Melulla is again a figure of parrot-like Balkan folklore

next to Venetian fire and Parisian ice — the strumpet as a prehistoric phenomenon; much more important in this opera romance is that it gives Casanova an opportunity for a guilty conscience and anguish, for us to see his childlike cleanliness, his abiding purity. Every man is born out of these two conch shells: an ideal and a strumpet — that is youth's leitmotif. Would it not be the same with Casanova?

103. Just as he knows how to defend the perfect embrace with Sophoclean darkness he is able to speak in the same tenor about his first attack of a sexually transmitted disease, although there is a touch of sweet humor in that as well. He senses the poisoned sources of life fermenting inside his body, perceives that as a big outburst of death and sin, and he accepts with a juvenile epicureanism for curses the role of Antichrist forced on him by Melulla. In the early fall he is cured: the dying lassitude of the Venetian September is equivalent to his inner birth. That is of major significance.

104. When he returned to Venice his life was again drawn into the sphere of the enchantment of symbols: he became a violinist, a tenth-rate, tin-eared, back-desk violinist at one of the leading Venetian opera houses, the Teatro San Samuele [129] — in a country where Marian churches answered to the name Venere and theaters to Holy Moses. Casanova was a very mundane European parvenu, twenty years old: a last

resort as a violinist. However much he may be bored by and hate it, it is as though out of sheer pedantry of fate he would not stand for anyone who was essentially Italian to climb into the grave untouched by the violin. For all that he is a low-class, penny ante scraper on the fiddle, music's Italian omnipresence shrieks before us in the even wilder colors of tragedy as if he were a second Mozart. The poverty, depravity, the drinking-house nihilism, the pit-like location of the sunken orchestra, the anonymity which were the substance of Casanova's life at this point in time — that somehow expresses even better the black magnitude, the passionate, strenuous tenor of Marcello-style,[130] baroque music-making in Venice. And don't forget that in Italy the kitschy and the masterpiece, ascetic Florence and hammy Capri, were always in incestuous proximity — the big joke in Casanova's sawing of the violin is that there is no chance of sensing the distance from Toscanini.

It may be empty blustering for effect or some cheap conceptual perversion, but when I imagine Casanova squeaking away in the orchestra lair by a half-burned candle and a score with a jumble of marks added by copying pencil, two words immediately spring to mind — Toscanini and Satan. Am I raving mad to bracket the greatest musical disciple and the off-key Gypsy fiddling of a tin-eared indigent? Maybe. But I sense the naturalness of Italian music in Casanova's sawing on gut strings; playing the fiddle is tantamount to living, despairing is tantamount to playing the fiddle, and it's all the same

whether I say 'all' or 'music', whereas even in the Floren-
tineness of Toscanini's performances I sense the plebeian
roots, the hurdy-gurdy, the useless beat-up violin of a
panhandling minor musician.

So what about Satan? There is something diabolical
in Casanova's destitution (here he was truly penniless and
proletarian for the first and last time; there is something
almost Russian and ritual in his nocturnal carousing, but
that is how it has to be, not in line with the precepts of
Baudelairean Satanic dandyism but because the mania
for discipline of the Italian Renaissance is a bloodily
logical function of a mania for indiscipline — stemming
from Brunelleschian Medici executioners, Toscanini
Antichrists, and Casanova ragbag outer-suburban fiddle
scraping of the harmonies. However, he not only plays at
the opera house; in the palaces of aristocrats at Carnival
balls he is much like a modern-day cadger in a tuxedo.
He lives by night — is there a night more nocturnal
than a Venetian night, where the dark water is a specially
condensed second night and the rotting houses are more
baleful than clouds before the moon. But it is good that
it is so: that is what it needs to be with sonatas by Marcello. The masks also proliferate; Punchinello fishes and
Scaramouch fishes topsy-turvy. Is not a notional accident
worthy of hypochondriac imaginations a fitting end to
this feverish violin-playing period? Between lanterns
and lutes, on dancing water, surrounded by indifferent,
non-scowling masks: one of the senators has an apoplectic fit. Conceptual agonizing in a lagoon at a midnight in

Carnival — that is the flourish, the amusical groaning on Casanova's accursed violin.

105. One needs to pause at the phrase *"herannahende schöne Jahreszeit."* [131] We know that is all; we know that Thomson was the only one of all the poets in the world who gave a poem a worthwhile title: "Seasons." [132] At 29, the commentator had still not seen spring; throughout his life Aprils only ever meant a wet month and Mays, frozen or scorched tatters of flowers, neither full sun nor full moon, only freezing, grayness, comic, green-with-envy leaves before a stormy sky, a Grand Guignol shrieking of birds in the early-morning frost — nowhere a cheery sun, basking in a meadow fit for a lizard. Yet one is not after history or gods, not women and wealth but the sun on one's skin, grass, the white cyclamens of the white clouds in the beetle-buzzing nothingness.

How essentially different must be love & one's general condition (what a dry word the latter, even though it is the only poetic one), where one can count on the approaching fine season, where the spring rises on regular gamma rays and is not up to its ears in muddy, snowy, sleety nothingness. Casanova counts on that spring as on an old partner who flies on light heels into his arms.

106. In Casanova there resides a primeval, ineradicable belief in occultism, while at the same time he is a swindler, ready to cheat people left,

right, and center with fake lucky charms, fortune-telling numerical pyramids, alchemical hocus-pocus. In point of fact naïve Italian peasant old wives' tales without which rationalist geniuses could never take a step — one need only think of "songe *de Descartes*" freemasonry, which is a concentrated 18<u>th</u> century mixture of colorless, odorless, abstract humanism and vulgar Isis & Osiris kitsch; and last of all the pure swindle, the money-fleecing, extortive lie, his turning a rich widow, marquise Madame d'Urfé,[133] duped to death by his resurrection scam. Some people will undoubtedly be surprised that even in the latter half of the 18th century, when that harlot who was painting make-up on her cheeks will be set up as *Raison* goddess on the cathedral altar, there was still such strong credence given to alchemy, spiritism, and all manner of absurd superstitions.

One cannot say that the Middle Ages was still an intact whole around Sans-Souci and Ferney, because the Middle Ages were simply unfamiliar with the above-outlined stupidities: then religion largely worked off any instinct for mystery, so that there was barely any need for that instinct to take all sorts of byways — the clipped trees of Versailles were necessary for alchemy at last, really and truly, to have its fling. Casanova would not have been the body of his century had he not thrown himself with the most innocent cynicism into a business which was worth millions. His cheating was grandiose and fantastic: by a cynical parody of the mythic he rouses a greater mythic shudder in the reader than any true myth.

The angel Paralis,[134] correspondence with the moon, the hypostasis of young Count d'Aranda,[135] liturgical embracing of the seventy-year-old marquise, impregnation under hypnosis, and in the end the death of the woman, who had previously received as an Elysian virgin, with incense and garlands, an Italian slut — all giddiness in the grand style, classicism, on the heights of magic.

107. The three elderly aristocrats who take twenty-year-old Casanova under their patronage are embodiments of the 18th century from precisely the above-outlined viewpoint: a unification of "Aufklärung"[136] and total superstition. What is there is like that to the end: Mozart just as much as Casanova, that is freemasonry just as much as the policy of French kings or the economy of London bankers.

That eternal tragicomic link between reason and mystification, Voltaire and Isis, anticlericalism and liturgical craziness needs to be fixed: after all, that is the essence of man, the background tone of every possible life, what makes a whole person whole. Away, away forever with all illusion that the two can exist separately — the freemasonry in *The Magic Flute* showed how comedy can be wrung from separate reason and superstition. And also how indispensably comic they are together, and that is how it will remain as long as man is man.

Freemason Casanova supplies the formula as if he were extracting the word from the mouth of Adam to God the Creator — "*sie waren Leute von Geist, jedoch abergläubisch.*"[137] Chimeras, occult sciences, *Universalmedizin*, ancestral spirits, diabolical souls, kabala, Delphic oracle, auguries, apocryphal Fathers, the Devil himself and a good few angels: the century contended against those while confiding in them.

108. There are situations which are not representative of this or that century but imply the 'good old world,' as opposed to a modern one imagined as being more tragic or more squalid. A weary burgher's thirst for idylls indulges itself in that, a nostalgia for sleeping caps and cozy hearths that it would be proper to ridicule according to the currently fashionable cult for heroism.

The relationship of a converted Jew, a great judge of paintings, who had purchased for the King of Poland the gallery of the Duke of Modena for one hundred thousand zecchini.[138] When dukes still bothered with such Jews and paintings! — the whole thing is like a porcelain-joke — aristocracy, Jewry, and art, what kinds of expressionist fits of epilepsy and dismal death throes did they undergo both internally and in their relationships to each other; what an odd mood it must have been when paper sociology and mass vengeance did not place themselves in garish colors behind dukes; when a Jew was a nice rococo caricature and not a 'problem' artificially enlarged to baroque dimensions; when art was a salon filler, a complement to the aristocracy and not a tussling of souls with ill-reputed gods. Pastel Jews;

pastel dukes; pastel still lifes — what an improbable souvenir.

109. In reaching a judgment of Casanova's character is it not crucial to consider what appealed to him in a new female face? To start with, for him the face was all — the notion of the 'figure,' which is the sole positive aspect of modern eroticism, was for him essentially not present in even vestigial form. So what did he look for on that face, alongside the banal requisites of beauty? On what was he keen? One example among a thousand: *"Adel, Schmerz und jene Unschuld der Tugend."* [139]

That Casanova (the Casanova of the *book*, & the Casanova whom I am styling, if need be forcibly, to my own Orphean image) — is the proletarian last-resort violinist who seeks nobility, elegance, the magic of formalism which redeems manner, not out of parvenuism but out of ingrained 18th-century culture, a Cyprus of uprightness, a Watteauesque nirvana of ascetic constraint; the cynical, cheating seducer seeks pain, self-weighting of the soul, the bottomlessness of lyric poetry, the lethal sentimentalism of a virgin; and lastly the guilty, the frivolous, the gigolo and freethinker: seeks innocence and virtue not out of gourmandism, or perversion, but out of a naïvely fresh sense of style.

No one sensed as well as he did etiquette, lyricism, and virtue as forming decisive parts of the external beauty of women — no one turned away with such immediate disgust from a woman if she lacked the style-decisive trait of virtue. The last consistent apologetic of female cleanliness.

110. In these 18th-century spiritual drills it is not unnatural, after so many exercises, that the piano, the other collecting point of music-making, should be granted a separate chapter. He buys a harpsichord for one of his lady loves and scores from which to play — characteristically carrying those and books in a *basket*.[140] In the harpsichord already there lurks Romanticism, instead of the Venice of the Marcello brothers that of Wagner, instead of counterpoint the patchwork world of harmony. Those keyboard pieces of music are just as distant among the linearities of violin music as seraglio odalisque romanticism beside the staccatos of salon embraces. Like Pandora's box: on the outside still rococo but inside treacherous chaos. For what did he buy it?

111. Signor Barbaro, a Venetian potentate, leads into his 'cabinet' a young Countess with whom he wishes to speak intimately. 'Cabinets' were places just as crucial in that century as were salons. There were no private & social lives — those are useless, scholarly jargonistic nonentities: there were salons, as one place, and there were cabinets, as another room or space.

Anyone who frequented Italian or French palaces always came across, among the large chambers and spacious rooms, fantastic and ridiculous little holes with flush doors or wainscoting — singular crosses between a closet, a light well, and a Byzantine reliquary with its enigmatic intimations of prayer, sin —, these were sanctuaries of private life where the up-to-the-minute crises of the souls of the age played out. Were there worthier sites for such souls than these one-foot-square roomlets — would not the whole human body became immediately confessional if it were stuck away with another in such a lair, with its whiff of perversion and intimacy? That is precisely the irresistible non-compulsoriness the way one straightaway chemically perceptibly, without transition, becomes oneself and a sincere only-soul and tearful only-confession: that was the secret of those opium dens. The soul is: a 'milieu' — in that kind of cabinet it is not the long-existing soul which opens up but the non-existent soul is born within a trice only again to become non-existent the moment it steps out of there. A cabinet gives rise to a soul in the same way as wine gives rise to dizziness or dampness does to mold — the soul was soulfully large, rich and material-mastering in places where it was known that there is an exact material technique to calling to life. The whole face of Europe would be different if the 'cabinet' had been retained — *inter alia* the shameful interlude of 'psychology' could have been completely sidestepped.

112. In his time as a musician he held orgies at night with the other musician scum; they would often listen together to the midnight chimes

of the church bells; sometimes they would play the prank of unhanging the bell from a campanile and lowering it from on high onto the stone flags of the square. What a lovely sound that must have made. That Venetian bell tolling always puts me in mind of a Debussyian cathedral sunk below the sea: the contrast of water and bell remains ever new. And the way those bells hammer, resonate, as if time were just a carousing convocation of intoxicated birds: the hammering may sound from the church, but it is godless; it is ringing midnight, but it is a heedless Carnival jape for its own sake. It is no 18th-century thing for sure — those are skew-eyed sounds from the Middle Ages. Two extremes: the soundless, hefty bronze breathing of the Byzantine basilica as if the cupolas were reverberating due to the moon's stinging; and hand bells, hung up like hams for smoking in the little gateways to towerlets the way they swing to and fro, sticking out their chattering tongues.

113. He makes the acquaintance of a count's son, who is handsome as a god of love and full of wit and aristocratic attitudes. In the midst of the many death sentences, the Venetian bell and nocturnal knifings, this ephebe does not signify 18th-century harmony but a German-favored withering of worldliness and otherworldliness as personified for us by Frederick II; the magic of the Ghibellines. There was also some Habsburg darkness about it, Spanish black-and-yellow. Casanova likes only women, but here he catches some-

thing: from the night, from candle pallor, male demons put together from Loyola and the Renaissance: an aristocratic blend of demoniac strength and decadence, something which is essentially not Casanova.

It is interesting that alongside that a thousand things should come to mind in connection with such a 'Spanish' death-hermaphrodite Casanova except that he is — a man. Casanova has nothing to do with any masculinity in a physiological, social, or practical sense: he is that abstract complement of a woman, a thought, a century, a big book, everything but masculinity.

114. It is perfectly understandable that where he presents a male figure that can only be enjoyed mythically but not socially in any way, there he swings into picking at myths; in one train of thought he even mentions the apple of the Hesperides. As with spying on the odalisques and the making a gift of a harpsichord, he is haunted by a shadow of later times as if here, in Velázquez's portrait of a boy, he were suspecting the subsequent Romantic plundering of myth instead of the game mythicizations of the 18th century.

Here one certainly cannot comprehend the apple of the Hesperides as a *giardinetto* ornament: what comes out of it is heavy poetry, a bearded Bachofen.[141] Twilight and fruit, Tarshish and Elissa,[142] hell and paradise, nirvana and fertility — what does Giacomo have to do with those opium humbugs? And for just a moment at that.

115. "*Oh, wie wird die Kunst immer hinter der Natur zurückbleiben.*"[143] A rupture needs to be drawn sharply, and to the utmost, between the two, so that life is everything and art: nothing. Not in the name of any old, naïve culture of life — there's not a word of 'culture' here; that would bring in the muck of art. No. All that is in question here is that when Casanova awakens in the morning to a cold, damp, overclouded May day and thinks back to his previous evening, that is separated from the morning by a quite short, restless or, if you will, poor sleep that is a hundred times more refreshing than any longer sleep, then the reddish hair caught on his nail that he had fortuitously brushed aside from the neighboring woman's brow when he had been seeking to tidy his own hair; the pale lilac shade of crocus in his nail varnish that, on the face of it, he protected out of mock-chivalry, but in reality with every fiber in relation to the lodge's other guest; that half-bathtub aura, half whiff of burning hay which emanates from his powder; that historical and physiological antithesis which results from the concave crest on a black signet ring and the crab's claw twitching of a bony finger (the coat of arms is a memento of a permanently dead culture, the wishy-washy finger is a bitter pledge of the dead and resurrection-mocking body); the little coronate swelling above the knee under the evening gown, which signals that the woman may not be wearing garter belts but squeezed the end of the silkworm net into a noodle in the way schoolboys do with

a paper strip in an *escritoire* game; the disproportionate alarm which seized him when he accidentally poked the Venetian ambassador's wife, sitting in front of him, with the tip of his shoe (that shoe tip was longer than that of a Flemish fool or a fashion-conscious French crusader at Nikopolis that certain "*Herbst*" [144]); those conspiratorial glances pieced together from witchcraft, children's playrooms, sentimentality, and quinine-bitter defiance that she threw at Giacomo whilst a Parmesan mezzo-soprano played wandering Orpheus on stage; the desperate silk that a genuine woman's skin signified for half a second when Giacomo was able to reach under her skirt — not in search of piquancy (even in his dreams Casanova would not know what that is) but the untheorizable, godless secret of beauty & death; the primitive movement with which the woman uses her hand to shield her neck from the May sleet when she turns down her collar with housewifely eagerness; that momentary tone of lamentation with which Giacomo seeks to seduce her back into his own little orphan-velvet and orphan-volatile idyll; the sweet pain with which he thinks of the woman's torments as that torment sought to color a greater love from his own self, pain for the woman and pain for Giacomo, so that the lilac of the 'lilac' should be evident — all that together, the objects and the minuscule cultivars of soul shards: that is reality, that is what one lives for: these are not Proustian delicacies, it is nonsense to speak here of nervous sensibility or nuances, these are breads & wines, big birds and rains, wild and Cyclops-style *natura naturans*: the musician is alone on the stage, Orpheus in the opera is crazy about himself, we do not live for art, not ever, but for these powder traces of ideas which have remained on our necktie.

Maybe once those had been 'delicacies,' and for precisely that reason intelligent and sensitive people were ashamed (at the time justly so) to declare solidarity with such 'nuances,' but today we know that precisely these are the raw materials of life, crude, bell-like masses, they have nothing to do with the cheap mist of 'mood': each one of them is 'object,' 'substance,' 'existential'; to revert once more to that adolescent lingo by way of parting.

Casanova is the 18th century embodied & thereby becomes almost a grandiose renegade: he quits his century, drops out of his Italianateness, out of history, out of Catholicism, and Voltaireanism — to become just himself in the redeeming infinity of tragic egoism, where everything depends on the hairs which catch on his over-long nails, where the tone of shoe heels is a religion, where the small change absent-mindedly left lying in the palm of a woman's hand is logic; where a scrap of an old word unexpectedly coming to mind during a morning bath is beauty itself: this where Tintoretto has to die, and with the carcasses he forgets Ariosto & all his own things as well.

116. In Casanova's rapture for virtue there are two contradictory and equally essential features: there is the 'paganistic' (perhaps one day there

will be a better adjective for this barely anything), where
virtue is not a moral concept but half sport, half-esthetic
— simply an individual's fateful private harmony, style,
nothing more nor less; and there is also the Christian,
the charitable, self-sacrificing, destroying whatever merits that for the sake of fellow-beings, because mathemati-
cally there is so little chance that a fellow-being would be
suffering from the same self-destructive mood in regard
to Casanova.

In female beauty he always enjoys this physique
turned into style — "*Diese Tugend wollte ihr Wesen darstel-
len*": [145] virtue here is not moral but the racial aroma of a
female race, a harmony of kidneys and cecum, the pure,
musical tonality of the personality. — For that matter
Casanova will assist everyone, sacrifice his last penny
for another; he is prey to swindlers, blackmailers, cheats,
gives away millions in gifts to gallows-birds, because he is
incapable of saying a bad word, because his entire fantasy
world is not set up in any other way than to imagine with
Italianate extremism the pain of those suffering. Casanova is a 'dupe,' in the most tragic and most Christian sense:
sometimes he is frankly Franciscan-bonkers, an outright
twit in his band of charlatans.

117. I cannot go on without
pausing on a sentence in which the two words "*Pantoffel*"
& "*Tod*" feature so closely together. [146] This is a symbol
of the 18th century: the knowledge of a bedroom stifling
with whispers and a fall's perpetual and alone damning

character. A pair of cothurns[147] and death? Nothing. Slippers and death? The sole part of humanism that can be turned into dogma.

118. Because the century knows what it has to know without running for Jeremiah, Calvin, or Aeschylus like the maidservants of lazy cultures run to a grocers for a ſpot of tragedy: Casanova remarks about one of his lovers that *"Der letzte Liebhaber, dem diese einzige Frau durch das Übermass des Vergnügens den Tod brachte."*[148] It should never be forgotten: at every moment Casanova is juſt a hairsbreadth away from the same fate, juſt as Mozart was not even that much away.

The quintessence of the rococo is the black mask & black domino amid gleaming candles, "the masque of the black death," as Poe would say. Half the correſpondence of the Spanish kings of old was made up of paternaliſtic exhortations in which the deaths from excessive debauchery were brought to the attention of the deranged infants: the youthful years of Charles, Philip, and Don Carlos were filled with these myſterious deaths, and Casanova conjures up before himself juſt as freshly such piĉtures in the biggeſt flower of a pretentious century. Casanova: beside all his loves a possible corpse; not a metaphoric death but a common or garden yellow or green ſtiff.

119. The ultimate embodiment and firſt opportunity of Casanova's worldliness; Chris-

tianity identified with Satan all those who varied this type. Satan is nothing other than a consistent lack of metaphysicality, the logic of material. Casanova also appears in such a transfiguration in that he wishes out of vengefulness to scare a person to death, & to that end he digs up a newly buried corpse at night in the cemetery and chops off an arm. When his enemy touches that piece of dead flesh in his bed, he is so terrified that he takes leave of his senses for the rest of his life and twitches spasmodically. For Casanova that Satanizing, which still belonged to what were still almost adolescent years, was predictable.

The worldly success that attended Casanova exceeds human measure & truth — it can only be Satanic. A suit was lodged against him — with the Venetian judiciary citing him to appear on a charge of blasphemy. Because his life, that rococo-sprite-rainbow, was truly a sacrilege: it equated with Satan precisely because it was *not* Dionysian and bestial. It was only a lot later that Casanova got to Spain, where the fandango boisterousness and hellish phantasms of people flit between royal asceticism and Aranjuezian revelry in the crudest and most implausible divergences — the world of El Greco, that of death torsions of Iris where damnation is a factor in politics and etiquette: 40-year-old Giacomo, of course, scoffs at all that as crazy superstition, yet in his own body and career he is a greater and more precise Satan than all those Judeo-Gothic-Arabic-Vandal hell-neuroses put together. For Casanova, as an absolute death and sin could not be just a game — they had to be sublimated into a veritable body snatcher and desecrator of corpses in order that 'this world' should be granted its most authentic portrait.

120. It is characteristic of this hell-grade 'laicism' that he prefers to carry his riches round the world in the form of jewelry and in rattling carriages rather than as ready money.

The two extremes of riches: precious stones are the most ancient, a raw Rheingold world; whereas securities are already fictive, abstract art treasure & artificial money. "… *meine Juwelen und meine Papiere wieder in meinem Koffer…*":[149] Casanova has no home, he lugs his wealth from country to country and, like a caravan driver keeping an eye on people's fingers, pays with rings & pocket watches, shirt buttons and diadems — all the gaucheness and nervousness of an upstart is evident in that scrutinizing of jewelry and voraciousness for jewelry.

For Casanova 'value' is not in money, which consolidated something — he had nothing to do with landowning and affluence; he even emphasized how little understanding he had for those: for him value resides either in a fabulous object, a naïve rarity, a 'solitaire' — or in a lie. A precious stone is just as much a Satanic symptom as chopping up a corpse.

121. It is so much all the same whether this is Roman stoicism, Greek nemesis, Christian hell-craziness, or Hindu fakir phantasm: the fact in

the end is that the essence of a wholly great life can only be grasped in relation to some kind of morality — our sense for logic wears out very soon in the course of life, and that is followed somewhat later by a healthy cynicism towards every aestheticism, so that finally there is nothing left except morality.

It is likewise morality which will pronounce a final judgment on Casanova, naturally, not the fussiness of a schoolboy's 'good boy'-'bad boy,' but one which glances at to what extent an ominously expansive personality realized in his career all of nature's most primitive and most paradoxical intentions: was he able to create a tragic harmony out of the jostling and all but mutually exclusive chaos of all life's forces, or was that just a pseudo-harmony, the kind of classicism which, seen from the viewpoint of life's magma of morality, will always be a lie and corruption.

At the end of the volume Casanova introduces La Fragoletta,[150] an old crone who dyed her eyebrows black, coated her face with rouge and powder, and reeked of ambergris: it is as if he wished to see and display the autumnal essence of all his loves in accordance with the bravado of medieval dances of death — as if momentarily the fate of Casanovan gold were disloyally to betray itself and in female nobility, etiquette, grace, and the whole rococo tenderness were nevertheless divining the fiendish asymmetry, ignominy, the betrayal of nature's quintessence.

As if, all of a sudden, the synthesis and harmonies were, after all, cacophonies and paper pretense — as if in Spanish otherworld superstitions and moonstruck banditry there were more inner morality or a closer connection with the roots of nature, i.e., the whole complex vegetation. At the end of the volume,[151] the miracle of harmony and absurdity of worldliness seeks to compromise itself: unearthed corpses and horrendously daubed harridans take over, starting up before us with unexpected vigilance the long-forgotten and scorned question: what if the Gothic were truly 'classical'? (La Fragoletta's nipples are separate, lilac- & red-painted little cork pyramids.)

122. From this unexpected Toledan viewpoint, the *"Naturalienkabinett"* of Antonio de Capitani in Mantua is no longer a charming or elegant synthesis, nor is it a collection of curiosities but a soiled burlesque of the human mentality.

In it there are saints' relics, books of magic, antediluvian coins, a model of Noah's Ark, medals of Sesostris and Semiramis, moths, lice, and the paraphernalia of Freemasonry. Until Casanova revealed his nocturnal bestiality at the graveside and the repulsive spectacle of La Fragoletta appeared before him: the museum may have been an idyll where the gobbling of God by religion became a tame glass cabinet of tidbits, and learning's pursuit of nature became gentlemen's *pasque* flower pressings between the pages of the weightier tomes in the library — and since we know full well that gods will never fit in our mouth however much we may gape, and nature is either demonic or dumb (both are plausible),

its essence will anyway slip out of the nickel-framed perspective of 20-dioptre eyeglasses: one happily celebrated
these attractive little museum collections as being, as a
matter of fact, the most of which a person was capable.

But the inassimilable gods and mask-flaunting nature are always able to revenge themselves at the last minute: the dead hand and La Fragoletta's flaccid bosoms,
drooping with creams, suggest that it is about something
else; the 18th century is nevertheless a lie and immoral
intermezzo beside some indefinable greater truth.

Though Casanova might justifiably raise his peruked
head amid grave clods, moons, and Venetian cypresses
and ask: why condemn the century, had not that century
created a counter-century as well, that grave, that Fragoletta, those sodomite solitaires? Was it not that century's
black light that within its own span was already able so
ruthlessly to cite in defiance its own condemnation to
death and intellectual fragility?

123. At the end of the volume a
pseudo-Mozart, pseudo-Don Juan ending, but, miracu-
lously, that pseudo-business does not in any way disturb
one — one takes it as being true; indeed, for that very
reason, more truthful. The situation: Casanova deceives
a peasant family in Cesena, lying that by declaiming all
kinds of nighttime hocus-pocus in the open air he would
recover huge treasures from the earth, the diamonds and
gold of Crusader knights, pixie kings and leopard count-
esses — and while he sets about the great bogus opera-

tion a genuine storm attacks with whirlwind, downpour, lightning, and thunder — superstitious Casanova is frightened to death, believing that God has tired of his blaspheming charlatanry and had indeed decided on his eternal damnation. To no whit was everything all Voltairean and duchess adolescent libertinage. It's true he lived until he was 73, but here he had already been condemned forever at the age of 23. True perdition could be terminated within a moment by confession and extreme unction which, on the occasion of major illnesses, he never neglected to receive, but that *symbolic* damnation would not be removed by anything. "*Gegen ästhetisch-bedingte Symbole kämpfen auch die Götter...*"[152]

At that last step the commentator pondered for a moment what was the most accurate and most exact interpretation of Casanova's perdition: what is meant here by 'scientifically' the *hell* which would swallow the 18th century. There could be only one hell, no other: *the inner world of the commentator himself.* Casanova's curse is that his century was wasted in a dirty mirror of the 20th century; that his loves became wedged into a subsequent mental mold; that his great consistency of action was exchanged for the dishonesty of ascension.

A 17th-century poet, Andrew Marvell, wrote a poem with the title *The Definition of Love*, the first verse of which contains the two lines: "It was begotten by Despair, Upon Impossibility." Who was your father, bastard love, if not cross-eyed Doubt, and your mother, whom he embraced in a corner, the withered Impossible?...

And in the second half of the strophe he declares something much more astounding and more lethal for Casanova: "Magnanimous Despair alone Could show me so divine a thing." Beauty and a divine woman could be cast to earth only by despair: only death is colored, only hell will save one, only insanity is intellectual, only illness has a thousand elements, only nonsense is worth the trouble, only the radically bad can sketch right down to a theme.

Those two quotes from Marvell are the inscriptions on Casanova's hell: the very person whose entire life was a happy series of achievable things was driven into the fiendish cell of a commentator, where every atom is imbued by a Marvellian approach: the essence of love was always an impossibility, something desperate. Let me eke out those verses from Marvell with some imaginary Marvellian comments, as if those too were running along in different-colored pencil markings in the margins of the manuscript that was then to be published only in a critical edition by École Normale alumni.

"... What a mysterious connection & fatal contradiction there is between a woman's exterior and interior? Between the uppermost layer of paint that she dabbed onto her cheekbone just now with the tip of a finger and the scriptural opening of her soul with which God invited the eternal Christian fate from non-existence into existence?" — Is that question not fiendishly comic from Casanova's point of view? Where the concepts of grace, nobility, and manners humiliate the threadbare concepts of 'bordello makeup' and 'heavenly spirit' into stupid pigeonholes.

Of course, here Marvell is viewing centuries: a woman's face, in its own diabolical, intriguing beauty, all detail in its barely feminine Richard III-ness, individual and an excessively singular something: although that is all that is in our positivist hands (love and positivism are kindred concepts), just because they are so specialist and accidentally unique: it is nonetheless truly impossible to believe in them completely. That love is a vision gained from a woman's face and nothing else is undisputed: but one cannot believe in that picture — stinking from accident to the grave (Abelard!). What about the soul which is behind this?

The soul is invisible, yet anyone who loves and is in love cannot believe in the invisible, even if they are a Christian saint. The woman in Marvell's life, it seems from the marginal notes, was someone who was externally treacherous, vindictive, and a merciless villain, a cat driven wild by woeful paint, but inside a lamb, an *agnus Dei*, self-sacrifice and childlike flexibility. Marvell, like any lover and poet, was only able to believe in the exterior, marveled in its brilliance of color, but he also suffered from its apparent wickedness — in vain did he know that the soul is something different, which did not help.

The soul: forever a fiction — a face: forever a chance absurd specialty, so in a woman there is not a single point in which it is worth believing. For Casanova external beauty was not a physiological accident (and thus a caricature) — nor was the soul an invisible hypothesis (and thus a certain lie).

Is it conceivable that one comes across a note like this with Giacomo: "The big suffering is not when a woman is in love with me, but when I cannot love her the way I would like — when I yearn to be enthusiastic and only the prickles of criticism and the leaf-litter of indifference are on my skin." This is the significant Casanova alienation: the constant knowledge that there is no convincing intellectual or physical or ethical reason, nor can there be, for love.

Marvell, just like the 20th century, is standing at the unluckiest spot in the world, a spot suitable only for playing satirical burlesques — between pure intellectuality and pure sensuality. One can make friends with the wild fact of woman only if one is an extreme rationalist, and likewise if one is absurdly brutish, but a mixture of the two is ignominy and farce, from which there is no exception. "Love *per se* is a problem": a sentence like that acts on Casanova like the steps of the stone guest do on Don Giovanni on the eve of perdition.

"Have I decided whether a woman is another *person*, or in other words just as much a man as myself — or less than even an animal, a *pictus masculus*, an esthetic rarity, in which it is not a question of badness and folly if that hurts me (after all, an inhuman picture has neither brain nor morals), but solely of objective nails and splinters, mold and knots. Maybe all the trouble stems from men handling women sometimes as a «man,» sometimes as a vegetative mass of phenomena seen from under a crystal, & with the most stupid inconsistency hop from the one perception to the other. For that very reason, there is no harlequinade more uncomfortable than when a so-called clever woman is completely right about a man. The objective truth is hanging in the air, but it is impossible to believe in it. It is not male vanity which prevents this; truth in a woman's mouth is always a joke, a plagiarism, a swan-song, decadent and scandalously uneven. When women, looking into my eyes, tell me a barely compromising truth, I want to break off with brutal impatience: not due to being uncovered (though that too saddens me), but because some idiotic and possibly tragic dilettantism has occurred in the order of nature. What can't I stand? Truths? Women? The two together?" Would that come to Casanova's mind? The insoluble contradiction of woman-*crystal* and woman-*person*?

Once, so it seems, Marvell's *'agnus*-démon' must have set about seriously defining itself before the poet, because in a sketch for a poem he writes: "This woman is something primitive, her soul is a transparent structure like an amoeba's or a crucifix's — a simple line like so and another crosswise, and there you have the complicated spiritual life: the outside, wild, gaseous, fantastic, I can only listen to it as a ghost's tale. If the soul is simple & the body a jest: how can she be right? Because «she is right.» From what part of her does the truth come? It is interesting that I long discounted all truths as being something which was in itself impossible, a matter suited for Aristophanes' quill: nevertheless now, in relation to this phantasm face and spiritual life the size and mag-

nitude of a plus sign, there seems to be a nobler matter
— which is why I cannot reconcile it with a female being.
Should I accept a woman's truths about me? Those local
truths from a woman who, in her entire body and mind,
is *par excellence* an untruth and counter-truth? I feel precisely the opposite: my whole being is of the nature of a
truth, but its every branch, vibration, and fragrance is a
lie. That would not be a bad joke: me bowing before the
accidental truth of the «woman-lie,» me, for the truth?"
That is the quagmire in which Casanova drowned; the
way half-mad Prince Metternich, Chancellor of Austria,
grasped a candle at midnight and pointed out to the
Duke of Reichstadt those portraits whose death was
awaited by the eaglets:[153] the commentator holds up this
Marvell-self before Casanova's pure rococo face — in
order to frighten, as a bogey and a hell. That is revenge.

"I feel two things equally when I am with a »lover.«
One variant is that every word I pronounce is forced and
mendacious, every gesture deliberate theatrical labor,
no fatefulness, no spontaneity, instead of love an «as
if it were» love — so why do I do that? At root there
is a primeval compulsion, cause and reality: the fact is
that I *have* to get married, that I *wish* to put on an act
shows that it cannot just be a case of play-acting or lying.

But there is also a second, inverse variant: I sit together with her, I hear her voice, I follow the shadow of
her hair on my coat sleeve, I keep an eye on the splinters
of brick in her lip gloss, I enjoy the oily melodies of my
confessions, the conspiratorial humor of the clinking of

glasses, the adjusting of my necktie, sniffing the rain and pouring sauce — then I know that only those details are the absolute and exclusive realities in love and — unlike with the first variety — the essence is precisely nothing: there are only the million contingencies of being together, but love itself is nothing. What is the truth? Is there a fundamental destiny between us above which luxuriate a million hypocrisies of psychology and circumstances — which is to say that there is no serious attraction within us, the root is zero, but above this abyss of humbug a million little concentrated realities entertain me?"

Casanova does not recognize a difference between 'shades' of reality and the 'essence' of reality: he had long left the Middle Ages, so that essences and substances should excite him — prime causes and similar, but on the other hand he was still so very much ahead of the 20th century not to be able to take into his power the devilish magic of nuances and thereby pose the commentator's Marvellian question: Is the detail true and the essence nil, or alternatively is the essence true and the detail eyewash?

Marvell, like all true poets: is in part philosophy and in part shreds the bloody-stemmed fruit of beauty from the trees of morality. That is why one finds lines like: "If I examine the whole of my amatory experiences I find in myself nothing but egotism and nihilism." The moralist is typically always a man of the brain: he notices something about himself, regularly something small; he gives that a name, and in that critical name-giving he already finds ecstasy, so he inflates the name, trumpets it, and in its honor performs self-annihilating grimaces with his whole body, but the essence is always an intellectual orgy and not moral.

Only *little* sinners will become big moralists, self-torturers, and merciless self-analyzers.

A big sin is attended at most by big repentance; but Marvells like that do not rue their little sins, they just inflate them intellectually and on a totally rational stage decry them with all the theatricality of analysis. Just as it is the statement: "I find in myself nothing but egotism and nihilism," already signals by its show-off stylization that Marvell is highly charitable and he must have been a devout person in a thousand things. If there was anything big within him those were not sins but more in the way of moral insanity. The major self-tormentors and moral philosophers are always composed of sentimentalism, hypochondria, infinite hunger for *raison*, analytical fury — and only then moral insanity. In other words, *no* characteristically moral streak of any kind is to be found within them even by accident! This is the "overmoralizing of the pseudomoralists," which is essentially alien to Casanova: he truly does possess sins in places where Marvell had only analyzed moods — and suspicions in places where Marvell had theatrical and *purely* intellectual games of self-torment.

For a woman there is no more accursed partner than this Marvell type of 'moral' being. He himself knows full well that these kinds of reactions of his have no conceivable connection with any true intellect or true morality; the whole thing is just physiological reflex twitching — on a slip of paper it states:

"If I moralize, if I pursue psychology, if I squint for the truth — all that proves only one thing: I have not yet cuddled a woman whom I love. What does poetry mean, along with all its rhymes, Shakespeare as an encore? Not beauty, not nature; just an absent cuddle. What is this psychology? An absent corpus. The psychological life in itself is not a stationary business; only if the body is without work does some sort of mold arise like on fruit sprawling idly in the sun or on moronic cellar walls: the soul (of course, here »soul« only ever betokens »modern psychologizing,« nothing else) is a function, it is only there when the body is not — illness, a very comic illness. The best thing about it all is that, on the other hand, no one is more bored with cuddling with a woman than I am. After that kind of thing I have no positive desires. In cuddling not even by lamp do I find a possibility of either myth or epicureanism; of either intellectual or esthetic good or pleasure. My sole remark about it: if it does not happen, »spiritual life« commences, but that is such a purposeless luxury of rotting that I would even rather cuddle a woman."

In another place he dashed off in green chalk the two words: *"corpus nolens,"*[154] under which is the note:

"How did I set about the whole thing? For what reason? In prime place was vanity. Of course, I am condemned to death & galley-boat psychology if such petty, shiftless prompting leads me to a woman. Most likely her body has to be desired — however much *materia* bores me in principle and in practice: if I had not started with that then I would be blowing bubbles in the night. That does not befit Andrew. My second motivation was sentimentalism: idyll after idyll, repugnant tears, sublimated from smeared corporeality, which become salted between corporeality and gospel, making a mockery equally of Aphrodite and Jesus. Love cannot be founded on that; one cannot dupe such health and cleverness as a woman into such a thing. The third motive? Esthetics? Lovely eyes, intriguing bone deformations, and hairwaves? If one holds those very firmly in one's eyes one cannot wriggle away from them but is stuck there in the way that even becoming immersed in some detail of a picture does not stimulate one to draw any conclusion in favor of action. No coupling will come of gawping — that should be present alongside all its uselessness, because a bigger zero is on its way: — in the modern sense » soul.« Vanity, mawkishness, artistic taste: those are killers of love."

"I wonder if, before I die, the question will be resolved as to whether I have been, at root, frivolous and unfaithful or tragically faithful in nature? At one moment I sense that I am a deceiver to beat all deceivers (needless to say a tearful and thus low-grade deceiver), as by and large I lie continually: by now I am even myself a lie, and there are always heaps of women rushing around me (quite rarely do big and healthy geniuses of love have parallel relationships: only cowardly amateurs have four lovers simultaneously). Undoubtedly that sort of thing ought to be called sordidness. Except, except! I am religiously faithful to those memories, dreams, & associations that women conjure up: is not that the essence? Is not the whole question of fidelity a trumped-up, forced, sickly, inadvertent and non-existing thing: or at least from that sphere? Is fidelity moral or just polite adaptation to the partner's bestial selfishness?... Why is there only body and soul, why not a much better third or fourth, and the whole faithful-unfaithful comedy would right itself. Meanwhile I was with other women — and so I deceived the first. However, I am tied to the first by my dreams, her beauty is the reality-core of my life, so it is possible that I deceived her. Did I cheat on the latter by, in the meantime, being nostalgic for the former? No way: with its whole material faith my body was only with the one who was present, not with any nostalgic feelings. The clown pranks are all over, if I want I am frivolous, and if I want I'm fanatically faithful — in this area there are not even any test touchstones in our hands."

Casanova knows that there are, indeed, quite rough touchstones in this area, and he derides all such sterile sophistry around us.

But can a person be anything other than sophistic who writes this about physical embraces:

"One thing certain about an embrace is that it is not pathetic. My woman, by contrast, is passionate, and she is shaken by tiny nerves and fatty gods if I just touch her with a finger or my lips.

The matter is much too insignificant, of course, to make it worthwhile wondering whether it is hysteria or theogonic big lyricism: it disturbs me, I wish to flee, maybe even to laugh, when I see it. For that reason I avoid encountering her like a cat avoids hot mush: I find it hard to take such Gomorrhean Quakerism. What is embracing after all? Partly humor, partly technique: just humorous, because it is technique. This has to be done, that has to be done, extinguish, light, button, mop, cover up, look for, close, lift — with those going on one cannot even play on the harp of the nerves, nor »mingle with the Universe«:[155] at best like a Swabian joiner's apprentice."

If one puts this 17th or 20th-century statement beside Casanova one feels something approaching blasphemy: that is what came of his classicism; the rococo harmony of nature, etiquette, poetry, religion, brightness, and darkness could have shattered thus — every Marvell word a shard of a Versailles mirror on the rubbish tip. But this last commentary wants precisely that: to see that Casanova had to incur damnation; Polycrates can only be a moment, love only the 18th century.

Let us continue the anti-Christian blaspheming: "...For me coupling and love are two essentially alien entities. Each one *per se* is a reservoir of *nihil* and transience, together they are like the pantaloons of the pagliacci of old, sewn together from legs of white and black. The fact is that love is nothing other than a negative, that there was, as yet, no coupling between the separate parties. What is embracing? Akin to the motion of primitive amoebas, something connected with the most bestial layer of animals: of course, that is neither a mythical merit nor a diabolical mistake; here, to embroil any values is asinine.

The body is not good and not bad, not valueless nor exalted nor a wretched, anonymous talent, outside the human phantasms of truth and morality. But right now it is not from those kinds of standpoints that the body is of interest; only from that of it being impossible to believe or trust in it: to establish a life form on it is madness: embracing is a function from which no consequence can be struck — neither practical nor of any other sort, a situation of the nerves resolved within boundaries of the nervous system, which are *sui generis* to the point of blindness, and that's that. But the fact is that man, to his profit or detriment (that is again a baby's toy, a matter of dispute), is more than that, infinitely more, or, to be more accurate — more different, much more different, than a primitive amoeba and unannotated nervous reflex. So, embracing, which is precisely just that, does not satisfy; no one can found any characteristically human thing on it, which is to say, in his relationship with a woman all that is left is colorless intermezzo, a bureaucratized, willy-nilly little mystery — it just *is*, and that's all there is to it. That is embracing.

If even that trifle is not there, though, then in its place there is the forced replacement product: love, with the stench of poetry, the mendacities of its psychological variants, and the sickness of its morals. The soul anarchy, sporulation, materialized sophistry itself, a *sui generis*, senseless flourish, death in melismatic form — a discreditable, pseudo- and chaotic entity. If a body is not worth a plugged nickel because in its plasma anonymity it is traveling so far from the human that this ungradable irrationality is virtually more tedious than even tedium — then the »soul« substitute is, for that reason, good-for-nothing and a *humus nullity*, because its rationalism is empty mechanism and forced automatism; every thought, whether it be Thomist syllogism or a Surrealist carnival of associations, is merely, with complete uniformity, sick prolificacy, somewhere in the region of pus and cancer. Love is precisely this: an accumulation of shadows on shadows, which might somehow be bearable in the fleeting moment of a Proustian canalization but prompts the partners like hell."

"I believe that the differentiation between a beautiful woman and a characterful woman may be the rule. However, if those two exist there is a problem with both of them; our sexual part, of course, is excited more by a woman with a distinctive facial profile and figure, but since love does not depend on physiology but on vanity, our constant desire is for the beautiful woman: she may often leave one cold in bed, but she is a much better decoration for one on the street. After all, one does not keep a woman for one's private delight but for boasting to others. An immediate drawback with an »ideally« beautiful woman is, therefore: that she cannot be seriously taken into account erotically speaking.

From that point of view, everything would be in order with the characterful woman but, on the other hand, through habituation her distinctive features become distorted into a caricature, and after a few embraces what was once a striking feature is seen as ugliness — the whole woman turns into an abomination within hours: precisely those features which had preoccupied one's body. You can choose between these two Elysian joys."

"Love has just *one* realistic and attractive form: the nostalgia-filled recollection of a long-deserted woman. There the trinity of reality, dream, and lack fuse into a single marvelous melody — everything is suffused by the secret of time and vision — that's love. Memory is the sole thing when I feel that I have a lyrical world — the current woman: a question, anger, boredom, vexation over sensitivity, I never felt those as being feelings. All our affection and wonder belong to the women of the past; it is only them one loves, they are genuine, they ennoble, they influence: the current one is neither more nor less than a mix-up, a raw, rough disorder. It must be something highly distinguished and practical when a woman roundly declares that a man's former lovers are of no interest at all to her — but the whole thing is nevertheless tantamount to her saying that a man's essence and sole aspect in realistic love is of no interest. What a worthless louse an active lover beside a deserted woman's burning peacock's feathers."

"And it is of no interest that it is precisely those sorts of men who look at the possibilities of relationships between men and women with the most deplorable pessimism who are able to give the two most magnificent things, in the face of the clipped ganders of optimism — by portraying love and woman as the greatest *poetic* miracles and the most crystalline sources of intelligence — precisely they are able to give women the greatest *happiness* in love for the odd moment or week. Only that bottomless nothingness flowers beauty out of love, only obdurate cynicism, mendacity, and deception renders women absolutely wildly happy. What monotonies and vile little tragedies male *believers* in love produce from day to day: within weeks they tear women to rags with their idealism, their fidelity, their morals, and their confidence. Because to take love seriously, to believe in it, for them means nothing other than pushing its most peripheral, most fortuitous contributions into the foreground, all sorts of strange materials that a mistaken female-male relationship only carries as silt in society out of necessity. Love is anyway unliveable, cannot be dogmatized about, is unrealizable: the whole thing is just an abstract staccato moment, then possibly a second, completely independent of the first, and then again an alien third staccato, but to make a connection, a legal legato, from it is to be: narrow-minded. Love is a fraction of a fraction of a second: a constellation of color, taste, and mood; it has no antecedent, still less a future; when that mode is at an end, then everything is at an end, and has to be begun again from the beginning.

There are isolated coexistences which are just about held together merely by external circumstances, so there is no natural blood circulation between two consecutive amatory encounters, but people fail to notice that clearly enough.

That every tear, eternity, and naïve faith of an »eternal« confession dates from the fact that on the meadow a pale-green maggot climbed into the girl's handbag, the woman started cautiously to hunt after it with bony fingers and hair spilled-forward, and altogether only this infantile look-out for bugs affects one to the extent that one starts talking about marriage, fidelity, and salvation: although these dreadful will o' the wisps are only symbols for games and half-second metaphors instead of maggot, handbag, and spilled-forward hair.

After all, one would sense straight away that the maggot had been reinterred in the grass and the handbag's buckle had been snapped too impertinently, and the woman has mercilessly tidied back her tumbling hair: one would sense precisely that marriage, fidelity, and the coral blather of eternity were already invalid, comical.

In love everything is bound to a thousandth of a single moment; if there are no enduring values anywhere, then they are not here. This is well known to a pessimist, who even exploits the moment: what is impressionistically exciting about the woman, body, clothes, movements, odor, shadow, thought — he will highlight it like nobody's business, laud it, define it, all of which will make the woman happy, albeit not like the precision

of the moment, but she will swallow it in the form of
» How that boy loves me. « The magnitude of love forever has just one touchstone: it can only last a moment."

"What is tragic lust, sacral-grade sadism in absolute deceit? Because, however naïve anything like
absolute deceit may sound, there are cases when one
deceives a lover with another woman in such a way
that one feels a mathematical completeness as against
other deceptions which are diffuse, non-Satanical.

The first black pleasure is that one sees the final destruction of love in one's own absolute deceit: it is clear
that the male-female business is nonsense, a vacuum,
if that total deceit is possible; that is the ineradicable
ascetic in me, who takes delight in such things, at the
same time. I expect that my infidelity will cry out to the
heavens — so monstrously symmetrical are my sins (e.g.,
when a woman is sick and expects that I will nurse her
I will go right away to another woman to whom I have
never as yet resorted and stay longer with her than I ever
did with the one who is now sick), that I think one somehow sees it in the air: the cheated woman can also see it,
and she lays destruction around for ever with her eyes.
My ethical mania all but thirsts for the open din of hell in
place of lurking damnation — let it come, swallow me up.

I enjoy with maudlin gourmandism the imagined
pain, which would be genuine in the cheated woman
if she knew that I was deceiving her with such system-
atic, blaspheming proportionality. If I did not cheat on
her, yet did so in a completely underhand manner, then

I would be unable to pity the poor woman, even though that pity would be marginally longer-term than sterile sparks of the momentary impression from the woman's point of view. Thus, in the long run it is in the woman's interest for me to cheat on her: that way I mollycoddle, protect, and cover her much better — against my own baseness. In the occurrence of such 'classical' deceptions that natural-history »*frisson*« makes me shudder — how is such simultaneity possible so smoothly? Therefore do the eyes, it seems, really see no further than the wall? The ears hear no further than the doorbell in the hall? Is it *possible* to commit a deception quite close in space and, as it happens, simultaneously in time?

When the next day I hear from the deceived and ill woman the details of her waiting for me and I know exactly what I was doing meanwhile — if a third person were to ascend a tower three hundred-feet high they would see the simultaneous deceit straight away, & it is only due to a physical chance that this tower did not figure. Is that not eerie? That it is *possible* at all? When the woman clambered out of bed to go to the phone and call me up, at the time I was talking with another: in point of fact the other woman was calling me to go to her for the first time. What does it signify that that is tolerated by nature, the telephone-mechanics, and a moral God?"

"So why am I talking so much about the impossibility of love — is there not affection itself in those very internal irrationalities, two friends, parents, and sons? What is affection? What does it mean that two people come under the sway of an emotional attraction? The question arises with such natural facility, because one's first impression about such a charitable emotional relationship, is that it is not necessary, *not* essential, however universal & inevitable — no more than an odd accident, an illness, a diabolical suggestion, a joke.

Why is the other person needed, though I do not see any, truly not any feature which makes her winning? Because God takes holding His counsel to extremes, His invisibility is substituted by another person's visibility and ostensible-salvational tangibility — all philanthropy is a variant of sacrilege, idolatry, clinging to man instead of to an invisible God. When a person has been selected, then in order to narcotize ourselves in order increasingly to numb one's sole natural thirst: the thirst for God. Two people are bored with each other, become habituated to each other, wonder at each other; the main point is that a fellow-being is always *faute de mieux*: God was needed, and instead of Him we get a physiological scarecrow like that: a fellow-being, an attractive woman, a good mother, an old private tutor. When we have become habituated to the cheap narcotic, no wonder it becomes an obsession.

It may be a reason or basis for affection, sometimes perhaps an appraisal as well: one acknowledges something in the buffoon known as »the other person« and one strives to possess that — and, since it is an intellectual affair, one invents the affection story, which is one of the constrained techniques or tricks of spiritual possession.

Even hypochondria may lead to affection: it lets one enter into the life of the other with an excessively nervous imagination: one's self-affection is so profligate that yet another puppet was needed so that it should not overflow onto the asphalt. The source of the affection is therefore, in the end, a matter of desperation, always a secondary consideration, a chance discharge of situations — nothing ancient in it, nothing pure: the whole affair is decadence. What would come of that if one were to graze on fresh sexual meadowlands !"

"Is it not comical, after all that, Andrew, that you nevertheless wish for people to like you ? What are you begging for ? What is a woman to like about you ? That, however attractive, however characterful, you are bored with her body and only desire it maybe once a year out of absent-mindedness ? Or maybe you should gain women's approbation by ranking any sign of intellectual life to the category of influenza with complications, seeing morality as a disease, fidelity as a fiction ? Do you suppose that is going to add hugely to your attractive power ? That as a rule you label it a peculiar fault, just a mass neurosis ? — Ought not such a one precisely be loved ? A person who is so dreadfully lonely and mistrustful ? Because once such a love-nihilist like that sees love in another it is destroyed through nostalgic happiness and gratitude. Perhaps it is not such a comic turn, after all, to like an Andrew Marvell." He himself gives the response: "a scribbler is not loveable; a scribbler cannot love."

Besides general complaints there are more special ones also — such as the following: "Women's desires and needs of a man are decidedly self-contradictory. My woman loves two things: poetic lunacy, assuming moon-struckness, the spirit of a hovering Ariel, yet at the same time money, success, political *arrivisme*, a don's chair at Oxford; she is not bothered that the two are generally mutually exclusive — the fact is, women are mixtures of an excessive thirst for romanticism and an excessive thirst for consolidation. My woman has the especially brazen luck to be acquainted with an Oxford don, whom I am in the habit of referring to as His Worthiness the Lunatic: he is both an eccentric poet and sober eager-beaver. She can always use that to rub in my face. Because I am not two individuals: a bohemian and a don."

"It will remain a constant riddle what leads people to make this distinction between a »fleeting flirtation« and »a momentous grand amour.« As the starting-point for both is the same, and in a love relationship one never gets further ahead — the whole game is constrained, always artificially, into the tiny autonomies of ever-renewed starting-points.

It depends on seemingly utterly insignificant externalities whether a woman will be an absentminded padder-out of trysting places or a sacred and eternal wife, a little card-game liaison or an Isolda of death. One thing that is perpetually sensed: when one jocularly flips the easy woman out through the door after use, and one subsequently catches the fragrance of her cologne in an unexpected place, it will suddenly become clear that every love myth, exalted fidelity, and poetic destiny is invested in this little token of a girl. And *vice versa*: when one's body, morality and, above all, time has fatefully knit together one always feels that it is not that the woman is so great and permanent, an externality is the only reason why precisely that variant is what became of her — it was raining and one had to escort her a long way, one particularly detested another woman in a gathering, and it was more a case of our seeking to flee her presence, etc. Destiny can also be a joke; flirtation a chance for destiny."

The interesting aspect here is that Casanova fortuitously was also familiar with *this* Marvellian distinction, with the enormous difference that for him flirtation and love were fixed variances like tin plate and gold — he could not even dream of a destructive chemistry which would deem to discover gold even in tin plate and tin plate in gold.

"It will turn out at the end that writers are writers. Is it not comic that while I am filling up these pessimistic margins I am impatiently glancing at the huge wall clock to keep an eye on the minute when I can meet with my love. People have no idea how immeasurable the discontinuity is between the freewheeling of thoughts *ad absurdum* and life. Otherwise how could I so often be happily in love? Moreover, happiest when I was able to *write* down accurately before a tryst the utter uselessness of every tryst — which is why I say that it turns out that it is useless, my writing. I still write, the naïve fact of writing a problem down in itself makes one forget it: and one twitters away as one races into the lover's arms — for glee, beauty, faith, and the happiness of May. And how stupid a »bright« woman can be: if she were to find these nihilist notations she would walk out on one like an express train leaving a milestone behind — yet for this, *formulated* pessimism is the one and only aphrodisiac: it is only once I have precisely anathematized the love out of me and to the point of exhaustion that I am to a T just as pleasant, passionate, practical, & mythical as the woman wished for in her most optimistic dreams."

"The most idiotic thing in the world in love is an occasion. In my whole life there was never a word about women or my desires, only about such occasions that, if I could not have exploited, I would have considered myself as being inept or a bad mathematician who was unable to accomplish even an easy task like that. It is a sin against God to leave that magnificent opportunity unexploited — one says, quite unconsciously expressing oneself in a highly pedantic fashion and in reality merely exploiting the opportunity: the woman in question being a seventieth-rank issue, indeed an explicitly disturbing and inhibitory side-factor which sullies the ideal cleanliness of the occasion. Throughout my entire life every such marvelous opportunity for a tryst has been spoiled by the woman who came along for it — yet all the same with some crazy animal consistency, if she is solitary and I hear of a bungalow entrusted to me, a rival who is going away and a shared boat trip, my heart beats faster from

joy, and only in the moment of realization does the grub-
by damage come to mind: i.e., that the woman has come
along for the occasion, and with that the happy abstraction is at an end."

"Lovers sometimes talk. The conversation is in every
respect a run-of-the-mill subgenre; superfluous either
because it is completely insignificant or because what we
have to say is excessively significant — the style for both
of us is silence. But lovers are crazy in the second degree
as well; when all is said and done, there are people within
craziness of the first degree. What do I customarily talk
about when by chance I have the opportunity of casting
my paradox routine for a female catch?

First of all, about all the things that sensitive impressionism dispatches to the brain: garish and immensely
broad green belts on very thin waists, about the radial
white stripes of a blue dress, a host of tiny externalities
which normally irritate women but it happens to be the
case that if one makes some banal global statement of
praise to a women she will take it as being individually
tailored and assume it, whereas if one analyzes her entirely individual traits, the woman will immediately suspect that the emphasis is not on her but on the male virtuosity of the analysis for its own sake. Despite being well
aware of that, I carry on stupidly analyzing further. — So
what about the second source of conversation? All kinds
of diplomatic tactics. The bulk of being together in love
is taken up with that — a thousand hypocrisies, traps,
watching, lures, and poses, an immense lacework of lies.

One is exasperated, wearied, by the source of all imaginable evil, but without it there is no man and woman. A third source of conversation — in contrast to that, lovers, taking a desperate, deep breath, want to recognize a completely honest, primeval, and great psychological truth in one another — but then is it possible to get into deep water where soul and truth are quibbling? ... Those are the invigorating brooks of cultivated amorous chattering. Have fun, Andrew Marvell."

"The main reason why I fussed around with so many women was my ascetic cynicism: I thought that if women trample around indiscriminately on my body and brain, they would sooner destroy the whole possibility of eroticism in me than if I were abstinent. Farce and filth, uncalibrated scandals, are a surer anti-Eros than fasting. So what became of the self-torture? I did not murder love within me with this witty technique, only the women: the ladies, my living fellow beings, truly agonized around me, & due to me — and I splash around in the esthetic selfishness — the ego, the self-tormenting, the sacred: I observe, psychologize, write poems. My patentable morality in vain ..."

"To those men, young and old, who thirst for passionate understanding and for lyrics intimating the most profound secrets of vegetation in a woman, I can only offer this one important piece of advice: never put your trust in deep consideration, fiery silence, chthonian swooning, and quivering trance — with a woman like that even sudden apathy, unexpected & unjustified lethargy, not to say every grayness and impudence of indifference, is always standing on watch. Every profoundly vital entity is barren, every typically vegetative thing is just a hairs-breadth from impotence and idiotic complete ignorance and apathy. Big sentiment and lyricism are essentially exaltations of another kind: that is unknown by these pseudo-pathetics belabored with biological pathos."

"There are two kids of humbug in the world: the comic sterility of mysticism and the comic sterility of rationalism. Chthonian humbug and Voltairean humbug: deep feeling and unprejudiced clarity of sight are the two classic parodies of mankind. That jive music during sex should not be forgotten. I referred just before to the use-lessness of a woman fluttering her eyes intensely, down to the vegetative base — and it is interesting how this type is always also a rationalist run wild: one extreme endeav-ors to counterbalance its sterility with another, unsuc-cessfully, of course. Rationalism is the sole thing which is able to compete with the naivety of an infant and the gentle trustworthy freshness of violets, which need not be taken amiss on that account alone. Jesus himself said to the Jewish mothers: »Suffer the rationalists to come to me.« Of what is the incomparable violetness of the rationalist woman composed (she is always the same as one who occasionally has chthonian whims)? Some-where a poem or piece of prose was once written with a title like » Les Quinze joies du mariage «[156] — at a time when a dithyramb about such girls could only be entitled » Deux joies du rationalism. « Such a woman, when faced with an action, will always find a surprising cause which lies in cheap antithesis to the action: the cause of action A is assuredly B, and that of action B is unsurprisingly A. Behind charity lies selfishness, behind humility, pride, behind impudence, cowardice, behind heroism, neurasthenia, behind asceticism, business, behind simplicity, artfulness, behind sensuality, impotence — the game is infinite and tedious. But girls of reason are not bored, every morning they pray to God to give them their daily grub for disclosure — and God is a merciful God.

The other joy, once their fingers have grown tired of the *causal* knickknacks: to see through the structure or internal mechanism of a new action: especially an action by men, or of the masculine character; once the structure, an outline of outlines, is in their hands, the second satisfaction is ready. That the structure is a lousier part of a man than a discarded coat hanger is by the bye — reason does not seek the significant and the true but the readily and speedily tangible, the evidence. Minor disclosures and evidence: that is all she lives off. Yet life's sensible and sensitive things happen to be *between* the two poles, just as far from vegetative pathos as from the pallid *logos*-narcissi of *raison*."

"Of what does the sort of »clever« woman who has become fashionable since Renaissance times consist? The previous pattern: of blind biological pathos and the opposed corners of continually grinding rationalism — that is the basis. If I wish to go somewhat beyond that pattern, one has to start out from that Narcissus frame of mind: from that deeply embedded, self-canonizing, tragic egotism, which estheticizes and moralizes its own desolateness and insensitivity towards other people." — The other element: a certain elegance, something coming virtually close to mundaneness but which, at the last minute, is not that after all — there is much more intelligence, starched and dogged taste, in belts and caps for it to be truly Vogue-like.

It is intriguing that women of so-called definite taste, however impeccable that taste may be otherwise, are not posh people — more rabid humanists who define their own Narcissus solitude with their belts, with a mix of impertinence and desperation, a still more eternal Narcissus. A real posh person has a freer, more changeable taste — in it there is more of a switch from poshness than from a fixation of the personality. But who in the hell would have the goal of becoming posh? — says the merely almost-posh woman on such occasions with a touch of resentful cockiness. Puritanism rages quite disastrously in her elegance, household, and morality, she does not like beating about the bush, shamming, the baroque — anything that is not evidence or primitive disclosure is to her already a lie, sickness. That, of course, stems from her loneliness, and her persecution mania has a naïve and harmless variant: she is scared of jumping into something, of being taken for a ride, and in her over-defensiveness she attempts to tarnish every more complex matter, to wear it down to a primitive pattern. Then there is less risk of being cheated.

On such girls until the day they die, whether they are ashamed, show it off, or are *blasé* about it, is an Ox-bridge shadow, that of Queen Elizabeth I, who conversed in Greek with her teachers and flattered easily deceived Asturian gigolos with Spanish heroic verse. The shadow of university: it is a strange thing on these women this just as much semi- or almost-something as the poshness. But without that Andrew Marvell would have been unable to approach them, that is for sure. When the Gothic faculty of St. Thomases in Paris reaches the point that a woman will have no more than an intellectual perfume — »*Quelque Thèses*,« on the model of »*Quelques Fleurs*.« The average breadth of reading, regardless of this university false pregnancy: with geometric precision, those books which are more than commonplace but less than extraordinary. A symbol of the literature that it forsakes with unerring accuracy is: my brother, John Donne. This *not*-Donne trait outlines this sort of woman quite explicitly. Naturally, her manner is a stylized, handmaidenly, babyfying Goliath, as a theologian friend of mine put it, expressing everything with the grimaces, intonations, and gestures of a child of five or six — thereby fleeing from the forced penchant that, their thoughts and emotions are too passionate or too cynical, and always inexpressible in the normal forms of social discourse, yet on the other hand she cannot lie, though not for ethical reasons but out of a nervous sensibility to reality.

In life she is guided by certain clichés of *raison* — the brain just as much as the heart has its own schematic courses, which in practice are very useful — and a woman is always highly practical; if she never becomes familiar with something, then it is thought of as a luxury.

If a writer sets down, with every tropical richness of analysis, how the rose color of a wild rose is a rose, that will leave her cold — that, as a proto-neurasthenic, she treats as proto-neurasthenic; if a writer of pulp fiction casts before her nose the poor bluff that a rose-colored wild rose is not, in point of fact, rose colored but white or lilac, or whatever, she will voraciously leap at the disclosure, because to her nose that has a down-to-earth, *savoir-vivre* aroma. In her mechanical shredding of illusions she is usually guided by a long-fostered big disappointment: a woman like that has always had some black experience with a man having deserted her, having almost died on account of an abortion, marrying on account of the poor mother, or a girlfriend became a star because she (the friend) made herself available to someone, whereas she did not, not on your life, never. They make up their mind about the experience, which is crushing them, and they choose for themselves the black shadow in which they will be seen by the world thereafter; they will be hard, supplanting the disappointment with a decorative & demonstrative sadism."

If Casanova incurred damnation, then so too did those magnificent women without whom there could have been no Casanova: this female portrait sketch by Marvell is, I believe, just as accurate a hell for the true women of the 18th century as Marvell was hell for Casanova.

"What do you mean that I can't believe in anything a woman does? This afternoon I saw one calling domestic rabbits and little chicks by pet names and this afternoon nursing a sick person. Both nauseated me. Why? What is so repugnant about her smelling a flower as she delights in a wood or thinks of the sea? Perhaps because nature belongs just to the two of them — the absolutely first-rate poet's and the absolutely backwoods peasant's. Somehow, they never enjoy, love, or delight in such things — they either subsist on it or they notice with a shudder how much of nature is a closed monstrosity, alien, how little it speaks to mankind.

Someone who loves nature is making a fraud cocktail out of therapy and esthetics but has not the faintest idea what is being played with. Woman and flower, woman and bird, woman and wood — those are mutually exclusive, repugnant: if they are together, muck is present. It is just as much a natural and logical error if the woman is good. Things like that always have some concocted, vulgarly professional character, some conceited parody of every morality. Was goodness itself possibly lacking in style from the very outset? Why did God not grant me the pleasure of being able to delight in flower-smelling and sick patient-pestering girls? Can one only truly believe in the mother with the rest being no more than suburban décor?"

"Every male-female antithesis is a variation of a fundamental antithesis: a woman seeks *via* love & through the man to arrive at, and settle down for good in, reality:

the man is the anchor selected in order to berth. The man seeks *via* love, and through the woman's help, to escape once and for all outside and to stay permanently outside reality (of course »reality« here in an utterly practical & non-poetic or non-philosophical sense); the woman is the springboard chosen for the purpose of escaping. That being the case, how would they wish for peace from each other?

There is no greater antithesis in the world than this: to run aground in prose or to lose one's mind in dreams, to crystallize sobriety or to push the luxury of luxuries into Art Nouveau. To a woman the man is: a goal; to a man a woman is: a means. A façade of non-existence unfolds before me like the gorgon-foul walls of Tivoli amid the cypresses: love must be abandoned."

Abandon love! That, that is the injunction Casanova must have been hearing when he felt constrained to write the lines: "*Meine Weltanschauung, die ich über jede Anfechtung erhaben glaubte, lag in Trümmern; ich erkannte einen Gott der Rache, der bis zu diesem Augenblick gewartet hatte, um mit einem einzigen Schlage mich für alle meine Freveltaten zu bestrafen und um meinen Unglauben ein Ende zu machen, indem er mich — vernichtete.*"[157]

HISTORY OF THE GENESIS OF THE ST. ORPHEUS BREVIARY

Mária Tompa

IN THE SUMMER OF 1937 Miklós Szentkuthy made a trip around northern Italy, which was when the plan for his work about Orpheus was seeded. An exhibition in Venice of the whole *oeuvre* of Tintoretto left an extraordinary impression on him, plentiful traces of which are readily discernible in his work *Széljegyzetek Casanovához* [Marginalia on Casanova], which became the first part of the *Fekete Orpheus-füzetek* [Black Orpheus notebooks], completed in 1938 and published in 1939.

In his 1976 memoir *Recollections of My Career*, this is how he refers to it: "Among the huge amount that I learned from Antal Szerb I ought to list my real acquaintance with the eighteenth century. It was he who inspired the Casanova commentaries of Orpheus … The structure of my commentaries was determined by the structure of the 1919 *magnum opus* of the Protestant theologian Karl Barth on the *Epistle of St. Paul to the Romans*."

In regard to the physical form of the *Black Orpheus* notebooks he considered it important to note in the series of interviews published in 1988 under the title *Frivolitások és hitvallások* [Frivolous Confessions]. "I even conceived of (but did not realize) an initial cover design for the *Black Orpheus* notebooks. I envisaged it as being of folio size, not knowing yet whether it would be a notebook or book. All I recall is that the inspiration for it were the very many relief tombs that could be seen on church pavings: a big rectangular marble or bronze in the center of which a deceased bishop was portrayed in relief with a legend running round in a rectangular frame. That was not what they became… but the big black notebooks do somehow tend towards my original idea… If anything inspired them it was utter simplicity: a few books put out by Jakob Hegner, the publishing house based in Cologne… on the spine of each of which, uniformly, was stuck a little vignette on which the title and author could be read. I felt that was extremely tasteful & elegant, and that was how I devised the cover of the Orpheus notebooks as well."

Given that this was a work about Giacomo Casanova, the infamous Venetian adventurer, the state censorship board and later the Hungarian Royal Court of Justice, condemned it virtually unseen, or at least only after a very superficial glance. Szentkuthy professed as follows in *Recollections of My Career*:

> To start with, the first novel (*Casanova*) had barely come out when something else — an almost illegibly typewritten scrap of paper — made an appearance at the Madách Gymnasium, where I was working at the time as the most novice of probationary teachers. It was an official document which communicated the heart-warming fact

that the public prosecutor's office was "laying charges" against my *Casanova* specifically for offending against public decency and affronting religious sentiment. (It was no mean feat, after that had been delivered to my hands, to go on and give two English lessons on the poetry of Shelley and Keats.) How had I offended against public decency? By the following: "The streets in Venice are narrow, windows are vast and thus, in mystic comfort [...] it is possible to spy in on a woman, into her home, her boudoir, her soup and her washing basin." In what way had I trampled on religion? By way of introduction, I ought to mention that in point 11 of the book I write about how, when Casanova was a child, it was customary in Venice (at New Year?) for the sermon to be given, in memory of Jesus' own childhood, not by an ordained priest but by a Venetian child, which tickled me to no end. At the place where I was open to prosecution I expressed this by, among other things, the following: "We cannot help but think that Casanova was entitled to deliver the sermon, and that what is happening here is perfectly logical, quite free of hypocrisy. It is God's will that the sermon should be delivered, not by St. John, bearded and in the wilderness, but by a lovelorn rascal..." So how had the newfangled censor and the public prosecutor's office turned that against me? "M. Sz. is teaching Christian Hungary that the sermons in church should not be delivered by professional priests but scoundrels." In my naivety I rushed off to get a defense lawyer, and naturally could find no one who was willing to take on my case, so that in the end the Attorney General's office had to appear on my behalf, a taking of my side that consisted of getting the charges against me dropped, but at the cost of having distribution of my book banned. In 1940-42, with the war in progress, I only had to submit to the censor a typescript of anything I wanted to publish, and to my no little surprise, they did not even bother looking at this but mindlessly slapped on, every 20 pages, the blue stamp authorizing publication, with the most eloquent "imprimatur" being given, for instance, to an imagined Chinese story that was a barely disguised scathing parody of Hitlerism!

Printed copies of the volume were impounded, so that it never reached bookshops, and nowadays only a few copies of it are to be found anywhere in the country... because, as Szentkuthy ironically remarked, those who knew that something about Casanova had been published but might be impounded quickly acquired it because they thought that it was some bulky and racy bestseller. In reality it is a reader's diary divided into 123 numbered sections that provides a picture of Casanova's personality extending to highly comprehensive, balanced, and minute psychological details. Szentkuthy gives an extremely detailed analysis not only with regard to his accomplishments in seducing women, but his intellectual and mental endeavors, his psychological and emotional stumbling blocks — much of it with great subjective vehemence.

Casanova wrote his memoirs in French but it was not possible to publish them in that language for several centuries and they appeared first in Germany (in six volumes, each of which was more than 600 pages long) before they were eventually published in France (1960 – 63). During the Thirties Szentkuthy was in possession of a German edition of the memoirs; that is what he read, and that is why so many German quotations can be found in *Marginalia on Casanova*.

The impounding and destruction of the work was not a calamity for Szentkuthy. His energy as a writer was undiminished. The next volume in the series appeared in 1939, and four more up until 1942, so that the six *Black Orpheus* notebooks comprised an independent part of the planned essay novel with the title *St. Orpheus Breviary*.

So that readers can more readily take stock of the position, what follows includes two programs for the entire work that Szentkuthy wrote (in 1939 and 1942, and a detailed chronology of the published parts).

The writing of the series of notebooks broke off in 1942 and it could not be resumed after the end of World War II due to the Communist dictatorship in Hungary under Rákosi. As a result, Szentkuthy had to wait until 1968 for an opportunity for a new edition of the *Orpheus* work. Csaba Sík, then the chief editor at Magvető Publishers, proposed to publish the books, but by then Szentkuthy already had as his aim publication of the entire work in a uniform edition, as originally intended in the 1939 program, with him writing the life of a saint as a preface to each single volume. Each book therefore would consist of two sections: 1) Vita (Life of a Saint), and 2) Lectio (Saintly Reading). The six *Black Orpheus* notebooks did not as yet have the "Life of a Saint" sections. He only set about writing those for the first six parts around 1969, & in 1973 the first two volumes published by Magvető appeared in the originally planned form. In the life of Alfonso Maria di Liguori there is to be found a reference to St. Silvester I, a life of which can be read at the start of the seventh book of *Orpheus: II Szilveszter második élete* [The Second Life of Silvester II, 1972].

In the end all 10 parts of *Orpheus* made an appearance in five volumes. Thus, over a span of 44 years the 10 volumes of the *St. Orpheus Breviary* planned back in 1939 were accomplished within the framework of a substantial cycle of essays.

On the other hand, one book that figured in the original plan was a reading diary with the title *Ágoston olvasása közben. Széljegyzetek Szent Ágoston » De civitate Dei « c. művéhez* [While Reading Augustine: Marginalia on St. Augustine's work *The City of God*]. He actually wrote that in 1939 but in the end, for unknown reasons, he did not incorporate it into the *Orpheus* cycle; it remained in manuscript and was published posthumously by Jelenkor Press (1993); soon after it appeared in French translation as *En lisant Augustin* (José Corti, 1996), and eventually also in Spanish (Subsuelo, 2013).

Already in the early Seventies Szentkuthy wrote two other works that he intended to fit into the *St. Orpheus*

Breviary but which to the present day have remained un-published (on the cover sheet he wrote: "of *St. Orpheus Breviary*, vol. IX and X: *Egyiptomi Mária és Amazonok római vadászaton* [*Mary of Egypt* and *Amazons on the Hunt in Rome*]"), though several excerpts from the latter were made available in journals.

Miklós Szentkuthy;
program set out in two prospectuses for the *Black Orpheus* notebooks

a) on completing the writing of *Széljegyzetek Casa-novához* [Marginalia on Casanova]
(the year before its publication in 1939)

I started the prospectus for the first of the *Orpheus* notebooks with the following text:

The work, larger continuous installments of which will appear quarterly, comprises an interlocking essay series. At the beginning of each chapter there will be a longer or shorter life of a saint, and, appended to that, historical essays, extracts from a novel, short stories, lyrical poems, and aphorisms that are connected with aspects of the life and times of the saint who stands at the chapter head. The designation 'Breviary' in the title refers to this man-ner of composition. The name "Orpheus" expresses the underlying conceptual tone: Orpheus wandering in the underworld is an eternal symbol of the brain straying among the dark secrets of reality. The aim of the work is, firstly, to portray the reality of nature and history with ever more extreme precision, and secondly, to display through variations in the history of the European mind an observer's every uncertainty, the fickleness of emotions, the tragic sterility of thoughts & philosophical systems. The reason for placing the epithet "Saint" before "Orpheus" is because the work seeks to portray both European history and the vegetative world of nature from an essentially religious, supernatural viewpoint. Although both the lives of the saints, as well as the other figures, famous books, and cultural manifestations of history are, in point of fact, nothing more than different features of a lyrical self-portrait, the various roles and masks of the author as it were, the work is in essence "religious," because from love to politics the emphasis throughout is on the battle of the body-politic of God and the body-politic of the world.

The part works, each approx. 100–150 pages in length, will not display the day-by-day arrangement of a breviary as this would pose technical difficulties with issuing what, as far as possible, will be notebooks of uniform length. One such notebook (in the same format as the present leaflet) will appear every three or four months at the price of Pengő 2.80* per notebook.

Széljegyzetek Casanovához [Marginalia on Casanova]; (A picture of the literature, society, and art of the eighteenth century via the *Memoirs*);

the next three planned notebooks are:

Ágoston olvasása közben [While Reading St. Augustine] (the antique myth, the Old Testament and Christianity, and finally the balance of European history);

Vázlatok Tudor Erzsébet ifjúkori arcképéhez [Sketches for a Portrait of Elizabeth Tudor of England as a Girl]

Orpheus tíz álarca [The Ten Masks of Orpheus] (i.e., 10 lives of saints)

b) on completing the writing of the last of the *Black Orpheus* notebooks: *Vallomás és bábjáték* [Confession and Puppet Show] in 1942

The aim of Orpheus is to find the human ideal and an acceptable lifestyle that a thinking cerebrum and a sentiment in search of happiness can wish for after the broadest possible circle of historical, the most universal religious, and the most profound natural historical experiences. The aim is thus an unmistakable humanist one: it seeks the man beyond every variant of cultures, all promise and failure of sciences and mythologies, the most distant periods and far-flung regions, the vast yet nevertheless finite shades of psychology. What remains of the masses of experience left behind? What can be utilized in the future? What is the play of time and what is the indispensable essence and possibly a permanent positive? A commonplace simile illumines the method of Orpheus: just as a human embryo before birth as it were recapitulates stages of its evolutionary development that after birth, including adulthood, are unnoticeable, so it is with the author of this book, before reaching the new human ideal set as a goal, first it will run through the most characteristic political, artistic, and religious figures of preceding eras, will with dramatic gusto fuse with them (with playful balancing of historical objectivity and lyrical personality) in order thereby to arrive at his own age and be able to give an answer to what — after Gothic and rococo, Greek myth and Reformation, Chinese painting and Spanish politics — what should the new man be like, & what should he do? As that is the goal and the method, in point of fact it belongs to the old genre of the *Bildungsroman*, a novel of a person's formative years, uniting the leading genres of the present day, the essay, & the autobiography in a common big framework.

Editions of the *Saint Orpheus Breviary*

1939 – 1942: *Fekete Orpheus-füzetek* [Black Orpheus notebooks]: Részletek Szentkuthy Miklós "*Szent Orpheus breviáriuma*" című készülő művéből / Extracts from Miklós Szentkuthy's work in progress under the title *Saint Orpheus Breviary*. Private edition, the six published notebooks of which were:

1) 1939: *Széljegyzetek Casanovához* [Marginalia on Casanova]
2) 1939: *Fekete Reneszánsz* [Black Renaissance]
3) 1940: *Eszkoriál* [Escorial]
4) 1941: *Europa Minor*
5) 1941: *Cynthia*
6) 1942: *Vallomás és bábjáték* [Confession and Puppet Show]

1973 – 1993: *Szent Orpheus breviáriuma*. Budapest: Magvető Kiadó (the prefatory Saintly lives were all written between 1969 and 1972).

1973: vols. 1 – 2, for the six works published in this edition see 1939 – 42 + II *Szilveszter második élete* [The Second Life of Silvester II]

1974: vol. 3. *Kanonizált kétségbeesés* (*'Kételkedő' Szent Hugó, Grenoble-i püspök élete*) [Canonized Desperation: the life of 'Doubting' St. Hugh, Bishop of Grenoble].

1976: vols. 1, 2 & 3 second edn. (700 + 732 + 458 pp.)

1984: vol. 4: *Véres Szamár, V, Szent Celesztin, lemondó pápa élete* [Bloody Ass: Life of St. Celestine V, the Pope who Abdicated] (568 pp.)

1993: vol. 5 (fragmentary): *Euridiké nyomában* [In the Footsteps of Eurydice] (149 pp.)

ENDNOTES

1 Alfonso set out his ideals of gentle, direct persuasion, rather than rigor, in his celebrated *Theologia Moralis* (1753 – 5).

2 Inmost theatricality of all entities.

3 Witchcraft. It should be borne in mind that Casanova's *History of My Life* first saw print in a German edition, between 1822 and 1828, and that was the text used by Szentkuthy (hence the occasional German quotations).

4 'will-o'-the-wisps.'

5 'Butterflying,' craving for variety.

6 Phrase used in a remark by Edgar in *King Lear* (I. ii).

7 "I set out *masked*." The English translation, and what follow in the endnotes, are the equivalents taken from Giacomo Casanova, Chevalier de Seingalt: *History of My Life*. Tr. Willard R. Trask. Baltimore & London: Johns Hopkins University Press, 1967, indicated in this particular instance: English vol. 1, Chapter 4, p. 102. (Masks were customarily worn during the theater season in Venice, from roughly late October to Carnival.) The German quotations (as in the very first published version of the *Diary*, which was written in French) are as they originally appear in Szentkuthy's *Szent Orpheus breviáriuma, I. Széljegyzetek Casanovához*. Budapest: Magvető Könyvkiadó, 1973.

8 Jean-Baptiste Greuze (1725 – 1805) won great popularity, especially for his pretty heads of young girls.

9 Also known as the "marble church," Santa Maria dei Miracoli is one of the best examples of the early Venetian Renaissance including colored marble.

10 "I must… I must…" Engl. vol. 1, ch. 4, p. 128.

11 "The murmur of water struck by the oars of a gondola…" Eng. vol. 1, ch. 4, p. 112.

12 Downgoing, or decline, as in Spengler's *Decline of the West* (*Der Untergang des Abendlandes*, 2 vols., 1918 – 22).

13 "I had read Plato." Eng. vol. 2, ch. 8, p. 205.

14 "Metaphysics… for this I don't care." Eng. vol. 3, ch. 10, p. 195.

15 "outcast forever, abandoned forever, destroyed forever be all ties of nature, rejected, abandoned & destroyed forever be all ties of nature…" (Act II, Scene I).

16 "Sleep and Poetry" is a 400-line poem, published in 1817 by John Keats, towards the end of which can be read the lines:

> "Petrarch, outstepping from the shady green,
> Starts at the sight of Laura; nor can wean
> His eyes from her sweet face. Most happy they!
> For over them was seen a free display
> Of out-spread wings, and from between them shone
> The face of Poesy: from off her throne
> She overlook'd things that I scarce could tell.
> The very sense of where I was might well
> Keep Sleep aloof…"

17 "...then fantasy finds new pleasures."

18 "delights of remembrance."

19 "Drunkenness and fear." "Eleven nights."

20 *The Complaint: or, Night-Thoughts on Life, Death, & Immortality*, better known simply as *Night-Thoughts*, is a long poem by Edward Young published in nine parts (or "nights") between 1742 and 1745.

21 "True love always makes one reticent." Eng. vol. 1, ch. 4, p. 124.

22 "This metaphysical curve seemed to me to be against nature..." Eng. vol. 1, ch. 5, p. 132.

23 Eng. vol. 1, ch. 5, pp. 136–137.

24 I.e., dry.

25 "with my two angels" and "my first love." Eng. vol. 1, ch. 5, p. 147.

26 Cf. Eng. vol. 1, ch. 10, pp. 289–293.

27 Cf. Eng. vol. 4, ch. 7, pp. 109–125.

28 This inverts a tag from Cicero's *De oratore*: *historia est magistra vitae*.

29 "The packet contained a piece of wax on which was the imprint of a key..." Eng. vol. 1, ch. 5, p. 143.

30 Dózsa (1470–1514) led a peasants' revolt against Hungary's landed nobility in the year of his death. On capture he was executed by being made to sit on a smouldering-hot iron throne with a heated iron crown on his head and a heated sceptre in his hand.

31 A "night-light with a dial."

32 The episode is recounted in Eng. vol. 1, ch. 5, pp. 144 – 146.

33 "My final act excitement."

34 "I buried myself in the woods to ruminate my grief." Eng. vol. 1, ch. 5, p. 149.

35 "Grief" — in experimental physics? And "to ruminate" —

36 "And the flower which alone could raise me to the rank of gods..." Eng. vol. 1, ch. 5, p. 149. This translates a line from Ludovico Ariosto's long poem *Orlando Furioso*: "e il fior ch'in ciel potea pormi fra i dèi" (canto 8, stanza 77).

37 "... I rejoined the lively company in the garden." Eng. vol. 1, ch. 5, p. 150.

38 'See-sawing.'

39 "... the prelate who was perhaps to set me on the road to the Papacy." Eng. vol. 1, ch. 6, p. 162.

40 Eng. vol. 1, ch. 6, p. 163. Szentkuthy reads this as "Liu family," though the notes to the English edition suggest that Casanova is actually referring to "Girolamo M. Lin (born 1690), member of a prominent Bergamese family that was given Venetian patrician status in 1681."

41 "Still a disciple of the demon of Socrates." Eng. vol. 1, ch. 6, p. 164.

42 "...he inspired feelings of the strongest friendship in me." Eng. vol. 1, ch. 6, p. 168.

43 "The wick is submerged in oil." Eng. vol. 1, ch. 6, p. 171.

44 The Teatro SS Giovanni and Paolo, owned by the Gri-

mani family, was the venue for the premières of Monteverdi's trilogy of operatic fantasies — *Il ritorno d'Ulisse in patria* (1639 – 40), *Le nozze d'Enea* (1640 – 41), and *Poppea* (1642 – 43).

45 "My sensitivity was so refined at that time." Eng. vol. I, ch. 6, p. 177.

46 The *Charities* (or *Gratiae* in Latin) were the personifications of Grace and Beauty.

47 "... Thinking of reality and imagination, I gave the latter the preference, for the former is dependent on it." Eng. vol. I, ch. 6, p. 197.

48 "I set off for my home with a joyful heart, regretting nothing." Eng. vol. I, ch. 6, p. 201.

49 Phryne (c. 340 B.C.) was a celebrated courtesan in ancient Athens. She served as model for, *inter alia*, the 'Aphrodite Anadyomene' of Apelles and the 'Cnidian Aphrodite' of Praxiteles.

50 "Angel of the Orient."

51 "Orient," "night," "balcony." Eng. vol. I, ch. 8, p. 213 & 215.

52 Mozart's 1782 opera *Abduction from the Seraglio*.

53 The phrase comes from Pope Pius XI's attempt in 1938 to distance Italians from their country's new anti-Semitic official stance on the grounds that a civilised country should not ape the barbarian German legislation, and he also attacked the Italian government for attacking the papacy: "Anyone who eats from the pope is dead!" (*Confalioneri*, 352)

54 The invented German title translates roughly as 'The World as a Turning Septemberish.'

55 "Nothing made an impression on me." Eng. vol. 1, ch. 8, p. 230.

56 Eng. vol. 1, ch. 8, p. 231.

57 The Greek islands of Kythera and Kephallenia.

58 Queen Plaisance of Cyprus (ca. 1235 – 61) was a daughter of Bohemund V of Antioch. She became Queen regent of the Kingdom of Cyprus and, until her death, acting Regent of the Kingdom of Jerusalem for her son Hugh II.

59 Mélisande de Lusignan, Princess of Antioch (1200 – after 1249), was the youngest daughter of Queen Isabella I by her fourth and last marriage to King Amalric II of Jerusalem.

60 Catherine Cornaro (1454 – 1510) was Queen of Cyprus from 1474 to 1489.

61 Theodora Tocco (née Maddalena Tocco) (d. 1429) was a daughter of Leonardo II Tocco, Lord of Zante, who was a younger brother of Carlo I Tocco, Count of Cephalonia and Leukas. She was the first wife of Constantine Palaiologos, who became the last Emperor of the Byzantine Empire.

62 Don Joseph Nasi (c. 1505 – 79) was in close touch with Rabbi Moshe Hamon, the personal physician of the great Sultan Suleiman, and moved to Turkey, becoming close friends with Selim II. When the latter met the Sultan on the death of Suleiman, one of his first

official acts was to repay his faithful Jewish friend for his services by making him Duke of the isle of Naxos.

63 Eng. vol. 1, ch. 8, pp. 234 – 6. This refers to a famous manufactory of arms in Naples.

64 At this point in the text Casanova writes: "The morning after I arrived in the capital of Calabria [i.e., Cosenza], I hired a small carriage & proceeded to Martorano. As I traveled I fixed my eye on the famous *Mare Ausonium* [i.e., the southern part of the Tyrrhenian Sea] and rejoiced in being in the centre of *Magna Græcia* [i.e., S.E. Italy], which Pythagoras' sojourn had rendered illustrious for twenty-four centuries."

65 Leon Battista Alberti (1404 – 72), a humanist polymath, in 1452 published a detailed work, *De re aedificatoria* (Ten Books of Architecture), which covers a wide range of topics, from history to town planning, and engineering to aesthetics.

66 "...he would be delighted to have me take chocolate with him in his library any morning..." Eng. vol. 1, ch. 9, p. 261.

67 Casanova's affair with someone named Bellino, a castrato, is interesting inasmuch as it was believed at the time that Bellino was a man, though from the start Casanova was convinced that Bellino was a woman; indeed, he eventually learned that she was actually a beautiful young girl called Teresa Lanti, who was posing as a *castrato* (cf. Eng. vol. 2, ch. 1, pp. 5 – 23).

68 Felice Salimbeni (1712 – 51), a *castrato* who sang some of Handel's roles, taught Bellino (cf. Eng. vol. 2, ch. 2, p. 26).

69 Marco Ingegneri (c. 1545 – 92) was Monteverdi's master. He published several books of church music & madrigals.

70 Cf. Eng. vol. 1, ch. 9, p. 267.

71 Lucrezia engages Casanova's attention from p. 250 to p. 296 in vol. 1 of Willard Trask's translation.

72 "In the most enchanting disorder."

73 "Look at that *little* demon."

74 "Secret of nature" and "protecting or tutelary spirit."

75 "I am convinced, there is a God…"

76 "…we penetrated the labyrinthine alleys of the Villa Aldobrandini." Eng. vol. 1, ch. 9, p. 279. Trask's translation at this point (Eng. vol. 1, ch. 9, p. 279) is at considerable variance with the German text used by Szentkuthy; thus the English wording used here matches the latter. The Villa Aldobrandini, near Frascati, was built around 1600 for Cardinal Aldobrandini, a nephew of Pope Clement VII.

77 Domenico Zipoli (1688 – 1726), who briefly studied under Alessandro Scarlatti in Naples, is remembered as the most accomplished musician among Jesuit missionaries of South America. He composed, among other pieces, a Pastorale in C Major for organ.

78 The close assonance in French, but not in English ('Temple of Time'), is used in the poem "Le cimetière marin" in Valéry's 1922 collection *Charmes ou poèmes*.

79 "The emergence of historicism."

80 "The individual thing is ineffable, cannot be expressed in words," which derives ultimately from Aristotle.

81 "*Les langueurs tendres*," Wq. 117/30 (H. 110) is a keyboard composition by C.P.E. Bach, which has recently been found to have been alternatively catalogued as "*Memoire raisonné.*"

82 "At the end of two hours, enchanted with each other and looking most lovingly into each other's eyes." Eng. vol. 1, ch. 9, p. 280.

83 This quotes the opening of the second epistle of Alexander Pope's 1714 work *An Essay on Man*, composed in heroic couplets: "Know then thyself, presume not God to scan; / The proper study of Mankind is Man."

84 "The birth of tragedy out of the spirit of *gossip.*"

85 "What a situation!"

86 "A new lust in obedience." Eng. vol. 1, ch. 9, p. 305.

87 "I stayed with them until nightfall. Then I went." Eng., ibid.

88 "Then I went?"

89 "this situation."

90 "... I must go to Constantinople!" Eng. vol. 2, ch. 2, p. 34. It needs to be borne in mind that in the Middle Ages Venice became extremely wealthy through its control of trade between Europe and the Levant, and it expanded into the Adriatic Sea and beyond. The Venetian fleet was crucial to the sack of Constantinople in the Fourth Crusade in 1204. As a result of the ensuing partition of

the Byzantine Empire, Venice gained much territory in the Aegean Sea, including the islands of Crete and Euboea. Later, in 1489, the island of Cyprus, previously a crusader state, was annexed to Venice.

91 "superstition" and "destiny."

92 The Old French device (*'Plus ultra'* in Latin), meaning 'further beyond,' was an ancient name given to the Strait of Gibraltar.

93 "The moment of happiness has arrived." Eng. vol. 2, ch. 1, p. 11.

94 "ragged philosophers."

95 "purses stuffed with money" and "vast horizon." Eng. vol. 2, ch. 1, pp. 14 – 15.

96 "Freak of nature"? Eng. vol. 2, ch. 1, p. 7.

97 "...when we are happy, the thought that our happiness will be followed by misery never comes to trouble us." Eng. vol. 2, ch. 2, pp. 36 – 37.

98 The quotation is from "To a Skylark." In English in the original.

99 "Greeks, Jews, astrologers and exorcists." Eng. vol. 2, ch. 4, p. 65.

100 "My curiosity to see Cerigo, which is said to be the ancient Cythera." Eng. vol. 2, ch. 4, p. 64.

101 "This magnificent *view* was the cause of the *end* of the Roman Empire." Eng. vol. 2, ch. 4, p. 68.

102 'magnificent' view & 'fate.'

103 Reference to Muhammad XI (aka "Boabdil" and "El Chico," or "The Little One"), Sultan of Granada (ruled 1487–92); he surrendered Granada to Ferdinand and Isabella and was thus the last Moorish ruler in Spain.

104 Evidently a reference to a volume containing Chapter XXXVII of *The History of the Decline & Fall of the Roman Empire*, in which the name of Leandro is briefly mentioned. The passage runs: "Leovigild, the Gothic monarch of Spain, deserved the respect of his enemies and the love of his subjects: the Catholics enjoyed a free toleration, and his Arian councils attempted, without much success, to reconcile their scruples by abolishing the unpopular rite of a second baptism. His eldest son Hermenegild, who was invested by his father with the royal diadem and the fair principality of Baetica, contracted an honourable and orthodox alliance with a Merovingian princess, the daughter of Sigebert, king of Austrasia, and of the famous Brunechild. The beauteous Ingundis, who was no more than thirteen years of age, was received, beloved, and persecuted in the Arian court of Toledo; and her religious constancy was alternately assaulted with blandishments and violence by Goisvintha, the Gothic queen, who abused the double claim of maternal authority [...]. Love and honour might excite Hermenegild to resent this injurious treatment of his bride; and he was gradually persuaded that Ingundis suffered for the cause of divine truth. Her tender complaints, and the weighty arguments of Leandro, archbishop of Seville, accomplished his conversion; and the heir of the Gothic monarchy was initi-

ated in the Nicene faith [...]. [Hermenegild] invited the orthodox barbarians, the Suevi, and the Franks, to the destruction of his native land: he solicited the dangerous aid of the Romans, who possessed Africa and a part of the Spanish coast; and his holy ambassador, the archbishop Leandro, effectually negotiated in person with the Byzantine court."

105 "all that Yusuf had said to me concerning the essence of God…" Eng. vol. 2, ch. 4, pp. 80 – 81.

106 "I then took a violin and played the tune." Eng. vol. 2, ch. 4, p. 90.

107 A *furlana* was originally a lively peasant dance from Friuli which became fashionable among Venetians in the 18th century.

108 Roscelin (born c. 1050; died c. 1120), French medieval philosopher and theologian. Taught liberal arts in Compiégne and later in Loches, where his pupils included Abelard. Only one of his works has survived.

109 Alruna (or alraun): a word etymologically connected with runes and used to denote a witch in ancient times; nowadays it denotes a herbal root found in human form (e.g., mandrake), or carved to be, and used as a magic talisman.

110 Literally "love always slays love, the heart of the heart tears out my life…"

111 "The shadow of a tree is more treelike."

112 An extremity, peak.

113 Presumably William, archbishop of Tyre (c. 1130–86),
a medieval chronicler (his work is sometimes referred to
as the "History of Jerusalem").

114 Before taking up a post at the cathedral school of Notre-
Dame in 1113, Abelard was taught for a while as a student
of theology at Laon by the venerable Anselm of Laon.

115 "a storm and stress after unreality."

116 It should be noted that Tintoretto's *Susanna and the Elders* is held by the Kunsthistorisches Museum, Vienna,
and the most important exhibition on the artist's work
in the past century was held at the Palazzo Pesaro,
Venice, in 1937.

117 Presumably refers to the Castle of Miramare (*Schloß
Miramar* in German) near Trieste, N. Italy.

118 Literally 'uncoupling' (i.e., R & R).

119 Pseudo-Heideggerian term translating roughly as 'in-
stances of the world growing to conform to the truth.'

120 Émile Verhaeren (1855–1916), Belgian poet and realist
writer who wrote in French, greatly influenced by Zola.
His critical writings on art included at one time widely
read works on Rubens and Rembrandt.

121 The Venice International Film Festival (Mostra Internazi-
onale d'Arte Cinematografica della Biennale di Venezia),
the oldest film festival in the world, was founded in 1932
and held annually on the island of the Lido.

122 "deepest worldliness."

123 "But do not call things by their actual names, that is what matters." Eng. vol. 2, ch. 5, p. 139.

124 "That is the most essential."

125 These are two persons who are encountered in Vienna c. 1767: Campioni (cf. Eng. vol. 10, ch. 10, p. 237 & 246), a man, and La Vestris (ibid., pp. 259–262), an actress married to the dancer Gaetano Appollino Baldessari Vestris.

126 "death" and "tenderness," "all pledges of affection," and "trifles." Eng. vol. 2, ch. 5, pp. 161–162.

127 "Do not betray love and truth!"

128 Cf. Eng. vol. 2, ch. 6, p. 172.

129 The theater opened in 1656 and operated continuously until a fire in 1747. A new structure opened in 1748 and in that century became increasingly associated with opera and ballet. The famous financial difficulties forced the closure and sale of that in 1770.

130 Presumably the more notable of two Marcello brothers — Alessandro (1669–1747), a composer, poet, philosopher, and mathematician, rather than Benedetto (1686–1739), a lawyer, writer, teacher, and minor composer.

131 "the approaching fine season."

132 James Thomson (1700–48) was the most celebrated Scottish poet of the 1700's until Robert Burns. "The Seasons" was composed 1726–30 and revised 1744–46.

133 Cf. Engl. vol. 5, ch. 5, p. 107 *et seq.* Jeanne Camus de Pontcarré, by marriage Jeanne de la Rochefoucauld, Marquise d'Urfé frequently styled Madame d'Urfé (1705–1775).

She had three children (b. 1727, 1732, and 1733) but her husband died in 1734, after which she spent a fortune on various alchemical and occult ventures, becoming involved with the likes of the Comte de Saint-Germain and the Comte de Cagliostro, and a series of other conmen as well as Casanova (1757 – 63).

134 Casanova became involved with a Steffani de Bragadin (born Giovanno Francesco Steffani, 1723 – ?), who was a simple clerk. He was at the time a member of the Rosicrucians and their occult beliefs, letting the parents of a dead girl believe he was in touch with her via a guardian angel he called Paralis (cf. Eng. vol. 2, ch. 8, p. 225 *et seq.*).

135 One of the impostures by which Casanova cheated Mme d'Urfé was getting her to believe that she could be transformed into a man by accepting the soul of a young Count d'Aranda (cf. vol. 5, ch. 8, p. 180, ch. 10, pp. 225 – 26, vol. 8, ch. 1, pp. 3 – 8, ch. 3, p. 51). Casanova writes about the failure of the first attempt: "…I thought it wiser to make the oracle reply that the operation had failed because the youthful Count d'Aranda had seen the whole performance behind a screen. Madame d'Urfé was in despair, but I comforted her by a second answer, in which the oracle told her that what it had been impossible to accomplish during the April moon in France, it could be accomplished outside of the kingdom during the May moon, but that she must send the prying youth. Whose influence had been so adverse, a hundred leagues from Paris…" (vol. 8, ch. 3, p. 51).

136 "Enlightenment."

137 "My three friends [their Excellencies Signor Dandolo, Signor Barbaro, and Signor Bragadin] were like the Holy Fathers [: seeing the divinity of my answers… they believed that my oracle was animated by an angel]." Eng. vol. 2, ch. 6, p. 197. The equivalent German text used by Szentkuthy does not include the phrase that he specifically cites: "[Meine drei Freunde schienen den Kirchenvätern zu ähneln.] Sie waren Leute von Geist, jedoch abergläubisch [und durchaus keine Philosophen. Indessen waren sie doch, indem sie meinen Orakelsprüchen vollen Glauben beimaßen […] meine Antworten lieber für die Eingebungen eines Engels zu halten.]" (Hu. p. 112).

138 Cf. Eng. vol. 2, ch. 8, p. 207. A *zecchino* (also called a sequin) was a gold coin minted in Italy.

139 "nobility, pain, and those innocent of virtue." Eng. vol. 2, ch. 8, p. 208.

140 Cf., Eng. vol. 2, ch. 6, p. 212.

141 Johann Jakob Bachofen (1815–87). Swiss jurist and anthropologist, who developed theories of the role of ancient 'Mother right' or Hetaerism (matriarchy) and The Dionysian (patriarchy).

142 Elissa is an alternative name used by some sources for Dido, Queen of Carthage before the 5th century B.C.

143 "Oh, how art will always be inferior to nature."

144 "Fall."

145 "Her virtue obliged her to portray it, as if it wished to tell her that despite her follies she had never strayed from virtue." Eng. vol. 2, ch. 8, p. 229.

146 The German text: "*Nachdem wir bis zur Erschöpfung alles durchgekostet hatten* [...] *meine junge Gräfin* [...] *zog ihre Schuhe an und, indem sie ihre Pantoffeln küßte, sagte sie, sie werde sich gewiß nur im Tode von ihnen trennen,*" which in English translation runs: "After dressing she put on her shoes, and she kissed her slippers, which she was determined to keep for the rest of her life" (Eng. vol. 2, ch. 8, p. 230).

147 A cothurn or buskin is a half-boot or, more specifically, a thick-soled boot worn by tragic actors in the Athenian theater.

148 "The last lover that this single woman, through the excess of pleasure, brought to death." Eng. vol. 2, ch. 8, p. 233.

149 "After putting my jewels & my papers back in my trunk." Eng. vol. 2, ch. 10, p. 280.

150 This is the grandmother of a ballet master and actor named Antonio Balletti, whom Casanova befriended in Mantua (cf. Eng. vol. 2, ch. 10, pp. 290–291). By coincidence the woman was an actress with whom Casanova's father, Gaetano Giuseppe Casanova, was involved as a young actor some time before meeting C.'s mother, Zanetta Farussi, the year before he had been born (cf. Eng. vol. 1, ch. 1, p. 42).

151 Viz. Eng. vol. 2, ch. 11, p. 293.

152 "The gods themselves fight against esthetically conditioned symbols."

153 Metternich thought of the son of Napoleon I Bonaparte by Marie Louise of Austria (created Duke of Reichstadt in 1818) as the Eaglet. The matters in question were dealt with by Edmond Rostand in a play entitled *L'Aiglon* (The Eaglet, 1900).

154 "The body is unwilling."

155 The phrase is taken from Lord Byron's long poem *Childe Harold's Pilgrimage*:

> There is a pleasure in the pathless woods,
>
> There is a rapture on the lonely shore,
>
> There is society where none intrudes,
>
> By the deep Sea, and music in its roar:
>
> I love not Man the less, but Nature more,
>
> From these our interviews, in which I steal
>
> From all I may be, or have been before,
>
> To mingle with the Universe, and feel
>
> What I can ne'er express, yet cannot all conceal.

156 *The 15 Joys of Marriage* is an anonymous late 14th or early 15th century French prose satire about the rows and deceits which may beset the married state.

157 "My philosophical system, which I thought was proof against any assault, lay in ruins; I recognized an avenging God who had lain in wait for me there to punish me for all my misdeeds & thus end my unbelief through — *annihilation*." Eng. vol. 3, ch. 1, p. 5.

COLOPHON

MARGINALIA ON CASANOVA was typeset in InDesign 5.0.
The text & page numbers are set in *Adobe Jenson Pro.*
The titles are set in *Charlemagne.*

Book design & typesetting: Alessandro Segalini
Cover design: István Orosz

MARGINALIA ON CASANOVA
is published by Contra Mundum Press
and printed by Lightning Source, which has received Chain of
Custody certification from: The Forest Stewardship Council,
The Programme for the Endorsement of Forest Certification,
and The Sustainable Forestry Initiative.

Contra Mundum Press   New York

CONTRA MUNDUM PRESS

Contra Mundum Press is dedicated to the value & the indispensable importance of the individual voice.

Contra Mundum Press will be publishing titles from all the fields in which the genius of the age traditionally produces the most challenging and innovative work: poetry, novels, theatre, philosophy — including philosophy of science & of mathematics — criticism, and essays. Upcoming volumes include Richard Foreman's *Plays with Films*, Elio Petri's *Writings on Cinema and Life*, & Fernando Pessoa's *Philosophical Essays*.

For the complete list of forthcoming publications, please visit our website. To be added to our mailing list, send your name and email address to: info@contramundum.net

Contra Mundum Press
P.O. Box 1326
New York, NY 10276
USA
http://contramundum.net

PUBLISHER
ACKNOWLEDGMENTS

Gratitude is due to that fateful night when, in a bar in Jyväskylä none too reminiscent of *Sátántangó*, we first learned of Szentkuthy Miklós, *Prae*, the epic *St. Orpheus Breviary*, and all else — the *cselszövés* all began then, in silence...

Now, thanks are due to Maison Gai Saber, Carole Viers, Andrea Scrima, and Cecile Rossant. To Filip Sikorski, we would like to express our *wdzięczność*.

Contra Mundum Press is especially grateful to Fenyvesi Kristóf, Szolláth Dávid, & Nicholas Birns for their magnanimous assistance with this publication, & to Orosz István for his *noblesse oblige*.

Finally, to Madame Fortuna, the benevolent ship that carried us through the dark ~

CPSIA information can be obtained at www.ICGtesting.com
Printed in the USA
BVOW05s0817230715

410068BV00006B/20/P